THOMAS FO
3 1308 00322 6362
W9-CAL-417

UNDER THE EMPYREAN SKY

The characters and events portrayed in this book are fictitious. Any similarity to real persons, living or dead, is coincidental and not intended by the author.

Amazon Publishing
Attn: Amazon Children's Publishing
P.O. Box 400818
Las Vegas, NV 89140
www.amazon.com/amazonchildrenspublishing

The lyrics on page 1 and page 67 are from "Harvest-Home Song" by John Davidson. Stedman, Edmund Clarence, ed. *A Victorian Anthology, 1837–1895*. Cambridge: Riverside Press, 1895. The lyrics on page 149 are from "John Barleycorn" collected by Robert Burns in 1782. The lyrics on page 287 are from "The Big Rock Candy Mountains" by Harry "Haywire Mac" McClintock, written in 1895 and first recorded as a song in 1928.

Library of Congress Cataloging-in-Publication Data is available upon request.

ISBN-13: 9781477817209 (hardcover)
ISBN-10: 1477817204 (hardcover)
ISBN-13: 9781477867204 (eBook)
ISBN-10: 1477867201 (eBook)

Book design by Sammy Yuen
Editor: Marilyn Brigham

Printed in the United States of America (R)
First edition
10 9 8 7 6 5 4 3 2 1

CHUCK WENDIG

UNDER THE EMPYREAN SKY

UNDER THE EMPYREAN SKY

CONTENTS

For Ben and Michelle,
who are my Heartland

PART ONE
THE DISCOVERY

The pleasure of a king
Is tasteless to the mirth
Of peasants when they bring
The harvest of the earth.
With pipe and tabor hither roam
All ye who love our Harvest-home.

—*"Harvest-Home Song," John Davidson*

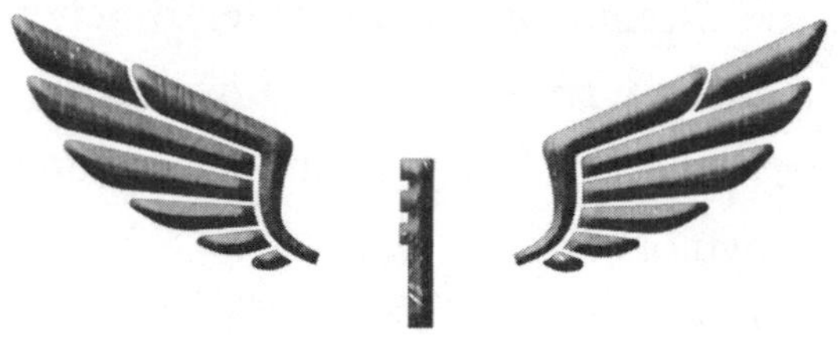

THE RACE

THE CORN REACHES for the land-boat above it, but the corn is slow and the cat-maran is fast. The stretching, yearning stalks hiss against the boat's bottom, making a white noise that sounds like pollen coming out of a piss-blizzard.

Betty, which is what Cael and his crew have nicknamed the long and lean cat-maran, sails buoyed by a pair of crackling hover-panels. Cael stands at the boat's fore, leaning on one knee, staring out at the line where blue sky and green corn merge.

Fifty yards to their left is Cael's opponent—a front-heavy, fat-chested yacht with a quartet of billowing red sails pregnant with wind. At the fore of the boat stands Boyland

Barnes Jr., the captain of the Boxelder Butchers. They're the number one scavenger crew in Boxelder.

Cael's crew, the Big Sky Scavengers, is number two.

But not anymore.

Boyland looks over, offers a dismissive shrug before making a jerk-off motion with his hand. His land-yacht eases forward yard by yard, outpacing *Betty* slowly but surely. Boyland's got a pair of small propellers in chrome cages posed at the back of his yacht—not cheap, but they give him a boost. Boyland's money *always* gives him the boost.

Cocky prick, Cael thinks.

Boyland laughs, a pissy squeal that doesn't match Boyland's broad chest or bucket-shaped head. Cael just waves. Then he takes the pair of blue-lensed goggles from atop his head and snaps them tight over his eyes to protect against the coming wind.

The Butchers have propellers. Wind power. Fine.

The Big Sky Scavengers have something else. Something *better*.

Cael gives Lane the signal.

Lane Moreau. Tall, lean, like a reedy tree shaken of leaves. Lane is *Betty*'s helmsman. Knows every inch of her. He plucks the pinched ditchweed cigarette from between his lips, pitches it over the side of the boat in a pinwheel of embers, and then reaches down and yanks hard on a newly installed lever sticking up next to the control panel. Cael feels *Betty*'s belly vibrate. The sound of the hissing corn is lost beneath the grinding of gears as his brand-new hover-panels tilt down and back—

A coruscating ripple of light bursts from beneath *Betty*, and she suddenly leaps forth like a horse with a nettle screwed hard in its ass.

Lane holds the ship's wheel with white knuckles. He howls like a hound. *Awoooooo*.

Rigo, the third mate in their crew of four—though today they're one light, what with Gwennie off getting ready for tomorrow's Harvest Home festival and the Obligation Day ceremony—hunkers down in the middle of the boat with a tube of maps under one arm, looking ashen and queasy.

Cael can already see, in the distance, the prize glinting in the sun: a defunct motorvator. Now just a flinty, metallic mote far off—but getting closer.

They heard the rumor this morning: someone spotted a rogue thresher out there, dead in the corn. Off its program. Off the grid. Didn't belong to anybody in Boxelder, either—must have come a long way from another town before its battery finally took a shit. That means it's ripe for the picking.

That's what Cael and his crew do. They pick. They *scavenge*.

That motorvator, they'll butcher it for spare parts, sell what they find. Provided they get there first—and Cael's pretty sure they're going to beat the corn off Boyland's cob on this one. Getting there first means getting first pick—same way the strongest, biggest vulture gets to have first bite of whatever dead thing it might find.

You get to the junk, you get the prize. You get the prize, you earn the ace notes from the Mercado maven. Easy peasy, cool and breezy.

It won't be long now. They'll be there in no time. Ten minutes. Maybe less.

Betty pulls ahead. Faster, faster.

And Boyland's land-yacht drifts farther behind.

Cael's heart leaps in his chest. They're going to beat the Boxelder Butchers. Beat them like disobedient urchins. He throws a glance back at Boyland, who stands at the fore of his boat, big, meaty fists on his hips. But something ain't right.

Boyland is smiling.

He gives a signal of his own: a fat thumb thrust up.

Felicity, his first mate, whips out a box with a long silver antenna. She pulls her conductor's cap tight over her tangled mane and then stabs a button on the box.

Atop the land-yacht's crow's nest, the third in their crew—a little towheaded ragamuffin way too young to be doing this gig—claps and laughs so hard his pale cheeks go red.

A flush of cold saline ices Cael's blood. *Something's up*.

He realizes too late: he shouldn't be looking at them. He *should* be looking ahead.

Rigo sees before any of them. He cries out, "Bounce it!"

Cael turns heel-to-toe and sees a rusty thresher bar from a defunct motorvator suddenly spring up out of the corn, rising over the stalk-tops. Lane hears Rigo's command and slaps a button on the side of the console, and the hover-panels shudder and emit a hard pulse, giving *Betty* a boost meant to carry them up and over.

But they're too late.

Betty runs fast over the threshing blades.

Then comes the sound of shearing metal and shattering glass as Cael's world goes ass over chin.

ABOVE AND BELOW

CAEL MCAVOY DREAMS of flying.

It's the same dream every night. He flies low over the endless corn, the stalks swaying not with the wind but because that's how the corn is: it drifts and shifts and twitches, leaves whispering against leaves, tassels like reaching hands. The sky above is a blue so pale it looks as though someone squeezed the color out of it, like a rag sitting too long in the sun, bleached by the light.

Cael has no hover-pads beneath his feet, no skiff beneath him, no wings. His body is unadorned; it flies free, without cause, without reason.

He wears no shoes in the dream. His toes can feel the wind prying between them like cold fingers.

Down below, a motorvator as big as a barn churns a diagonal line through the corn. It's an older model—a Straw-Walker 909—and it's gone off its program, the program that keeps it on the grid. But nobody's watching as it slices a hard line from corner to corner, its toothy metal maw chewing up the cornstalks. Cael can hear the growling of the rasp bars, the grinding of the augur, the loud *bangs* as cobs of corn punch into the back of the open box-bed.

Behind the motorvator lies a wake of dead straw.

Cael flies over it, past it. He opens his mouth, lets the air inflate his cheeks like balloons, and he tucks his arms flat against his body as he speeds up. The air stings his eyes, makes them tear up, and he blinks it away. *Higher*, he thinks. *We can always go higher.*

A shadow passes over him, a vulture's darkness.

Above, one of the Empyrean flotillas drifts out of the harsh light of the white sun. It's too far up to see which one it is—not that Cael would ever know that, but dream logic is a logic all its own. *Maybe it's the* Woodwick Miranda Mader-Atcha, he thinks, *or the* Gravenost Ernesto Oshadagea. The flotilla—a never-ending series of ships and homes and platforms strung together with chains fatter and rounder than the average grain elevator, comprising an area as big as a hundred towns—bobs lazily across the sky. Cael turns his head just so and can hear the hum of the engines, can see the contrails of white smoke.

He looks away, tucks his chin to his chest, and keeps flying. Up there they don't give a rat's right foot about him. They don't even know he exists. So he offers them the same courtesy and pretends they're not even there. But he wonders what it's like to live up on one of those great floating beasts among the lucky and the privileged. He tries to imagine winning the Lottery.

At that moment he hates everyone on the flotillas. Hates how much they have. Hates how they always fly above the Heartland—as if they're so much better.

But then in the next moment he wants to *be* one of them. Rich. Superior. Impossible.

Cael flies like this for a while. Sky above. Corn below. Always and forever.

But it doesn't last. He hears a *pop*, and across the flat plain of cornstalks the loud report tumbles over the rows and fields. Something hits him; it feels like a ball bearing cracking him in the breastbone. He touches his hand to his chest, and it comes away wet and sticky—his blood bright red, *too* red—and a surge of anger and regret churns through him.

He's angry because now he remembers; *now* it hits him: He remembers that the dream always begins and ends the same way.

It begins with him flying.

And it ends with him falling.
Cael falls.
Toward the reaching corn.
The endless corn.
The everything corn.
Cael dies, and with him the dream.

GODSDAMN YOU, BOYLAND BARNES, JR.

CAEL THINKS, *I'm flying! Holy shit, I'm actually flying!*

Then he hits the ground, his ass coming up over his head. He crashes through the cornstalks, the razor edges of the leaves slicing his skin like a dozen paper cuts. His back smashes flat against the hard earth. The air escapes his lungs in a gasp.

His ears are ringing: *eeeeeeeeeeeeeeoooo eeeee*.

His first attempt to get up fails. Cael can't get a breath. Instead, he rolls over on his side, curling up around himself, trying to figure out what the hell just happened.

All around him, the cornstalks twitch and shift. Bending toward him. Shuddering suddenly, as though excited.

Somewhere, he hears Rigo moaning. But Lane, Lane doesn't make a peep.

Cael's pancaked lungs suddenly inflate, sucking in a reflexive draw of air. He coughs. Rolls over on his hands and knees.

When he lifts his head, he sees the wreckage.

Betty is stuck in the ground, her aft thrust up in the air like a big middle finger. The mast is snapped, the sails barely attached—and as Cael watches, one pale sail blows free and drifts over the corn-tops, billowing out of sight.

But the worst is the hover-panels. Those two panels—round and big like the lids of an old trash bin—now sit skewered on the rusty blades of a thresher bar likely stolen from a busted motorvator. A thresher bar that looks to be rigged up on a pair of remotely triggered hydraulic jacks.

A trap. A trap set by the Boxelder Butchers.

Shit. *Shit!*

Cael spent every last ace note they had on those panels. An investment, he told the others, to give them the edge on the Butchers.

And now here he stands. Arms slick with blood from tiny cuts. Ears still ringing.

Whatever edge they had, gone with the sail, dead in the dirt.

For a moment Cael feels a twist of hope. One of the

panels is hopelessly borked, its tempered glass bottom shattered, the coils crumpled. But the other still glows and pulses with faint power. But then—*bzzt*—the panel flashes with purple light that leaves a seared spiral swirl in Cael's vision, and the panel shatters in a spray of sparks.

Godsdamnit!

Cael wipes blood off his arms and swats away a stalk of corn that has bent down toward him. They say the corn can't smell blood, but Cael doesn't buy it. He kicks past stalks heavy and pregnant with cobs. He zeroes in on Rigo's moans and finds his pudgy buddy lying on his back. Rigo's got a knee pulled up to his belly, and he's holding it.

"What happened?" Rigo asks, wincing.

"Boyland happened," Cael says, and spits. More corn drifts down toward him, like a nag's head dipping toward a puddle of water. He swats it away, careful not to get another cut. "He borked us. Rigged a trap, that sonofabitch."

"That means he knew. About the panels."

"Damn right he knew."

"The maven."

Cael cranes his head back, looks into the bright sun. Growls. *Of course* the maven. She's in the mayor's pocket. Boyland is the mayor's son. It adds up to such an easy equation, he's pissed at himself for missing it. Maybe he didn't miss it. Maybe he just didn't want to admit it.

Rigo sits up, jerking his head away from a leaf of corn that's seeking out his ear hole.

"You know what I'm going to do?" Rigo's eyes narrow. "I'm gonna kick Boyland's crap-can. I'll break bad on him. I'll break bad on him; on that girl, Felicity; and that little rigger rat-bastard they got running around with them. What's his name? Mouse?"

"Mole."

"Mole! I don't care that he's a little kid. I'll fight him. They gotta learn respect, Cael. That whole crew, every last Boxelder Butcher, is going down. I'm going to punch them so hard, they'll piss their pants. Way I hit 'em, they can't *not* piss their pants."

Rigo. Imagining him "break bad" on Boyland's crew is like picturing a feed-stuffed squealer fighting a starving dog. He tries to stand, but as soon as he puts pressure on his left leg—the one with the knee he's been rubbing—he yelps and goes down on his butt.

"Just . . . stay there for a minute," Cael says. "I'll go find Lane. And don't go to sleep! That corn will be all over you by the time I get back, and I don't feel like cutting you free."

Cael heads off to find Lane. He passes the wreckage of *Betty* again. It breaks his heart.

He finds Lane on the opposite side of the cat-maran. His friend's just sitting there. Lane has a cob of corn in his hands, one he's wrenched off the nearest stalk. With nimble fingers and long nails, he pops kernels out of their mooring and thumb-flicks them away.

"Lane," Cael says. "You okay?"

Lane turns. He's got a cut across his brow. Not a serious one, and it's already crusting over. But a grim trickle has frosted his right eyelid with a rime of darkening blood. "Oh, *sure*."

"You don't look fine."

"I'm just tired of it," he says, screwing a stubby cigarette between his lips and lighting it with a red-top match. "This is how they get you, Cael. This is how they keep us down."

"The Butchers?"

"*The Empyrean*. They make us fight each other over scavenged scraps while they . . ." His voice trails off. "Whatever. Assholes."

"Rigo's hurt," Cael says.

"Yeah. I heard him moaning."

"Long walk back to town. We better get him."

"Guess we better."

It's then they hear the sounds that crawl inside Cael's ears like a family of weevils: the hiss of the corn-tops, the buzz of propellers in their wire cages, the cocky piggish laugh.

The Butchers' yacht slides up over the corn about ten yards off.

Boyland fake-pouts. “Uh-oh. Did widdle Cael’s boat fall down and go *boom*?”

Cael sneers. “You did this, you dirty shit-britches.”

Mole clings to the mast like a possum, giggling. Along the back, Felicity just stands, arms crossed, mean scowl plastered across her mug.

“Such accusations really hurt me,” Boyland says, and then the other two in his crew whoop with laughter. But Boyland keeps a straight face. “I’d never do that to you. It’s just—you’re reckless, McAvoy. One day, if you’re not careful, you’re gonna get yourself killed.”

“That a threat, buckethead?”

Boyland just laughs.

In a flash Cael has his slingshot in his hand, a ball bearing palmed into the pocket. But Lane’s got a steady hand on Cael’s chest and a look in his eye that says, *You really want to go stirring up that soup pot right now?*

Boyland winks, says, “That’s right, McAvoy, listen to your girlfriend.” Then the captain of the Butchers makes a lasso motion with his index finger. Mole turns the sails toward the wind, and Felicity cranks up the props—the land-yacht goes drifting off, faster and faster, until all they can see again is the wall of corn before them.

• • •

As they walk side by side, Rigo limping between the other two, Cael watches a pair of pink-brown moths—corn borers by the look of the wings—flirt and frolic in midair, a mad dance as they circle ever closer to the corn. Bad idea. A nearby stalk shudders suddenly, and a leaf uncurls and lashes out, slicing one of the moths in half. Two wings separate from the body and drift down to the ground. The other moth, still alive, hightails it the hell out of there.

A corn leaf tickles Cael's ear, and he pulls away. "I hate this shit. Stupid plant. Stupid crop. Damnit."

Rigo shrugs. "I dunno. Been like this long as I can remember." He hobbles along on his one good leg.

"Corn's how they control us," Lane says. "It's like your pop says, Cael. Corn wasn't like this back when he was a kid. Used to be you plant the seed, that's where it grew. Now it goes everywhere. Got a mind of its own."

Way Pop told it, the Empyrean crossbred the corn with a handful of other plants: kudzu, flytraps, some kind of nightshade. Called it Hiram's Golden Prolific. Right now, Cael couldn't give a whit about any of that.

"We're out of money!" Cael says. "Guys, we don't have anything left. Spent all our damn ace notes on those hover-panels. Now they're just a pile of junk." *Like the stuff we scavenge.*

Cael swats at a corn leaf, but it doesn't seem to care. It

twists toward him, and he grabs it and rips it off. The stalk recoils as though in pain.

"We'll figure it out," Rigo says. "We always do."

Cael's not so sure. But it's his *job* to figure it out. He's the captain of this crew. He's out here every day earning ace notes—or trying to—for his brat sister, for Pop, for his poor, bed-ridden mother. Responsibility, he decided long ago, sucks. It sucks the shine off a brand-new motorvator. If only they got lucky, just *one time* . . .

"Those hover-panels were our ticket," he says. "Our way to beat the Butchers. To find that one big haul and set us up for life."

Lane makes a *pssh* sound. "It doesn't work like that. I told you. You have to put it out of your mind, Cael. Out here it's all just different shades of brown. You're like those people who count on the Lottery year after year."

"Hey, shut up," Rigo says. "The Lottery's the real deal."

"The Lottery's bullshit," Cael says. "But my plan isn't. Whoever has the ace notes has the edge. The mayor's on the Empyrean's teat, and that means he gets the biggest mouthful of milk—and that means Boyland's got a taste, too. But how do you think Boyland the Elder got to be mayor? I bet he bought his way in. And if we had enough money—"

Lane claps him on the shoulder. "Cool your heels, dude. One day at a time." He offers Cael a hand-rolled cigarette, but Cael waves him off—he doesn't smoke any of that ditchweed. "Let's just focus on getting *Betty* back up and running."

"Gwennie will know what to do next," Rigo says.

Cael cocks an eyebrow. "Gwennie's not the damn captain."

"But she's the first mate."

Lane adds, "And let's be honest: she's the brains of this operation."

Cael gives him the stink-eye. "We need someone to send a tow-tractor out there to haul *Betty* back to the barn. And we need to do it soon, because if we leave her out there too long, the damn corn's gonna grow up all over her. Then we'll have to pay for a chop-top to go out along with the tractor just to chain-saw through the stalks."

"That'll cost ace notes," Lane says.

"Ace notes we don't *have*," Rigo points out.

"We'll have to scrounge." Cael sighs. "Or take out a loan from the maven."

Lane shakes his head. "That's how they get you. They get you stuck in the mud, and every time you try to pull out . . . the deeper you sink."

Cael's about to tell them both to shut up, because none of this is helping—but then his eyes catch movement. The other two don't see it, but that's why Cael's the head of this crew: he's got vision like a hawk. Or an owl. Or some kind of hawk-owl hybrid that the Empyrean scientists are probably working on just for shits and giggles.

"Shuck rat!" Cael hisses. Then he breaks from the other two, his slingshot already out of his back pocket and in his hand a ball bearing ready to fire.

THE SHUCK RAT'S LITTLE SECRET

CAEL CRASHES THROUGH the stalks. The rat darts ahead of him, squealing.

This shuck rat is, like all shuck rats, fat—but that doesn't mean it can't run. These rats have longer, leaner legs: they can stand up at the stalk like a dog begging for food, their long tongues searching out low-hanging cobs to pull close so they can get a nibble. Cael sees a flash of the rat's banded tail, a tail that looks like the Carruthers rat snake, a serpent introduced about ten years back in order to control the population of shuck rats. Back then the shuck rat's tail was pink and wormy. Then the snake came along, and a year or two later, the rats start popping up with a different kind of tail. The tail confuses the snake, makes the snake think it's chasing one of its buddies, and so it gives up the hunt and the rat gets away. (And as a result, the snake has to change its food source, which means the Carruthers rat snakes decided to go ahead and eat up all the birds.)

The thing about survival, Pop always says, *is that it's not about who's fastest or strongest but who can adapt to changing situations.*

Right now, Cael aims to disprove his father's words and show this rat who's stronger and faster. Killing this shuck rat will put food on the table tonight and maybe tomorrow.

Cael sees another glimpse of the rat's tail and shoulders his way through the corn, chin to his chest so as not to cut himself up further. He's got the slingshot in his hand, a ball bearing from an old, broken-down motorvator pinched between thumb and forefinger in the pocket of the sling. His forearm is tensed.

The rat darts right, then left, zigzagging. Cael struggles to keep up.

He sees a flash of gray—how'd the rat get over there?

He hurries after it. Then another flash of gray to his right. *How the hell?*

Then he realizes: he's tracking a *pair* of them.

Dinner for *days*! His mouth waters, and he bounds after the animals.

Cael skids to a halt as he sees the two rats come together

in a clearing. He has the slingshot drawn, the ball bearing ready to let fly, a second metal marble already tucked in the palm of his hand—

And he stops. His jaw slackens: a look his father calls his "flycatcher" look.

"Whoa," he says, a smile spreading across his face.

One of the rats squeals—a sound that always cuts to Cael's marrow when he hears it, like fingers on a chalkboard but so much worse because it's coming up out of the throat of a howling, screaming mangy-ass rat—and bolts for the margin of the clearing. Cael's so stunned that he misses the shot, but the second rat isn't so lucky. Cael's brain catches up with his hand, and he opens his thumb and forefinger. The metal marble *thwacks* the rat in the head.

The rat gives him one last sad look before toppling over.

Cael laughs. Then he calls to his friends. Because they're going to want to see this.

The first thing that draws Cael's eyes are the red bell peppers, fat and swollen like breasts. They hang so low they're almost touching the ground. But soon his eyes move to see the bulging green beans, the jaunty onion tops, the round cabbage so richly purple it matches the iridescent back of a caviling grackle bird.

"Ohhhh" is all Rigo can say.

Lane is more verbose. "It's a garden. A glorious, no-shit, shouldn't-be-here, how-the-hell-can-it-survive garden."

Cael laughs, nudges the dead shuck rat aside with his foot, and grabs a red pepper. He twists it, and it pops off the plant. Then he takes a deep bite.

His teeth puncture the tough skin with a *pop*, and his mouth floods with the pepper's juices. It's sweet and bitter at the same time. Wet, crisp, crunchy—as refreshing as anything he can remember. Cael closes his eyes, listens to the corn rustling and whispering. Feels the warm sun at the top of his head and the cool breeze brushing across his brow. A moment of bliss. Then he's jolted out of it as Rigo hops over and snatches the pepper from his hand. His friend takes a big chomp.

Rigo breaks into a spasming dance of happiness. "Oh my gods oh my gods oh my gods, it's so good. It's like, it's like—it's like one of the Lady's angels is tongue-kissing me right now." Rigo cups his hand around the back of the angel's invisible head, and his tongue waggles in the open air.

"You're an asshole," Cael says, laughing.

"Not just an asshole," Lane says. "A weird asshole. *Really* weird."

Rigo's eyes roll back in his head, and he continues his blissed-out hobble-footed boogie.

"A garden," Cael says. "*A garden.*"

Gardens like this just don't grow anymore, not unless they're grown in a greenhouse on board an Empyrean flotilla. Around here—around *everywhere* in the Heartland—the only thing people are allowed to grow is corn. And they don't so much *grow* it as *manage* it, since corn grows anywhere it damn well pleases now, whether it's up through a barn's floorboards or shooting through cracks in those old asphalt roads that haven't yet been shellacked with plasto-sheen.

You can't even get the seeds for other crops. The Empyrean control all seed distribution, and they no longer distribute *any* seeds to *any*one down on the ground. Not that it would matter. The ground here is so degraded by erosion and chemicals, the only thing that grows is the corn. Cael heard the ground used to be grade A, river-bottom soil: a deep, rich topsoil that soaked up rain like a hungry sponge. But this ground rejects the rain (when the rain comes at all) like everything's covered in a sheet of oiled leather.

Food like this just isn't something farmers see anymore.

"What I don't get," Lane says, "is how the corn hasn't squashed this stuff. The corn doesn't let anything grow."

Hiram's Golden Prolific is not a fan of competition.

"This isn't random," Cael says. "Someone planted this. Right?"

Rigo wipes pepper juice from his chin. "Not necessarily. Maybe a caviling grackle stole a seed bag from one of the flotillas. They bring stuff down here sometimes—last week Henry Duggard's dad found a little grackle nest in his silo, and half of it was made of shiny thread and marbled buttons."

As Rigo's talking, Lane pokes his head through the corn on the far side of this little patch. "Guys. *Guys*. Look at this."

They hurry over and look.

Ten feet through the corn, another pepper plant grows.

And ten feet after that, a tomato plant has gotten cozy with a cornstalk, a plump green tomato hanging in the shade.

It keeps going. A trail of vegetables.

"I wonder how far it goes," Cael says, truly in awe.

Rigo shrugs. "Seems to be just as aggressive as the corn. Maybe this is some high-class Empyrean biology."

Lane heads back into the clearing. He kneels down, reaches out with lean fingers, and plucks a green bean. He bites it in half. He doesn't lose himself in a fit of delight like Rigo, but he breathes slow and deep.

"The question of all questions is," Lane says, "What do *we* do about this?"

"What do you *think* we're gonna do with it? Have a food fight? Make little red-pepper puppets and put on a show for the shuck rats?" Rigo says. "We eat it!"

Lane clucks his tongue. "That's your response to everything."

Rigo flicks Lane in the ear. Lane puts Rigo in a headlock and noogies the shit out of him.

"You guys said it," Cael says. "We need ace notes. Here are our ace notes. This is it. This is our *ticket*. We harvest these vegetables; they're better than gold."

Rigo, turning red in Lane's headlock, scowls. "This food isn't *legal*. We get caught with this, the Babysitters—"

"So we don't get caught with it."

"No, no, I like where you're going with this," Lane says. He noogies Rigo again.

"Ow *ow ow ow*." Rigo wriggles free and hobbles to the left. "Dude. Ow. My head feels like it's on fire." He turns to Cael. "Guys, you remember a few years back when Jessie Redstone raised a couple squealers in her barn and didn't feed them corn? Need I remind you what happened when the Babysitters found out?"

Proctor Agrasanto paid a special visit. Killed both of those piglets, put them in plastic bags, and shipped them away as if they were sick with something. Two weeks later, the whole farm burned down, and Jessie ended up on the spray-down line at Boxelder's processing facility. A year later the sprayer nozzle got gummed up, and a stray jet of separator chemical hit her in the side of the face. Now she's a permanent guest at the Grummans' farm next door, laid up in their attic bedroom, breathing through a tube. Nobody talks about her anymore.

"I got to see those piglets," Rigo murmurs. "I snuck into her barn. Man, those little pigs were cute. They were pink. No scabs or sores. Running around like a couple of happy idiots instead of just lying there in their own mess." He stares at a far-off point. "The bacon from those squealers would have been like nothing we'd ever tasted. Can we at least talk to your dad about this?"

"Uh-uh. No way. Pop doesn't need to know about this. We got our own thing going. This is crew business. Pop doesn't get a vote."

"So," Lane says. "We vote."

"Yep. And I say we sell it."

"Me, too."

"Wait," Rigo says. "What about my vote? And Gwennie's?"

"She's not here. And you're outvoted."

"Fine. *Fine*."

Cael thrusts his slingshot into Rigo's hand. Gives him a fistful of ball bearings, too. "Protect the garden. Lane and I are heading back to *Betty*'s wreck to get some bags. And the beacon emitter." That way they'll be able to track back direct to the garden. "We can't harvest it all in one go, and Lord and Lady only know how far the trail goes. But this is a damn fine start."

"Hey, just don't eat everything while we're gone," Lane says to Rigo, laughing.

Rigo scowls.

As Lane and Cael trudge back through the corn toward Betty's wreck, Lane blurts out, "So. Gwennie."

Cael knows where he's going with this. "Don't want to talk about it."

"Tomorrow's Harvest Home."

"I said, *Don't wanna talk about it*."

Lane snaps his fingers. "I bet she cleans up nice for her Obligation."

"It's not like that."

"It's *totally* like that."

"It's luck of the draw. Nothing I can do about it." Cael scuffs the hard earth with a ratty shoe, kicking up a puff of dust.

"You have, what, a ten percent chance? Not the worst odds. Better than winning the Lottery and getting a one-way ticket off the ground."

Cael stops. Meets Lane chin-to-chin. "If I have a ten percent shot, then so do you. You're just as likely to end up with her as I am."

"Oh," Lane says. He gets quiet.

"You didn't think of that, did you?"

"I actually didn't think of that."

"Anybody *you* want to end up with?" Cael needles.

"I don't want to talk about it" is Lane's retort.

"Then we're on the same page."

"Good."

"Good."

And the two of them keep walking.

THE BOXELDER BLUES

LATER, THEY FIND themselves standing at the crux of the old, shattered Boxelder Road. Lane and Cael each carry a sack bulging with pilfered vegetables. It takes all their willpower not to sit down here and now and have a feast.

The shuck rat will have to do.

The old Cemetery Road crosses their path, with corn rising up on all sides. Rigo lives one way, and Lane lives the other. Cael has to walk through town to get to his house. The Cemetery Road has an enamel of plasto-sheen on it so the corn doesn't grow up through it. The way the afternoon sun collects on the plastic coating gives it a glossy brightness; look at it the wrong way and you'll catch a blinding eyeful of white light.

They do their not-really-that-secret handshake: shake hands, then transition into locking elbows before moving into a manly, shoulder-clapping hug.

"Godsdamn Boyland," Cael says.

"Godsdamn Boyland," the other two say in unison.

"Least we got the garden." Rigo pats the side of one of the sacks the way you might the side of an old cow.

"True," Cael says. "I'm gonna head home first since it's on the way, but then I'm taking these to the Mercado right after. Fresher they are, better we get paid, I figure."

"Then I guess we'll see each other tomorrow," Lane says.

"You're not coming to eat?"

Lane's got nobody. Father dead. Mother off in some town, Lord and Lady know where, serving as a Babysitter for the Empyrean. Sending a few ace notes and provisions home now and again. Lot of nights Lane ends up at the McAvoy place for dinner.

But not tonight, apparently.

"Nah, I . . ." Lane shrugs. "I'm not hungry."

Cael nods. His palms go slick. "Obligation Day."

"Not for me," Rigo says, looking grumpy. He's only sixteen, a year behind.

"You still get to enjoy the rest of Harvest Home. Besides, count yourself lucky. You've got a couple pretty girls coming up at next year's Obligation. Summer Beaumont, for one."

"Whatever." Rigo waves them off. "Cael, don't get caught with those vegetables."

"I won't," Cael says.

"You get caught, we all get screwed. They'll be our ticket, all right—a ticket on some Empyrean work detail for the next ten years."

"I said *I won't*."

And then the three friends go their separate ways.

Get closer to town and the corn starts to die off—or, rather, it starts to get killed off. Boxelder sits like a tick on skin: a little dot in a clear, slightly raised-up circle. Cael waves to Bessie and Burt Greene, both wearing backpack tanks of Queeny's Quietdown, an acrid brew of herbicide that hoses down the invasive corn and keeps it from swallowing Boxelder whole.

Around here they just call it "the gravy."

Burt and Bessie don't wear much protective gear: old cracked plastic goggles and fabric masks held over their noses and mouths with fraying elastic. Bessie's okay except for a fatty shoulder growth, but Burt's got skin like a hot sausage casing: glistening, taut, blistering crimson, the flesh striated with pale stretch marks. Bessie says when he moves it hurts, but you'd never know it. Burt's all smiles, all the time. It's just how he is. Bessie watches Cael's mom once or twice a week—more when Cael's sister is off on one of her unscheduled adventures.

Burt points to the dead shuck rat. Cael holds up the rodent, its mouth open and baring pink incisors. Burt gives a bright red thumbs-up.

It's not unusual to see Cael with a kill. Whether it's a shuck rat, a Ryukyu rabbit, or a two-headed snap turtle, he'll thwack it on the head with a steel ball bearing and give it to Pop to cook for the family. One time Cael even saw a fell-deer out there—he felt bad shooting it, given it was the only one he'd ever seen around these parts, but that fell-deer was in misery. Half the animal's neck hung fat with dark tumors, and on those tumors the fur had rubbed away. Cael killed it, but Pop said most of the meat wasn't safe to eat. He cut away a helluva lot of the animal, and what they ended up with wasn't more than what you'd get out of a pair of shuck rats.

But, Lord and Lady, was it good.

Boxelder isn't much to look at. A handful of buildings on one side, another handful on the other, and a ripped-up plasto-sheen ribbon of road cutting it right down the middle.

Over there, the Tallyman's office sits elbow-to-elbow

with Busser's Tavern. That causes no end of moaning and groaning. The Tallyman—in this case a Tallywoman, Frieda Wessel—is all business, and her business consists of keeping up production and ensuring that the corn gets processed and that the Empyrean gets its due. The tavern is where the folks go to get goofy on bottles of fixy and chicha beer. Frieda likes it quiet. The taverners like it loud—in part *because* Frieda likes it quiet.

They all say, "To hell with the Tallyman."

Behind the tavern on a small berm is the jail—a dingy, cement-block structure where the Babysitters lock up the drunk and disorderly from time to time. Got a couple of holding cells in there and not much more. Empty right now, far as Cael knows.

On the other side of the street is Doc Leonard's (the only doctor's office with a diner counter in the back); Poltroon's motorvator shop; and, at the far end of the row, the provisional store. Not that anybody goes in there much. The Empyrean sends out weekly rations to every farmer and worker in the Heartland, and any ace notes over and above that are likely spent at the *real* market, the Mercado, just north of town. The goods in the general store are about as desirable as a wandering hobo. Last time Cael was in there, he bought a pouch of jelly beans. They tasted like sweet-flavored dirt nuggets. When Cael complained, the store's keeper, Weston Sinclair, just shrugged and went back to rereading that ratty old chapbook with the faded image of the pretty girl in the arms of the bare-chested farmer.

All around are the signs of tomorrow's Harvest Home. Hammers falling, people cobbling together wooden booths. At the far end of town, men drag pallets to make the stage. Chairs are being unloaded from hovering motorvator carts chugging black smoke.

But as Cael walks through town, the mood is not one of celebration. The air is still and somber. He sees that a small half circle of folks have gathered outside Doc Leonard's. From beyond that wall of people he hears a woman weeping. He's not sure of the voice, but if he had a pocketful of ace notes, he'd bet that it was Carrie Marshall.

Carrie Marshall. Couple years older than him. She used to be Carrie Tremayne, but when she turned seventeen, it was time to marry the man to whom she was Obliged: Stanley Marshall.

Wasn't but a year after their marriage that she ended up with child. And Cael knows she was coming up on being due.

Across the street at the tavern, the bartender, Tom Busser, stands out front, arms crossed. For a moment a wind kicks up, and a sheen of hazy dust separates them; but when it passes, Cael sees Busser waving him over.

"Believe that?" Busser says, lifting his chin in the

direction of the doc's. Busser smells of the sour mash chicha beer; he doesn't drink it, but he serves it most of the day.

Cael looks over, and finally he sees the crowd part a little. There's Stanley Marshall. Cheeks dark with stubble. Eyes low and sad. In front of him sits Carrie. She's got a bundle of something in her arms, and she wails like a ghost.

"Baby didn't make it," Cael says. It's not a question, because he already knows.

"Boy. Stillborn. Sixth one this year. Almost as many broken births as healthy ones." Busser looks Cael up and down. "Where's your boat? What were you flying out there, a pinnace-racer?"

"No." Cael feels a surge of anger like a hot wash of poison. "I was working with a cat-maran Pop and I put together."

"So why you walking through town? Pair of sacks like that should be in the back of your ride." He's already leaning over and trying to get a good look at the two burlap sacks. Cael turns away.

Another whorl of dust leaps up in front of them.

"Piss-blizzard's coming," Busser says.

Piss-blizzards wreak havoc on everything. The winds pick up and bring with them a choking tide of corn pollen. The air turns yellow. The pollen clogs up the motorvators. Folks can't work, so they stay inside, seeing as how they don't feel like breathing in that stuff. Even the bar shuts down because the promise of a taste of fixy isn't enough to get you outside. Which ensures that Poltroon across the way is the only one happy when a storm comes in.

Busser says, "Seems like the piss-blizzards come around more and more every year. Get worse every time, too."

"Just in time for Harvest Home." *For my Obligation.*

"Might miss us. Or come late."

"Like we're ever that lucky."

Busser laughs. "And yet we're told to keep on smiling with shit on our teeth. You want a beer?"

"Ain't I too young?"

"Sure. Good thing, too, because I wasn't going to give you one anyway." He claps Cael on the back—it's hard, it hurts, yet somehow it remains affectionate. "What's in the bag?"

Cael's heart kicks in his chest. "Nothing."

"Well, it's something. They ain't just holdin' fresh air."

"It's private."

"Okay, don't sweat it, Cael. I'm not digging a hole where nobody wants one dug. I'm just making small talk."

"I gotta go." Cael shifts uncomfortably from foot to foot. "Later, Busser."

"May the rains wet your face, boy."

As Cael passes Doc Leonard's office, he sees Carrie drawing the bundle tighter to her bosom as Doc Leonard—a man so bony you might describe him as rickety, like the way a scarcecrow looks hanging on a busted cross—tries to take the child from her.

A few eyes fall to Cael as he passes. He nods. Keeps walking. What else can he do?

Times like this, when Cael is walking alone, it feels like the only answer is to tear it all down. Burn the cornfields. Blow up the barns. Knock out the Babysitters. Escape.

Escape where, though? The flotillas won't have them. Unless you win the Lottery, they don't want you. Refugees from the Heartland? Please. They'll kick a refugee right off the edge. Let him fall to the earth and fertilize the corn.

If not to the flotillas, then to where? What lies outside the Heartland?

They're all like shuck rats trapped in snares.

Boyland used to play this game in school where he'd grab a fistful of your hair and then whisper, "Don't move, and it won't hurt."

This is like that. Like the Empyrean is saying to them, "Don't move, and it won't hurt."

Well, hell with that, Cael thinks. *Hell with that.*

On the way back out of town and toward Cael's own farm, the corn once more rises up. Small stalks give way to the bigger, woodier stalks, the ones that support the "prolific" part of the plant's name, since a couple dozen ears of corn on the stalk tend to weigh it all down.

And there, ahead of him on the road, is one of the town's two Babysitters, Pally Varrin.

Suddenly, the vegetables are a heavy weight in Cael's hand. If the Babysitter finds out he's carting around fresh vegetables, no telling what will happen. Pally might take them for himself. Or he might confiscate them and jail Cael. Or, given how spiteful Pally can be, he might just stomp on them.

Rigo's voice haunts him suddenly: *Cael, don't get caught with those.*

Pally stands there with his rubicund cheeks and patchy beard. He's got the top half of his uniform unzipped and tied up at his waist. Underneath is a sweat-stained wife-beater—Cael can see his ribs through the fabric. He's got his sonic shooter out and is taking careful aim at the signpost marking Creamery Road, the same road Cael uses to get home. *The only road.* Cael thinks suddenly to turn around and hightail it back toward town. Pally pops off another sonic shot—a buzzing, warbling blast of sound and air—that hits the sign and makes it spin like a loose weathervane in a hard wind.

Technically, Pally and the others are called Overseers.

But everyone else just calls them Babysitters.

"Shuck rat," Pally says, twirling the pistol. He's clumsy enough that he almost drops it.

"Yeah," Cael says. "Taking it home."

Pally tucks his tongue in his cheek, bulging it out. He's thinking. Whenever Pally thinks, Cael imagines a single pulley guided by a rotting rope inside the man's head. Whatever it's pulling up to the surface never seems to get there all the way.

Finally, Pally says, "Nah, you're not. I want the rat."

"No, you don't."

Pally's chest puffs out. "I said I do, and I do. And I want what's in those sacks."

Shit, shit, shit.

"This is a sick rat. Got into a tank of gravy. We're gonna eat him because we have to, but you get better provisions than us. You really want the rat?"

Please say no. Please just go away. I need what's in these sacks.

Cael prays this is enough to send Pally off the scent, because who the hell would want to eat a poisoned rat? Well, besides half the people in town. But Pally is bored. His cheeks grow redder.

"Fine. Don't want the rat. But what's in the sacks?"

"Fresh vegetables. Bell peppers. Tomatoes. *Green beans.*"

The misdirection works. Pally spins the sonic shooter.

"Uh-huh. That's real funny, shit-bird."

"We wrecked our boat," Cael says. "This is just some of our provisions. Some hardtack. A bundle of mouse-eaten rope. You don't want any of this."

"You're right, I don't." Cael's heart lifts. But then Pally smirks. "But I'm still going to take it, because I think you're a shit-bird."

"That's not gonna happen," Cael says, and the words surprise even him. Before he knows what he's doing, he's already dropped the rat and the sacks onto the road and brought the slingshot to his hand. "No helmet. Uniform unzipped. I got a clear shot." The Babysitter uniform is a kind of plastic mesh meant to absorb heavy blows and diffuse impact, but a white wife-beater won't help Pally.

"Put that slingshot away. I got my shooter out. You want to tangle with me?"

"You should be the one who's worried, Pally. You hit me, I get knocked back, bruised up, probably sick for a few days. I hit you—and I will—I'll put that eye out of your fool head."

Cael widens his stance, trying to look tougher, meaner. He's bluffing—he's never been shot, but Cael has heard it's pretty awful. Besides feeling like you just got hit by a drug-pumped bull, the blast leaves you dizzy and imbalanced for days. Unable to stand for long. Throwing up every couple hours. Busser once said it was like being drunk and hungover both at the same time.

"These are my crew's plunders," he tells Pally. But he knows it's coming. The way Pally's hand tightens around the shooter, the way his finger seeks out the trigger, Cael knows he's about to get hit dead in the chest by a sonic blast. Once that happens, he'll be rolling around on the ground, throwing up on himself—giving Pally the perfect opportunity to go rifling through those sacks.

"Hey!"

It's the other Babysitter, Grey Franklin. Jogging up behind Cael from the direction of town. Pally looks like he's been caught with his hand in the till. Though Grey is not his superior, he's damn sure mentally superior.

Pally suddenly laughs and his hand drops, his pistol with it.

"What's going on here?" Grey asks. Franklin's built like a bulldog, with a mean hunch and a hard underbite. The sides of his head offer thatches of gray hair, hard and bristly like a boot brush.

"Nothing," Pally says, waving it off. "I'm just giving Cael here a hard time."

"Leave him alone. Get back to town. Folks are getting riled up, what with the Marshall kid dying. We want to make sure we're both there. Just in case."

"Yeah, yeah, sure, sure," Pally says. As he passes Cael, he mutters, "Hope you eat that rat and you get the trots so bad it pulls your guts out your bunghole."

Cael's about to open his mouth, but Grey plants a hand on his chest. A gentle shake of Grey's head makes it clear Cael shouldn't say a thing.

"Go home, Cael. Say hi to your pop."

Just this once, Cael does as he's told.

PISS AND WISHES, BROKEN DISHES

THE HOMESTEAD ISN'T much to look at. Horseshoe gravel driveway. Old red barn falling apart. The skeleton of a silo out back. Pop's got a workshop above the barn, a place he calls his "fortress of solitude"—a term he took from some old flimsy rag about a goof in blue-and-red tights who flies around and fixes problems in a long-ago world. Smack dab in the middle of all of it is their home: an old white farmhouse with a slight leftward lean and a back porch with a roof that sags like a caved-in skull.

The air, Cael notes, smells of cloying fragrance. Strong and floral.

His father comes around from the back of the barn, a pump-sprayer in his hand with a dirty plastic tank hanging below it. He pulls the trigger on the nozzle in his hand, spritzing a mist across the little corn shoots that keep trying to come up through the driveway's loose limestone gravel. He's not wearing a mask, so Cael knows it's not a chemical spray he's using. Pop won't take his rations of Queeny's Quietdown—a fact that earns him a small measure of suspicion from everybody else in Boxelder.

Then Pop sees Cael, and he hobbles over. The limp favors his left leg. The right one works okay—it's the hip that's the problem.

"Cael," he says, nodding. He sets down the tank with a slight groan and then pauses to push his round-rimmed glasses up the bridge of his hawk's beak nose. His father's not a big man. Cael has already outgrown him by a couple inches. Someone in town once said he looked "academic," which is appropriate given the fact that Pop was a teacher once upon a time. "Not a bad-looking rat."

Cael nods. He hands the rat to Pop.

"What's in the bags?"

Cael doesn't want to say but knows he can't just dodge the question. "Motorvator parts," he lies. That seems to satisfy his father.

The two of them stare at each other for a while. An uncomfortable silence. It wasn't always this way, but lately a gulf has grown between them. Cael knows when it happened, but he doesn't want to shine a light on that dark space.

Finally, he says, "That stuff. What is it? It smells . . ." He wants to say, "Like someone ate a bunch of funeral flowers and crapped them all over the driveway." Instead, he goes with "Strong."

"Lavender. Well, lavender oil. Natural herbicide. Doesn't kill the weed so much as inhibit its growth. Or that's what it's supposed to do anyway. The fight against the weed continues, and we must remain ever vigilant." He shakes a fist and offers a wink.

Pop calls corn "the weed."

Part of Cael wants to rail against his father, tell him that "the weed" is how most people in this town make a living. Who is Pop to think he's better than them for not accepting the corn when they don't have a choice in the matter? It's what the Empyrean demands. Heartlanders grow corn so it can be made into fuel, plastic, food additives, and drugs. They're not even allowed to keep any for themselves or to eat it. Well, not that you'd want to—Hiram's Golden Prolific has about as much nutritional content as a palmful of the driveway gravel underneath their feet. Plus, it's all so goofed up with chemicals and twisted DNA, it's not even safe to eat.

Then again, what food is? You might end up like Carrie Marshall's baby. Or Pop with his hip. Or . . . Cael's mind drifts to his mother, but he can't think about her now. Later, later, always later.

Or worst, you could end up with the Blight. You get that, nobody will talk to you. They'll run you out of town on a rail. Maybe even bash you over the head with a shovel and plant your ass in a pocket of dirt somewhere, see if you'll grow.

Pop's eyes narrow. "Cael. Where's the cat-maran?"

Cael stalls, kicks a few stones. "Uhh. Took her to Lane's. Got a crack in the hull. He's got some mender's paste. We put *Betty* up on blocks in his barn."

"You should have said something. We have a whole tin of mender's paste here in the barn."

"Yeah. Well." Cael changes the subject: "Shouldn't you be at work?"

Pop works at the local processing facility. Once a teacher of children, now just another cog in the Empyrean machine. Mayor Barnes gave him that job like he gives out all the jobs. The Barnes clan has had it in for the McAvoys for a long time now.

"Got back an hour ago. Will be heading back there soon."

Cael nods.

Pop sucks air through his teeth.

Another yawning silence. Another uncomfortable void.

Pop holds up the rat. "I'm going to go skin this and

start on dinner. We got a new box of provisions in from up above—even ended up with a couple of knobby apples and a bundle of worm-eaten collards. Can you head out and milk Nancy?"

"No." Cael says the word and realizes too late that it comes out harsh, like a hammer-blow. It's just that Cael doesn't want to waste any time. He hurries to say, "I need to get to the Mercado, after I visit with Mom. Can I get Mer to milk the goat?"

Pop's smile is sad and strained, but it's there just the same. "Sure, Cael. Sure."

Her room is always kept dim. Curtains drawn so that only a glowing frame of daylight creeps in around the edges. The room smells heady. Verdant. Fungal, even. It doesn't make sense, really, given that his mother doesn't suffer from the Blight. Still, when Cael smells the air in her room, he can't help but think of Pop's old textbooks, of pictures of faraway jungles and rain forests.

The first thing he does in the room is listen for her breathing, because he fears that one day he'll come in and she won't be breathing at all. (And he hates himself for thinking that day will be a relief, in a way.) But he hears it: a slow, whistling wheeze as she inhales, then a small puff of air as she exhales.

She's just a dark shape on the bed. Never moving.

It's the tumors, in part. Her whole body is covered with them, and they lie against and atop one another like tar paper shingles on an uneven roof. They remind Cael of calves' livers. A heaping mess of them. They're heavy—a burden on skin, muscle, and bone. Because of them, her arms and legs and back have all atrophied. She cannot stand; she can't even sit up.

Maybe the tumors are also inside her body and her brain, or maybe the weight of the growths is more than skin-deep. Maybe it pulls on her mind above all else. Maybe there's not much mind left.

Cael can't think about that too long: On the one hand, he hopes her mind *is* ruined, because then maybe she's away from the prison that is her body. Trapped in a place of dreams or even nothing . . . that has to be better than here and now. On the other hand, this is his mother. He can't abide thinking about her not being *in there*. Somewhere.

She knows he's here, at least. That speaks something for her mind. He knows she knows, because when he sits, she makes a sound—it's like the way the wind whispers through the corn.

"Hey, Mom," he says.

His mother keens a raspy breath to greet him.

He goes about the ritual: He's gotten a short bucket of water from the well-pump outside, and he sets that by the bed. Then he opens the side table drawer and pulls out all the accoutrements. He dampens a hard, dark sponge that softens with water, and he dabs it against the layer of tumors that comprise her brow, washing the top and underside of each. She doesn't have much regular skin anymore; it's almost all taken over by the bulging bladder-like tumors.

When he's done there, he lifts the flaps from around her eyes and deposits a couple of wetting drops into her eyes. The eyes don't focus on him, not really; he's not even sure how good her vision is anymore, what with how the tumors keep her in the dark most times.

He wets her lips. Cleans her ears. Brushes back her hair. Her hair is the color and consistency of corn silk—thin and soft—and in this light an almost golden green. Her scalp is the one place the tumors never manifested. He doesn't know why. Nobody does.

Nobody really seems to know anything anymore. Maybe they never did.

Normally he'd talk to her. Light, polite conversation: *Heard a twister hit Guster's Grove couple days ago, piss-blizzard's coming, Lane and Rigo are good, got a portion of squealer meat a few weeks back, Pop's okay, so's Mer, got a shuck rat for dinner, everything's pretty fine, don't worry one lick about anything.*

He'd feel like a real monster telling her all the things that are really going on. All the things he's feeling. *Hey, Mom, I know you're trapped inside that thing you call a body, and while I got you here, maybe I could burden you with* my *problems? How's that sound?*

Today, though, he's got to hurry off. Got to get Mer to milk the goat and then head to market.

He kisses his mother on her brow, just where the tumors recede—he's not grossed out by them anymore, but he hopes she still has some sensation left beyond the cancerous margins.

Cael leaves the room. But then he hears a creak and a squeak—not from the hallway but coming from inside *his* room. Is Mer in there again? *Damnit, Mer.*

He turns heel-to-toe and marches straight into his room. He's about to start yelling at her to keep the King Hell out of his room—

A shadow runs fast toward him. A great darkness falls upon him; and before he knows what's happening, he can't see anything, and his hands are tangled. He can't see; he can't move.

Cael, whispers a female voice. *The Maize Witch has come for your soul.*

And then the darkness is gone again in a rippling flutter of fabric. Gwennie stands before him holding a blanket—his blanket, from his bed, which she clearly has just thrown over his head.

"Damnit!" he says, and feels the heat in his cheeks. *I'm such a damn donkey.*

Gwennie cracks up. When she finds something really funny, she snorts and doubles over, doing this little stompy shuffle with her feet. "I had you going there, didn't I? I mean, Maize Witch? Seriously?"

He folds his arms over his chest. Embarrassment bubbles up inside him. A wind blows into the room, and the edges of the blanket in her hand shift and squirm. The window sits open: Gwennie's entrance point.

It's then that he notices her hair. She has pale cheeks, a dusting of freckles across the bridge of her nose, hair like strawberry water. But her hair is done up—nothing pretentious or showy, not in an Empyrean way or anything, but braided and then wound in a circle, as though it were a wreath of laurels. Like the Lady wore when she was Obligated to the Lord in all the old stories.

"Stupid, isn't it?" She picks at her hair like she's looking for bugs in it.

He swats at her hand. "Quit. You're gonna mess it all up."

"Oh? You like it?"

"I might." Another blush rises to his cheeks.

"Captain, are you coming on to me?"

"I . . ."

"Do the others know?" she always asks.

"They do not."

"Good." She laughs then—this time no snort but a happy giggle that calls to mind porch chimes ringing in a slow breeze—and attacks him. Her mouth finds his and his hands find the small of her back, and they backpedal into the room doing the dance they've been doing for months now: a clumsy but earnest tango to which nobody else is privy. They tumble onto the bed, hands and fingers seeking.

"You messed your hair up," he says. His head is lying on her breast like it's a pillow.

"I didn't like it anyway."

"But that's the way you're supposed to wear it. For tomorrow."

"Tomorrow." The way she says it is laced with poison. "Hell with tomorrow."

"Maybe it'll all work out."

"Maybe it won't."

"Lane says we got about a ten percent chance."

Gwennie rubs her eyes. "That means there's a ninety percent chance it could go the other way."

"I didn't think about that." He didn't *want* to think about that. "What happens then? If that happens, I mean. Not that it's going to!"

"You know what happens. It is what it is. We're already taking a risk doing what we're doing. If my parents caught us . . . if the *Empyrean* caught us? We'd be run out of town on rails."

"Nobody knows."

"And nobody's going to."

She pulls away from him and sits up on the bed. He plants a hand on the small of her back, a pale expanse that calls to mind a puddle of milk. And then she stands, leaving his hand wanting.

But something tickles at his brain stem.

Milk. *Milk.* Goat's milk.

"Aw, *shit,*" he says, hopping up and then falling back as he trips over his own trousers. He races to get them up on both legs, kicking his feet up in the air like an upside-down weevil. "Gotta milk the goat. Gotta get to the market. Shit, shit, shit."

Gwennie pulls on her own trousers and shirt, and shrugs. "Go to it, Captain."

"Come with me," he says.

"Already late. They're wanting me to be there so they can fit the dress." What she means is, *I don't want to get caught.*

"I gotta go," he says.

"So do I. I'll see you tomorrow."

Tomorrow. And like that she's out the window. His gaze hangs there a little while longer. For some reason, his heart aches.

Mer's room looks like what he figures Guster's Grove looked like after the twister came through: Her clothes are on the floor, not in the drawer. Her bedsheets are off the cot. A knitted blanket is bundled in the corner. A couple of plastic-headed, fabric-bodied dolls lay arranged in a lascivious position atop the old swampwood dresser.

And there stands his sister, her dark hair tucked under a broad-brimmed farmer's hat. She's shoving clothes into a long canvas bag. Her window is open to the south roof of the house, a breeze blowing in.

"I heard you two" is the first thing she says, and a blush rises to Cael's cheeks. He crosses his arms and takes a step backward. That's Merelda. Good at disarming him. Him and anybody she's ever met. She doesn't even look over at him. Just keeps shoving stuff in that bag.

"You're running away again," he says.

She shrugs. "You weren't supposed to be home. *Pop* wasn't supposed to be home. I thought I had time to just . . . sneak out."

"So don't go."

"I have to."

"Shut the hell up. You do not."

She spins toward him. "I don't want to be Obligated. I don't want to be forced to marry someone I don't love."

"You have a whole year before you're Obligated, and another year after that until the ceremony makes it official. *I'm* the one who's on the hook this year."

"And are you happy about it?"

"No, of course not, I . . . I—"

"Then come with me."

He scowls. "And leave Pop? And Mom? I don't know if anybody told you this, but we have responsibilities here, girl. Work. Jobs. Ace notes to keep everybody alive. Pop would say—"

"I don't care what Pop says. He doesn't care about us anymore."

"That ain't true. And stop interrupting me."

"Besides," she says, setting down the bag and walking over to the old oaken rocking chair sitting in the corner of her room. "I have a plan to keep up my end." She snatches her old teddy bear: a one-eared, button-eyed bear named Mister Shushers, named not on account of the ear but rather because nobody ever seemed to have stitched him a mouth.

She's never taken the bear before. She loves that bear.

"Don't do this," he says.

"Got to."

"Damnit, Mer!"

She hops over to her brother, as light on her feet as a seed puff skipping across the dry earth, and she throws her arms around him. Mer always gives big hugs. Lung-crushers, unexpected for her sprite-like size.

He feels the warmth of her cheek against his.

Then she presses a small note into his hand. "A note. Saying bye to you guys. Give it to Pop. If he even cares."

"He cares—"

"Bye-bye, big brother."

"Don't be gone long, sis."

To this, she says nothing. Mer goes and grabs her bag, hoisting it over her shoulder. Starts to climb out the window. She waves one last time.

"Pop's not gonna be happy," he says.

"That's life in the Heartland."

And then she's gone.

• • •

Pop's outside by the garage at the stump—the remains of a tree struck by lightning when Cael was very young. Now it's a kind of butcher's block. Pop does a lot of cooking right there next to the stump, puts a kettle or a skillet over the fire pit only a few yards off.

By the time Cael walks up, the old man's just finished "shucking the shuck rat." The skin's off. Next to the grayish-pink carcass sits a little tray of blood, feet, and entrails. Some of that will go into tomorrow night's soup, and it's already expected that Cael will have Lane and Rigo come to share in that evening's meal.

Cael's about to hold up the note, tell Pop what his sister did *again*, when he sees that the two sacks he brought home are sitting on the ground. Empty.

And just past the stump is an old wooden tray of vegetables.

All of them cut up. Diced pepper. Chopped tomatoes. Green beans destemmed and broken in two. Cael feels the blood pound at his temples.

"Lord and Lady, Pop!" he cries out, hands balling into fists. "What did you do?"

Pop gives him a sideways glance. "Just cooking dinner, son."

"The rat, yeah! But those vegetables. I told you not to look in those sacks."

"What you *told* me was that the sacks contained motorvator parts. Which I found curious, what with the way the sacks were not clanking together. Decided I'd take a peek. Discovered that you lied to me and figured that you were just trying to surprise me by bringing home dinner."

Cael's mouth twists up. "That wasn't what you figured, and you damn well know it. You *stole* something from me. I was planning on taking that to the Mercado, to the maven—"

"And then what?" Pop wheels, the skinning knife in his hand. "Get a bundle of ace notes? Live high on the hog for a couple weeks? Maybe rub it in Boyland's face?" Cael tries to answer, but Pop doesn't let him. "Food like this isn't *legal*, son. And the maven is no friend to the McAvoys. She's in the mayor's corner, and you damn well know it. You walk in with a bounty like that, and it's like handing her a gun. A gun she'll point at your head and use to take you down, making sure that Boyland Barnes Jr. never has to contend with the likes of the Big Sky Scavengers again."

"Just the same, you had no right. *No right*. That was my choice to make."

The tip of the skinning knife punctuates each of his father's words. "And plainly you are not yet mature enough to make that kind of choice."

"You treat us like kids," Cael says.

"You and your little sister *are* kids."

"Yeah, well, maybe she feels like you should trust her more, too. And you don't. Maybe that's why she ran away again." And with that Cael flips the note toward his father. It flutters to the ground as Cael storms off.

He doesn't bother to see what his father thinks about it.

At the very edge of the horizon, Cael can see a faint golden hue intruding on the late-afternoon sky. It means one thing: the piss-blizzard is on its way. Maybe it'll come and swallow Obligation Day whole. Gobble it right up.

Cael is standing out back by the silo when Pop finds him. Staring up at the sky. Watching a pair of Empyrean flotillas way off in the distance pass by each other, silent and steady.

"She'll be back," Pop says, quiet. "She always comes back."

"What? That's it? She'll be back?"

"Way I figure it, yes."

Maybe the old man is right, Cael thinks. But he's not so sure. Mer and Pop have been fighting more and more. She stopped showing up at Molly Goggin's, where she works as a seamstress—a day like today could have earned her more than a few ace notes, what with the Obligation Day dresses needed.

On the one hand, Cael gets it. If he could run away, he

would. But the family has debts. And each member of each family is responsible for carrying that burden. Merelda runs away like that, she's no longer contributing. She doesn't want to end up marrying someone she doesn't love? Doesn't want to one day end up working in one of the processing facilities? Shit, *who does*? That's life in the Heartland. Wish in one cup, piss in the other, see which one fills up first.

Pop's brow tightens. The lines across it look like furrowed earth. "I suppose that means Mer didn't show up at Molly's again today." He holds up the note. Peers at it like he's trying to see something that isn't there. He pockets it. Adjusts his glasses. Nods as if he's come to some conclusion. "She's probably been gone since the morning. Surprised Molly didn't send someone over to let us know. But she'll be back. Like I said."

"Pop!" His father's sense of obliviousness when it comes to his sister is bordering on epic. For a moment, all Cael can do is make this stammering sound—"Eh? Whuh? Unh!"—because he can't even find the words. "You gotta be shitting me, Pop. Mer's gone. She ran away. *Again*. That means I gotta work harder. That means *you* gotta work harder. Never mind the fact she's not *allowed* to run away. You don't get to leave town without an Indulgence. I mean, godsdamn, Pop. Godsdamn!"

"Cael, watch your language—"

But Cael's not even looking at his father now. He's got his hands up in the air like a pair of startled crows, and he's pacing back and forth. "Oh, and let's not forget that *tomorrow* Proctor Agrasanto's going to show up here for Obligation Day. I'm sure she'll be totally fine with Merelda going off the reservation. Mer gets special exceptions from you, so why wouldn't she get one from her?"

"Cael. Calm down, son."

"Calm down. Calm down? *Calm down!* Mer's gone! We're on the hook for it now, and we'll be hanged even higher when the Empyrean catches wind of it. And you don't give a shuck rat's ass!"

"*Cael.*" It's the voice. The voice like a fist pounding down on a sheet of scrap. Cael freezes. The look on his father's face is one of confusion, as if he almost doesn't recognize his son. Finally, Pop asks, "Why are you so angry, son?"

Cael doesn't know what else to say except what he's thinking, so that's exactly what he says. "What I don't understand, Pop, is why you're *not* angry."

Pop looks stung. And before Cael really realizes what he's doing, he's moving in for the kill. "You're not angry about anything. Not angry when Mer goes against the family. Not angry about Mom lying in that bed every hour of every day. Not angry about how the Empyrean just keeps sticking it to us worse every year. Not angry about how Mayor Barnes makes life difficult for you or how his bucket-head son does the same for me. You let it roll right off you, like rain off a rat's back. You're content to let us just bend over the barrel and take what's coming."

With every accusation, Cael feels as if he's punching his father in the kidneys. It's not a nice thing he's doing, and it doesn't give him any satisfaction. But by the time it's done, it's too late. Pop sags a little, leans up against the stump.

"That's how you see me," Pop says. A statement, not a question.

Cael just shrugs. He can't take it anymore. He walks away and heads back into the house.

Later he'll try to find Pop, he thinks, maybe to apologize or at least shoot the breeze.

But when he looks, he can't find Pop anywhere. *Maybe the old man's gone back to work*, Cael thinks. *Maybe that's all it is.*

PART TWO
THE HARVEST

The thresher with his flail,
The shepherd with his crook,
The milkmaid with his pail,
The reaper with his hook—
To-night the dullest blooded clods
Are kings and queens, are demigods.

—*"Harvest-Home Song," John Davidson*

LANDMINE

IT'S ONLY BEEN a day since they wrecked the boat and found the garden—and Cael's itchy to get back there before anyone else finds it. Only upside to today being Harvest Home is that *nobody* else is out there. Everybody's here to eat, drink, watch the youngins get Obligated, and then finish the night with a Lottery that none of them will likely win.

Cael walks to the festival with his father and several other families who live down the old Creamery Road. John Redskirt and his wife, Lula Belle. Ed and Sigma Tyrus with their baby, Nicolaus, whose left eye is already given over to a milky cataract. Burt and Bessie Greene, smiling as if this is the first day of a brand-new earth, bless the Lord and the Lady and all their works.

They share stories as they walk. All Ed and Sigma want to talk about is the "hobo problem." She keeps hearing reports of vagrants and vagabonds rising up in the Heartland. He says they're probably joining up with the Sleeping Dog raiders—after all, wasn't the town of White Truck hit just a few months ago by the Sleeping Dogs? She says hobos are like cockroaches and shuck rats: once you find one, you'll find a dozen more living in the corn, eating your life's work. He says if left long enough, hobos will resort to killing folks and just eating them right up.

And that, Ed claims, is where the Blight comes from. "Proven fact," he says as though saying this makes it so.

John, who sometimes works as a mechanic down at Poltroon's, says that Proctor Agrasanto's skiff has already landed at the pad south of town. And Burt and Bessie just want to talk about all the festival food they're going to eat. ("We've been saving up our ace notes!") But they can barely get a word in edgewise around the other two talking about the hobo menace.

Cael isn't saying much. Neither is his father. A polite word here. A barely listening "uh-huh" there. They perk up, though, when Burt sneaks over and says, "Hey, where's Merelda?"

"She's ill," Pop lies.

"Snuck off again, did she?" Burt asks quiet-like. He pats Pop's shoulder, and that's the end of that conversation.

By the time they get to town, the festival's in full swing. Everybody's happy to have a day off mandated by the Empyrean, a day when they can gather on Main Street and hawk their handmade wares and drink gallons of chicha and fixy (sometimes together in a single glass, in what the old hands call a "land mine"). Smells of sweat and popcorn and tamales mingle together and crawl their way up Cael's nose. From somewhere down the street comes the drunken twang of a pair of guitars. The sun's a bright white eye in the sky, periodically diffused through a blowing curtain of fresh pollen.

The piss-blizzard isn't here—not yet—but it's damn well on its way.

Cael should be happy. Hell, he should be hungry. But he's not. All he has is that sour feeling nesting between his heart and his stomach and a vinegar taste in his mouth. Because it's not just any Harvest Home.

Everyone gets Obligated in the Heartland at age seventeen. That's just how it is. A young bride and a young groom, matched together. One year to learn about each other, to prove their loyalty to each other, even though they don't have the steel rings on their fingers that mark them as married. Till death takes one or the other. Empyrean claims it's a "family values" thing. Lane, though, says it's just one more way they lock down the Heartlanders. Just another pair of shackles.

Whatever the reason, today's Cael's day.

And he wants to throw up.

"You good?" Pop asks.

"Aces," Cael lies.

"I'm going to go take a walk around." Pop sounds . . . not sad, exactly. A bit lost, though. At most Harvest Homes he'd set up a book-cart and sell books. But this year the Empyrean decided that wasn't "in the spirit" of the day and denied him the privilege.

Pop musses Cael's hair and wanders off, leaving Cael to ponder his own fate. If he doesn't find the others in his crew right away, he thinks he might go crazier than a shit house owl.

As Cael wanders through the crowds, a hard elbow connects with his ribs. He jumps. Gwennie sidles up next to him and winks. She hands him a small bowl.

"Chicha beer," she says. He takes a smell of it: The odor neatly matches the sour feeling in his middle, and he has to concentrate hard not to throw up in his mouth. "Doc's special brew. He's selling it from his counter, which doesn't make Busser happy. They're in a little tiff, those two." She eyes him up. "You don't look so hot."

"Nah," he says, and musters a grim smile. "I'm fine."

"You've got the pallor of a grave rock."

"Allergies. Piss-blizzard's coming in, don'tcha know."

"Uh-huh." Gwennie raises an eyebrow. "Heard your sister took off again."

He shoots her a look and hisses: "Shhh."

"Oh. Right. You better hope nobody finds out. They find out—"

"They'll dock our provisions. I know."

"Bingo." Gwennie sips from the bowl. *Slurrrrrup*. Then she shakes and shudders. The first sip of chicha always sends chills skittering up your spine and out from your shoulders.

"So how'd you con a bowl of corn beer?"

"My usual charm."

"Meaning you stole it."

"I totally stole it!" Her eyes light up. Cael didn't think she was the type to get all giddy about narrowly dodging trouble—she's usually the sensible one in the crew. "First I bought a bowl of jellied pig's feet. Then while Doc Leonard was ranting and raving and trash-talking Busser, I did this kind of behind-the-back move and let Artie Mecklin's funky mutt steal those squealer-steppers out of the bowl. Then I quick snatched somebody's cup of chicha off the counter and dumped it in my bowl. And here I am!"

"With moves like that, you should join up with the raiders."

"I know, right? I'll be the Raider Queen of the Sleeping Dogs before the year's out."

He tries to picture her as a raider. But he just can't do it. The way he hears it, the raiders are filthy vagrants: rags and burlap and dirty cheeks. Cups and bottles clanging at their sides. Corn knives or sickles in hand. Bindles full of dry meats over their shoulders with mean cur-dogs trailing behind. Hobos, really. Except, unlike most hobos, they work together.

Not that he's ever seen a raider—he's only heard stories.

Gwennie's too pretty for that. Today especially. Her hair has been rebraided and wound on top of her head. She is wearing a simple but form-fitting yellow dress with a powder-blue cornflower over her ear. It's not like her to dress like this. She's usually got oil on her hands or dirt on her cheeks. *Hell*, he thinks, *maybe she would make a good raider.*

"So," she says, "you're freaked out about today." As she says it, she waves to her father, Richard Shawcatch, standing across the street talking to John, who works at Poltroon's garage—Cael notes he hasn't seen Poltroon all night, a man who usually gets drunk early and slinks away late. Richard's oblivious to it, probably—he forever carries around that "Aw, shucks" vibe with him. Nearby, her mother, Maevey, tries wrangling Gwennie's little brother, Scooter, who's probably jacked up on some kind of syrup candy. Gwennie turns back to Cael. "You don't need to be freaked."

"Aren't you?"

"This is it, Cael. This is the deal we get. This day was always coming. We knew that."

"I need you." There. He said it. It's not everything he's thinking, but it cuts to the quick.

She laughs. Not an encouraging sound. "You don't need me. You want me."

"I do."

"And I want you, too. Maybe that'll pay off. Maybe if you want something hard enough—"

His turn to laugh. "What? It just falls in your lap?"

"Who knows?"

"I say, you want something, you have to take it."

"Well, you sure took me yesterday." She winks and darts in for a quick kiss on his cheek. He wants to scold her—*Did anyone see?*—but he liked it too much.

"Don't," he says, but he doesn't mean it.

"That's not what you said yesterday."

"That could be it, then. Last roll in the hay. Last kiss on the cheek."

She tenses. "Could be."

The voice of Gwennie's mother carries over the crowd, calling her name. That means it won't be long now. They get the Obligation out of the way early in order to move on to the celebration (or, for some Heartlanders, the mourning period).

"That's you," he says.

"That's me."

He wants to grab her by the shoulders and drag her out behind Busser's Tavern, where all the piles of junk and boxes of old bottles stand stacked up; and he wants to hold her there and kiss her like they're dying, like tomorrow is a dream and not a promise. But instead, all he can do is stand there with a fear-struck look on his face.

Gwennie squeezes his hand, and she's gone.

Lane's lit up like a string of bulbs. Drunk as a brain-diseased badger.

"Puts the *fester* in *festivities*," he says, bold and blurry and loud, as soon as he sees Cael. He grabs Cael's face and meets him nose-to-nose, forehead-to-forehead. "Drink with me, Captain."

He pats a barrel next to him not far from one of the popcorn stands. The *rat-a-tat-a-tat* of Hiram's Golden Prolific popping fills the air. The stuff isn't edible unless you turn it into popcorn. Cael's father says even then not to eat it. Says not to eat *anything* with the corn in it if you can help it.

Across the street, Cael spies his father talking to a votary—one of the Lord and Lady's preachers, stuffed tight into his black dress, big white beard lying over his chest. The votary plucks something red and round from his pocket—an apple—and takes a big bite before shoving it back in his dress so nobody sees.

Cael's about to say something to Lane, but then Lane almost falls off his own barrel before steadying himself. "Sit, I said. Sit."

"You're piss drunk," Cael says, still standing.

Lane squints while pulling a half-crumbled cigarette from his shirt pocket. He licks the end and then smashes it between his lips.

"I can't find a match. Lord and Lady can go diddle each other. Damnit." He spits the cigarette into the dirt, wasting it.

"You do know that today's your Obligation."

"I know it."

"And you don't care."

"Nothing to care about. They're going to match me up with someone I don't give two hog's tits about, and she probably wouldn't piss on me if I asked her to."

"Maybe you'll get matched up with Gwendolyn."

"For fuck's sake, McAvoy, don't start with that again." Lane staggers off the barrel and nearly face-plants. Cael has to steady him. "You know what? I'm tired of your mopey hullaballoo. Let us seek out our other cohort, Mr. Rodrigo Cozido. He's always good for a laugh."

Before Cael can answer, Lane leans forward and tumbles forth in an awkward, if determined, walk. He pushes his way through the crowd, and Cael follows after.

The crowd is thick. Elbows and knees. Fixy breath and clouds of gnats. The sun is getting hot now, and Cael can feel sweat beading up on his brow—sweat that already collects pollen in yellow blobs and droplets. Once in a while the wind will blow and cast a streamer of pollen down from the sky, like a string returning to earth without its kite.

It isn't long before Cael spots Rigo's round head and squat shoulders moving through the crowd toward one of Busser's fixy stands. Cael has to grab Lane's elbow and direct him that way.

"Oh, a glass of fixy. Good idea, Captain, *good idea*."

Rigo hovers not far from the bent back of one of the Poltroon sons, who stands idly staring down at a motorvator part and talking business with John Redskirt.

"Rigo!" Cael calls.

Rigo looks over.

Two things happen almost at once. First, Cael sees the knobby knot just below Rigo's hairline. A bruise hides beneath the skin, not yet fully formed but red enough that it'll soon darken to the color of old meat. Second, Rigo's father, Jorge Cozido, steps out in front of Rigo, waving a brown bottle.

"Get out of here," he says to Cael, spit-froth flecking at his lips. "This is a family day." He reaches into the crowd and pulls the arm of a small, cowed woman with darting eyes hiding beneath a dark brow. Rigo's rarely seen mother, Cristiane.

"*Hey*. Rigo can come out and play," Lane mumbles, staggering into the mix.

"You're drunk," Jorge says.

"*You're* drunk," Lane retorts.

Cael thinks that if he found a match and struck it, the fumes coming off the two of them could blow the lot of them ten feet up in the air. Already, an explosion isn't entirely out of the question: Lane's stepping forward and so's Jorge, both drunk enough to take a swing.

It's the mayor who saves them.

The voice of Mayor Barnes—loud, jowly, lightly slurred, and amplified by an old microphone—suddenly calls out over Main Street: "If the lovely young Harvest Home candidates could double-time it to the stage, we would like to begin the"—he poorly stifles a chuckle—"obligatory Obligations. Come on, lads and lasses. Chop-chop."

Suddenly, everything seems hyperreal. The hairs on Cael's neck and arms stand up. His palms are cold and damp. "That's us," Cael says, pulling Lane back from the brink.

Lane acquiesces. Only barely. Jorge grumbles and grabs his wife and drags her back to Busser's counter. Cael meets Rigo's stare and mouths the words, *You okay?*

Rigo gives them a thumbs-up. He means it. This isn't new for him. This is his life.

Not that it makes it any better. You're with who you're with.

That's life in the Heartland.

TAKE THE STAGE

MAYOR BARNES COMES back on the mic and starts with some half-poetic horseshit about Harvest Home. He's saying something about how farmers once harvested the corn by hand and not by motorvator, and how this day is just like that, and how all the "beautiful young girls" and "handsome gentlemen" are like mature plants whose "fruits must be reaped." Even as he's saying this, Cael's not thinking about reaping corn but about the hand of Death sweeping down with a sickle so big it blocks out the sun. Here it comes, chopping off legs right at the knees. As Barnes (a man who's stuck his mayorly bits in Lord knows how many ladies) is going on about how an Obligated marriage is the bedrock of the Heartland, Cael and Lane are already moving toward the stage.

Cael sees his father out there. Pop offers a small nod. Cael doesn't return it.

Lane laughs and jogs up onstage. Most of the other boys are there. Rajit Werner. Dilly Brim. Little Wyatt Sanderson.

And Boyland Barnes Jr., standing close to his father. The mayor's big like his boy, but these days most of his muscle has gone to fat—or as the saying goes, gone to seed.

Cael steps past Boyland. He's looking up in that sonofabitch's eyes, which is the wrong place to be looking. Before Cael realizes what's happened, Boyland's foot thrusts out and catches Cael, who falls to one knee—the whole stage bangs and shakes. The audience gasps. Everybody sees it.

Godsdamnit godsdamnit godsdamnit.

"Gotta watch yourself," Boyland says, helping Cael up. "You aren't more careful, one of these days you'll wreck your boat. Hey, by the way, how's your sister?"

Cael thinks about hitting him right here. Hauling back and breaking that fat nose.

But then, as though on cue, up on the stage walks Proctor Simone Agrasanto. Dark hair hanging in waves around her shoulders. The prim, sharp-angled suit in the Empyrean colors of ruby and gold. Emblazoned on her chest is the sigil of the Empyrean, a pegasus whose long, sharp wings hang back over the beast's haunches.

The way Proctor Agrasanto looks around at the boy candidates for Obligation is the way a Heartlander looks at a vagrant; it's as though they all give off a *smell* they have long gotten used to.

Other proctors might get up, give a speech like Barnes did. Maybe talk about the Empyrean's "commitment to the Heartland and its people." Not her. She just snaps her fingers and her attaché—a wiry, twitchy man not much older than the boys onstage (Cael wonders if those on the Empyrean flotillas must submit to Obligation)—hurries up and hands her a stack of paper certificates. The mic, clipped to the podium, is still on, so everyone hears when she says "Get the girls."

The attaché scurries off.

Cael's blood churns so loud he can hear it in his ears like a river and so fast he can feel the fluttering pulse in his neck. His mouth is dry. His hands are wet. His toes are curling in.

The other boys must feel the same way. They all shift nervously from foot to foot. Or fidget with their hands. Or quickly wipe the wrinkles out of their loose, button-down shirts.

Boyland, on the other hand, does nothing but stand stock-still, chest puffed out, chin thrust high, a smirk on his concrete drainage block of a head.

As for Lane, he looks like he's about to lose his lunch. He's gone green as a corn husk. He stares ahead with big bug-eyes, as though he's afraid of what he's going to see but won't dare look away.

"You good?" Cael whispers.

"*Fine*," Lane hisses.

The girls begin walking up on the stage one by one. They're all in their Obligation Day dresses, with their hair worn in the braided crown as the Lady once did when wooing the Lord.

First is Alia Polycn, a blond little slip of a girl. The proctor makes no ceremony of it. The audience goes dead quiet as Agrasanto hands the girl her paper. Alia's eyes rove quickly over the assembled lot; and Cael finds that, even though Alia's a nice enough girl and certainly pretty, he can't help but hope *not me*, *not me*, *not me*.

And it isn't him. She drifts over to Wyatt Sanderson, a small smile on her face, and the gathered festival-goers all clap. He looks relieved. A few *awws* come from the crowd.

Holding hands, the two leave the stage, ushered by the proctor's attaché.

Next up: Marissa Ruhlman. She's paired with Daffyd Kelly. Neither of them looks particularly happy about it. She's got a mouthful of dead teeth, the poor girl. He's got one arm that looks like a withered tree limb. They go off together, the unhappy couple. Uncertain applause follows them.

Then it's Hetta Busser, niece to the tavern man. She gets her certificate and her eyes light up and then fall to Rajit, who gets a smile on his face so broad Cael wonders if it'll cut his head in half. The two race to each other. They kiss. This is what they wanted.

The crowd loves it. Above the din, Busser hoots and hollers.

Francine Goggins. Her father is a factory worker. Her mother is Molly Goggins, the seamstress who employed Cael's sister. She's as plain as butter, this girl, a little broad in the hips and not a swipe of blush to her cheeks nor paint to her lips. With a trembling hand she takes her certificate (not seeing how Agrasanto scowls at her), and once more Cael wishes *no, no, no*. But then her eyes find his, and the voice inside gets louder: *no! no! NO!* But despite his wishes, here she comes.

She reaches for Lane.

Not me, Cael thinks. *Not me.*

Her pleasure is manifest. Lane's enough of a catch. No physical deformities. A good job. Lane, however, wears a mask of disdain and disgust. He sags like a tent with a broken pole. He doesn't even bother giving Cael a look before she and he hop off the stage. Then a tiny question in Cael's mind: *Who did Lane want to be with?*

He doesn't have time to think on it. Because:

Here comes Gwendolyn Shawcatch.

Cael's pretty sure he's not breathing.

Please.

Agrasanto hands her the certificate. Gwennie takes it. Turns it over.

Please, by the Lord and Lady's grace, please.

She looks to him. His heart leaps. She smiles. He takes a deep breath.

And then she crosses the stage and stands before Boyland Barnes Jr.

That smile, it was a sad smile. A *consolation prize* smile. An "at least we had what we had" smile.

And it kills him. It slices a rift in his sail so the wind passes through. He feels like he did when *Betty* crashed just a day before: the world gone end over end, his lungs unable to find air to breathe, a loud ringing in his ears.

He can't look as they leave the stage. Hand in hand. The mayor with two fat fingers in his mouth, trilling like a factory whistle.

Gwennie and Boyland.

Obligated to be married in one year's time.

Cael's so dazed, so dizzy, he doesn't even realize what happens next. Before he knows it, a shape comes out of his peripheral vision and tackles him with a smothering hug. He feels the dry kisses of Wanda Mecklin on his cheek and her gangly arms around him. Wanda's giggling and crying and stroking his hair, but all he can do is move her aside and look once more for Gwennie. He catches a glimpse of her ducking between townsfolk. He finds her by looking for Boyland. Her future husband.

ALL WET

IT'S NOT THAT Wanda isn't attractive. To someone, she probably is. And Lord and Lady both know that she's a damn nice girl.

But Cael just can't hack her. Something about her rubs him the wrong way. Maybe it's the way that all her parts don't seem to match: Her nose is a little too small, her ears a little too big, her hair a little too sandy. Long arms, long legs, chest as flat as a barn door. The teeth are white and small. And he can see her gums. Makes him think of an old nag chewing on a bundle of hay or an old man gumming a pebble.

The fact that she's nice doesn't help, because she's *too* nice. She doesn't seem to have a single mean bone in her

body. Wanda Mecklin's entire existence is geared toward making other people like her, and in a thick dose of irony, that's the one thing that keeps everybody from liking her. She doesn't just want it. She *needs* it.

And the way she *talks*: nonstop, an endless, rattling prattle as she trails after Cael drifting listlessly through the festival-goers. "So nervous for today, but I knew the Lord and Lady would look after me. Momma and Poppa always *said* the Lord and the Lady knew my heart and that Old Scratch wouldn't win this day, no sir, and sure enough it was truer than true. Cael McAvoy! I am a lucky girl, a lucky girl indeed, Obligated to the captain of the Big Sky Scavengers—who, if you ask me, hasn't a thing on Boyland's Butchers, and I have full confidence you'll one day be the top crew in town, not that you can stay a scavenger forever; eventually you'll have to get a proper job of course—"

On and on. Yammer jabber gibber. It just becomes noise to Cael. He pulls her along by her hand, not because he wants her with him but because she won't let go. They move past the fixy counter and the two competing chicha beer stands. He moves through a cloud of steam and smoke coughed up by the fry-bread griddles. Hands clap him on the shoulders, and voices offer the two of them congratulations.

Eventually it happens: Lane appears out of nowhere. Alone, with Francine Goggins nowhere to be found. Lane grabs Cael by the collar of his shirt.

"Wanda," Lane says, "if you'll excuse us for just one hot second?"

He drags Cael in an awkward waltz toward the game booths. Colorful wheels are ticking, balls are being thrown at old metal milk bottles, wooden shuck rats are tottering this way and that as Heartlanders take shots at them with oversized rubber band guns.

"Don't you even dare complain," Cael says.

"I have every right to complain."

"Francine is a very nice girl—a little homely, but I bet she cleans up nice—"

"I don't like—" Lane blurts, then pauses, takes a deep breath. "I don't like her."

Cael growls. "Did you even *see* who Gwennie ended up with?"

Lane blinks.

"You didn't, did you? She ended up with Boyland, Lane. *Boyland.*"

"Jeezum Crow. Him?"

"Him."

"*Him?*"

"Him!"

"See? This is what I'm talking about, Cael. The Empyrean, they lock us all down, man. Close up our schools. Make sure the only money we have is a currency they invented just for us. Force us to marry like it's some kind of . . . enforced breeding program. You know what we need to do? Do you?"

"Don't say it."

"We need to join the raiders."

This again.

"The raiders. The violent criminals who rob and pillage Heartland towns."

"Yes. The raiders are heroes. They're not striking at the Heartland. They're striking at the *Empyrean*. We can run away. Tonight. While the festival's on and the proctor's mind is elsewhere. Shit, look over there—Pally Varrin is doing the damn *apple-dunk*."

"We're not running away; we've got responsibilities here. . . ." Cael's words drift off as his eyes search out the apple-dunk. Sure enough, there's Pally Varrin. Sitting on a platform with a small, round, wooden bull's-eye to his left and a tank of rusty, dirty water beneath him. Nobody's lining up because nobody wants to piss off one of the Babysitters. Little good can come of that.

Cael steps in line. The booth barker is R.J. Biddle, a literal half man who's just an upper torso in a red-and-white striped shirt. He tilts back his black cowpoke hat and waves Cael closer.

"Cael McAvoy, as I live and breathe," R.J. says with a surprisingly booming voice for a body missing its legs and lower torso since birth. "You going to be the first?"

Pally sees Cael. He squints and scowls. Shakes his head. The message is clear: *Don't you dare, boy; don't you dare.*

But Cael is having the worst day of his life. He damn well dares, all right.

He fishes around in his pocket for the one ace note he's got floating around. He thought he might spend it on a churro, but this is better.

Biddle plops three rotten apples into a bowl. They're from the remaining few apple trees up in the black orchard, trees long twisted into an arthritic curl. The fruit off those trees turn worm-eaten and misshapen long before the apples hit the ground.

"There you go, son. Three apples."

Cael nods. "I'll only need one."

He knows the drill. The target doesn't move on a breeze; Cael will have to hit it *hard*. Last year Busser did the apple-dunk, and he reached out and swatted the apples away as if it were a game of handball. Nobody dunked him.

The apple is cold and squishy in Cael's hand. Even if it's mushy, though, it has a hard core. A worm crawls out and inches up his finger; he flicks the critter to the dust.

Pally continues giving him that look—teeth clenched so tight Cael wonders if they might crack and shatter to dust.

"Cael," Lane says, "I don't know if this is such a good idea."

"You want to get back at the Empyrean."

"Cael, c'mon. That's not what I meant."

"Grow a pair, Lane. Because this shit is happening."

Cael winds up and lets fly.

Pally leans out and tries to swat away the apple, just like Busser did. But the apple flies hard and fast—and Pally's clumsy swipe catches naught but pollen-dusted air.

The apple *thwacks* against the bull's-eye in a spray of rotten sauce.

Pally's plank seat disappears from beneath him, and he plunges into the filthy water. His head immediately resurfaces, his mouth gasping for air.

"You're dead, McAv—" But he speaks too soon and catches a mouthful of foul water. He gags and splashes. "*Ghlurghglag*."

Worth it, Cael thinks. If only for the temporary lift in spirits.

Night falls and the pollen falls with it. It blows in streamers and trails, whispering across the ground like wind-swept snakes. The festival is lit with colored bulbs that hum and snap, and the Heartlanders are drunk; a lot of them are catcalling and yipping like dogs and dancing to fiddle music up and down the street. Now that the Obligation is over, a lot of them are buzzing about the coming Heartland Lottery, which will be announced in a handful of hours when the town clock strikes the midnight bell.

And it's then that Wanda whispers in his ear, "You wanna go under the water tower?"

An Obligation Day tradition. The newly betrothed couples, all of them hornier than a Capote water ox with two dicks instead of one, go beneath the water tower to the east of town in order to get to know each other better.

Cael doesn't want to. But he's mad at Gwennie. And he's a little bit drunk from drinking with Lane. So before he even knows what he's saying, he agrees. "Yeah, let's go."

And he waves on Lane and Francine, too.

"No," Lane says, "I dunno about that. . . ."

But Francine smiles sweetly and pulls him along, and Lane goes with it.

They leave Main Street and all the light and noise and descend into the ring of darkness around town, corn pollen whispering against the hard earth.

And soon a massive shadow darker than the gloaming appears. The water tower rises before them, shifting shapes and silhouettes hiding within the cradle of its wooden legs. Every time the wind stirs, the tower groans and stutters, eliciting an excited gasp from those beneath it as though it could come tumbling down at any moment.

Francine leads Lane away. Wanda's hands find Cael's chest, and she holds her palms flat against him. "I don't know what to do," she says.

"I don't know either," he lies.

"Maybe we should talk. We could just stand here. For a while. And talk. We don't really know each other. I'd like to know you better. Wouldn't you like to know me better?"

There it is again, that sense of desperation coming off her. The fact is, he *doesn't* want to know her better. So instead, he just leans in and kisses her. He feels her teeth clack hard against his. Their noses smash together. Her tongue finds his, and it's like a dog licking a mess off the floor: wet and inelegant. Cael thinks, *Ugh, get off of me*; but he doesn't move and neither does she, and there they stand for a while, groping each other inexpertly while Cael tilts an ear and listens to the others do the same.

He's listening for something. Some*one*.

For one of Gwennie's telltale moans. Or sometimes she squeaks. Like a little mouse.

It isn't long before footsteps approach and he hears the

murmur of familiar voices. A new pair of shapes emerge—one smaller shape arm in arm with a much larger-bodied blockhead.

Cael pulls away from Wanda.

"Did I do something wrong?" she asks, following after him. But he's not listening. Not to her.

"*You*," he says, stepping in front of the shape that resolves into Boyland Barnes Jr.

"Yo, McAvoy," Barnes says. With a snort, he adds, "Wanda Mecklin, huh? Here at the water tower? You lucky dog."

"Sonofabitch—" Cael says, and he steps forward with the full intent to tear that bastard's head clean off his neck and shove it back up his ass. But Gwennie steps between them and catches the full force of Cael. She's strong. Always was. "Gwen, move!"

"Don't be an ass," she says.

"He sank our boat!"

"That's not what this is about."

Boyland plays dumb. "I didn't— What? What's he accusing me of? I'd never."

"Go to hell, Barnes! May Old Scratch steal your liar's tongue." Cael tries to spit on him but misses.

Gwennie grabs Cael and hauls him away from the water tower. She lowers her voice. "This is over. It has to be. You can't do this."

"Boyland," he says, the name like slug's ichor dripping from his lips. "*Boyland?*"

"Like I picked him?"

"And yet here you are with him. Under the water tower."

"And here *you* are with Wanda Mecklin. I could say the same thing about her." She mimics Cael's blustery incredulity. "*Wanda? Waaaanda?*"

"I was here looking for you!"

"Did you think your tongue would find me down her throat?"

"I was hoping you weren't here. And yet you are. With him."

Her voice drops to a hissing whisper. "You think I like this? He's a *skunk ape*, Cael. But he's my husband. Or will be. I figure the best thing I can do is keep my head down and take the ride."

"You've changed," he says. "You never would have gone along with it before. You always did what you wanted. Those days are over."

"Maybe they are." She hesitates. "Maybe they have to be."

"Yeah. I guess so." The words suddenly come out of him, a bubbling, bilious concoction that he wishes he could swallow, but it's too late: "You're no longer first mate of the crew. You're out."

"*What?*"

"You heard me. Go with him. I can't have a person on my boat married to the enemy."

"You're an asshole," she says.

"At least I'm not a slut." It quiets her like a slap—but, really, it's worse. Those words plunge deep like a knife. Did he even mean them? He stammers, "Gwennie, wait."

But she pulls away from him and storms back to Boyland.

"C'mon," Gwennie says, pulling Boyland underneath the water tower. On the way she pauses by Wanda and says, "Congratulations, Wanda. Good luck with that one."

And then their shapes merge with the shadows.

Wanda comes up, asks him, "What was that all about?"

But Cael doesn't even open his mouth, because he's afraid of what will come out.

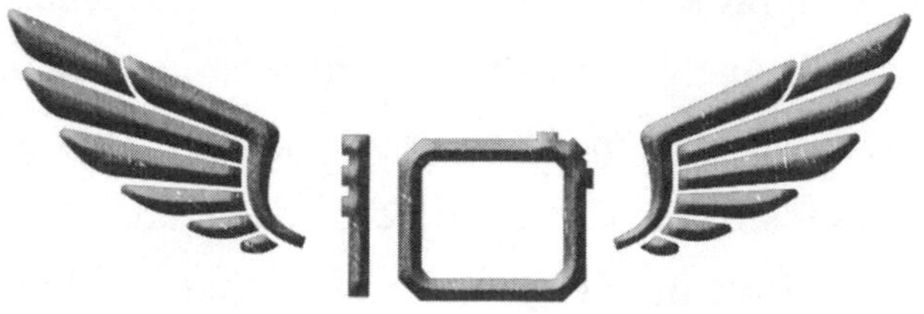

THE HOWLING POLLEN

MIDNIGHT IS WHEN they'll announce the Lottery. An hour before, the street starts growing tighter with people, gathering in the hopes that they'll be the winner. The pollen drift picks up and the winds start to howl, and all around are those allergic to the storm—blowing their noses into paisley handkerchiefs or rubbing their swollen red eyes. But they gather just the same because, above all else, they want to win.

The Lottery goes out across the Heartland. Once a year the Empyrean randomly selects a family, and that whole family ceases to be Heartlanders. Instead, they get a one-way trip to an Empyrean flotilla, to go live among the skyward elite. A reward, it's said, for their "mighty toil." Rumor has it that the

winners are highly sought-after guests to all the biggest parties. Lane says this just proves that the former Heartlanders are a hick circus act brought in to entertain the cackling harpies.

Cael stands there, lost in the crowd, looking toward the stage, a stage on which he stood earlier that day. He doesn't see his father, or Rigo, or Gwennie and Boyland. Wanda's gone now; he sent her away, off to be with her family. Like she should be. (Like *he* should be.) She was just standing there, behind him and to the right, queerly subservient and keenly afraid to speak lest she set him off. He hates that this was her first impression of him, but what can he do? "That's life in the Heartland!" he wants to scream in her ear.

Proctor Agrasanto, her attaché, and Mayor Barnes alternate between milling about the stage and hovering over a visidex computer. The glow from the single handheld screen bathes their faces in an eerie blue light. Cael feels a presence at his side, and there stands Lane. Looking grim.

"It's all bullshit," he says. His pinched eyes and hangdog face suggest the ghost of his fixy drunk still lingers. But he's got a fresh jar of the liquor pilfered from somewhere, and he passes it to Cael, who takes a sip. "I'll tell you, Cael. The Lottery. *Pfft*. It's how they keep us on the hook. How they keep us fish from flopping around."

"Uh-huh," Cael says. He's heard this speech before. Every year, actually.

"No, really. Everybody thinks, 'Ah, yeah, okay, I can be rich one day, and not rich like the mayor rich, not rich like the Tallyman. I mean flotilla-rich. *King Shit of Shit Mountain* rich.' We don't say boo against them because we think that one day we might *be* them. Right? That's what you think is gonna happen to you. To us. We're gonna get rich, and when we do, that's the key that unlocks our endless happiness here in this dead dog of a town."

"It's true. Ace notes make the world go round—"

"No—the Empyrean make the world go around. Being one of *them* is all that matters, and there's no way to ever be one of them. Not through money, not through the Lottery. The only way it gets better is if we tear it all to the ground. Like the Sleeping Dogs want."

"You're drunk." Cael takes another swig because he wants to be drunk, too.

"Ayup." Lane snorts. "Nobody from town will win anyway. Last year it was someone from . . . where?"

Cael thinks back. "Tremayne, I think."

"Yeah! Tremayne. Third time in ten years. I smell something fishy."

"You and fish," Cael starts to say, but just then a still-wet Pally Varrin comes up from behind Lane and shoves a finger in Cael's face.

"You little snot," he says. "You dunked me."

Cael tries not to laugh. Lane doesn't even seem to bother: he just brays like a mule.

Pally's not having any of it. He grabs a fistful of Cael's shirt and shakes him. "You laughing at me, boy? I notice your sister's gone. *Again*. How convenient that the proctor's here in town—guess I'll just have to tell her your sister's gone hobo again. They'll dock your provisions. Maybe more this time. Maybe they'll throw you in the hoosegow. Or drag you and your damn daddy away from Boxelder once and for—"

Suddenly, a man steps between them. Grey Franklin, once more. He plants big, broad hands against Cael's and Pally's chests, separates them like a wedge.

"Merelda's taken ill," Franklin says, giving Cael a look.

"Horseshit," Pally barks.

Gray shakes his head. "You're just mad 'cause someone sunk your butt. Now go on and get some dry clothes. The pollen'll stick to you like burrs on a dog's ass."

Pally sneers but slinks back into the crowd.

"Thanks," Cael says finally.

Gray shrugs. "I do what I can. But you better find that sister. They will cut your provisions. Or worse, if the proctor gets involved."

"I know."

Grey musses Cael's hair then heads off after Pally.

Lane shrugs. And laughs again. Carefree. Or just careless.

Suddenly, those gathering at Busser's beer stands and Doc Leonard's beer stands begin to sing competing verses of the "Harvest Song":

"Here's health unto our mighty Lord, the founder of the feast,
Here's health unto the Lady fair, the tamer of the beast.
And may heaven's doings prosper, whate'er takes in hand,
For we are Heartland servants, ever at command.
Drink, boys, drink!
And see ye do not spill.
For if ye do, ye shall drink two!
The Lord and Lady's will.
Now harvest it is ended, and supper it is past.
To the health of Lord and Lady, boys, a full and flowing glass,
The heavens rain upon us all and grant us all good cheer.
Here's to the Lord and Lady, boys, so drink off all your beer.
Drink, boys, drink!
And see ye do not spill.
For if ye do, ye shall drink two!
The Lord and Lady's will."

It's hard for the mayor to be heard over the raucous, drunken chorus, but he eventually thwacks the mic with his open hand and sends a feedback shriek over the whole crowd, quieting the song.

It's still an hour early. Why is he talking? And where'd the proctor go? Cael suddenly doesn't see her or her attaché anywhere.

"The Lottery is being postponed," the mayor says. A chorus of boos and hisses rises up to meet him, and he has to raise his voice so he can be heard. "The piss-blizz—ah, the pollen drift is too bad, and it's not just here; it's across half the damn Heartland! The proctors have to—"

More boos. And hisses. And stomping of feet.

"I *said*, the proctors have to head back to the flotillas before they get grounded here for a couple days—" Clearly the proctors wouldn't get caught dead tooling around the Heartland for longer than a day.

Someone throws a glass toward the stage, and it shatters.

By now Barnes is holding up a folder to protect himself from both the pollen and the threat of getting hit by something. "They'll draw the Lottery in one week! They'll announce it over the Marconi! One week! Now go home! *Go home!*"

Mayor Barnes ducks and darts toward the back of the stage and, like that, he's gone—and, just then, the pollen kicks up *hard*. For a moment it's tough to see more than a few feet. It stings the eyes. A tickle itches inside Cael's nose—like a spider crawling there.

Then the wind dies back and the curtain parts anew, and a great cloud of grief-struck incredulity washes over everyone. In one long minute the crowd's anger has deflated into a kind of collective depression.

The crowd breaks apart like a clod of dry earth as the Heartlanders disperse. Lane just shakes his head and mutters, "Suckers."

But Cael's anger hasn't deflated. "Now what?" he asks.

Lane shrugs. "Guess we go home."

Cael takes another pull off the fixy, hands it to Lane. "I say we make our own damn Lottery."

Lane gives him a look.

"Let's go get those vegetables."

"Tonight?"

"Yes! Tonight. Lane, here's our shot. Nobody's going to be paying attention to what we're doing. Hell, nobody can see their hands in front of their fool faces. This piss-blizzard isn't a problem. It's a damn *opportunity*."

"It's a crazy, godsdamn idea is what it is," Lane says. "You should not be allowed to drink, Cael McAvoy."

Cael grabs him by the wrists. "I'm going out there tonight. I'll walk if I have to."

"Cael, if this is about Boyland and Gwennie—"

"Hell with them! This is about us. This is about taking what's *ours*, Lane." Cael snatches back the fixy, takes another pull until it's gone. "Besides, once she sees what we've done and how we're rolling in ace notes, she won't be so quick to cotton up to the mayor's son."

"She's Obligated, Cael."

"Fuck the Obligation! I'm going. Either you're coming or, or . . ." Cael thrusts out his chin. "Or you're not on the crew anymore."

"You can't do that!"

"I'm the captain; I can do whatever I please."

Lane narrows his eyes. Licks his lips. "Fine. *Fine*. Let's get Rigo and do this."

"I ain't ready to leave yet, godsdamnit!"

They're at the top of town, near to the spot where Gwennie offered Cael a taste of chicha beer earlier that day. Folks are starting to leave, a herd-like movement urged on by the fear of getting caught in the throes of a full-bore piss-blizzard.

"*I still need another drink.* I said, I still need another— *What*? What are you looking at?"

They recognize that perpetually slurring, ever-growling voice. Cael grabs Lane by the belt loop and drags him toward the voice as another whipping gale rises, sending forth a whorl of golden pollen.

There, out behind one of the fixy stands, away from the crowds, is Jorge Cozido. His son trembles before him. Rigo's got a paisley handkerchief held up against his head because the more he breathes in the pollen, the worse off he'll be. He won't die. But he'll bloat up like a chigger-worm fat from feeding.

"Got your little mask on, do you?" Jorge bellows, hoarse and boozy.

"I need it!" Rigo cries. "My allergies."

"Your damn allergies. C'mere." The man makes a grab for Rigo's face and swipes the handkerchief away—just in time for Rigo to catch a face full of stinging pollen. He sneezes, coughs, sneezes again.

All the while, Rigo's mother stands behind his father. Hands folded tight under her armpits. Looking like a scared little mouse. Cael can't stand her. She's weak. She's doesn't have the grit and the stone needed to be a proper Heartlander. Then again, maybe she had it once. Maybe that husband of hers—a husband she didn't choose—beat it out of her long ago.

Rigo tries to reclaim his handkerchief when his father pretends to hand it back, but then Jorge yanks it away as soon as Rigo jumps for it. "You little pussy. Like your damn mother, pussy. I don't care about your allergies; I want another *drink*—"

Rigo reaches again for the handkerchief, but Jorge shoves him.

Then Jorge rears back with a fist. Rigo cringes, anticipating the blow.

But before it comes, a ball bearing *thwacks* hard into the back of Jorge's hand, and his arm recoils like a snake hit by a stick. Ammo from Cael's slingshot rarely flies false, not as long as he's the one doing the shooting. This time he didn't pull the pocket all the way back—if he had, Jorge's hand would be hanging limp by his side with all its delicate bones broken.

"You sonofabitch!" Jorge wails. He tries to step forward and come after them, but all he does is fall to his knees, cradling his hand. Blubbering like a drunken old fool.

Lane waves Rigo over. "Rigo. Rigo!"

Rigo looks to his father, looks to his mother. She turns away.

He hurries over to his friends. Cael gives him his own handkerchief, and they rush to join the exodus of the crowd. They all pray to the Lord and Lady that come morning, Jorge will have blacked out—again—and forgotten how he hurt his paw. Small prayers never hurt. Though Cael wonders if they ever help.

• • •

The handkerchief is soaked through and shellacked with snot. Rigo's eyes bulge with white froth pooling at the corners—it looks as though they might pop like corks any minute now.

They hurry along in the crowd of Heartlanders heading north out of town. The crowd thins as folks turn off toward their roads, toward their farms. All the while the wind blows harder, and with it the blinding sheets of pollen. By morning the piss-blizzard will have paralyzed the town. Gumming up motorvators. Dirtying windows with golden grease. Nobody will earn ace notes tomorrow. Nobody.

Cael isn't thinking about that, though. All he's thinking about is Gwennie. And Boyland. And those vegetables.

Cael pulls his two friends close.

"I'm going after the garden," he says.

"Jeezum Crow," Rigo says. "Cael, I can't—I can't do that. I don't feel good."

"My sister ran off again," Cael says. "Did you know that? She just packed a bag and hightailed it out the window. She's off living the high life somewhere, and we're stuck here. Well, I'm tired of being the responsible one. Tired of sucking hind tit and liking it. I want those vegetables. Lane's in—"

Rigo shakes his head. "You won't make it. The storm's getting—" He rears back and sneezes so hard he almost concusses himself against Cael's forehead. Cael barely manages to dodge the inadvertent head-butt. "*Worse*. And we don't have a boat!"

"We'll hoof it," Cael says. "Like we did earlier. We'll track the beacon and—"

"In this mess?" Rigo asks.

Cael looks up. "Now, hold on a minute. I have an idea." Cael points, and through the pollen they see the offshoot of Orchard Road.

"No," Lane says. "No, no, no. That's cruel. You're not that cruel."

"They have a boat."

"That's *cruel*."

"I don't want to be mean. But I have to do this."

"Fine, we're coming with you," Rigo says. *Fide, we're gumming wid you.*

"Shit," Lane says. "Fine. *Fine*."

The Orchard Road stands before them. And Cael heads toward it.

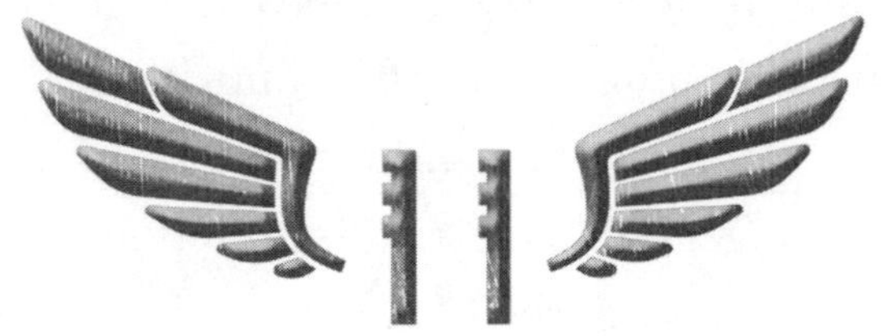

THE BLACK ORCHARD

THE NIGHT GLOWS golden. It would be pretty if the pollen wasn't stinging their eyes so bad. The wind snarls and keens through the corn, casting streamers of pollen into their eyes and mouths. They can't see ten feet in front of them: It's all just a yellow haze, the air suffused in a dandelion wash.

It turns out that Rigo *could* get worse. His skin, normally the color of an over-milked coffee at Doc Leonard's diner counter, is now beet red. His face is so swollen it looks like a fat cherry. Even Cael is feeling the effects: The edges of his eyes are starting to crust over, and his sniffles have kicked into high gear.

Cael starts to feel dizzy. A tiny ember of fear burns inside him, becoming a match flame, then a campfire. Everything out here is corn and asphalt, and it's all behind an eye-blistering curtain of too-bright pollen. With the wind yowling like a chorus of lonely cats, they can barely even hear one another. Cael knows where they are, but it still feels as if his bearings are lost, as if they could be anywhere in the Heartland.

As they stagger forward, Cael sees something.

A ramshackle lean-to. Cael knows it well. It's the Burkholders' old farm stand. Cael remembers it from when he was a kid, from when you could buy things like red peppers, green beans, and heads of cabbage from other local farmers. Those days are gone. So too are the Burkholders. Otto was the first to go, with a skin cancer on his back that reportedly looked like a blackened biscuit. Then, only a few weeks later, they found the Burkholder boy, Peter, down in the well like a gopher. Hard to believe that he fell in; most say he took his own life. Missy, the mother, well . . . they found her a year after, sitting in a rocking chair, still rocking, dead as a doornail. Nobody can say for sure how it happened, but they all *know*. Heartbreak is a powerful thing in the Heartland, sharp as a corn sickle, mean as a twister.

Still, the Burkholders knew how to build things. The

farm stand holds mostly together, even with the climbing stalks of corn slowly trying to mash it into the earth. It's there they stop for a while. Mostly just to clean up Rigo a little.

"This is still a bad idea," Lane says. Outside, the piss-blizzard rages.

"It's the only idea," Cael says.

"Fine, then it's just plain *mean*."

"It's not mean!" Cael says. "It is what it is. They'll say yes because they're nice people. And it's our only shot."

"I'm drowning in my own phlegm," Rigo says.

He's not. They ignore him.

"Then what?" Lane asks. "What will you do once you get to the vegetables?"

"I . . ." Cael can't find the words. "We'll sell them. Not to the maven, though—you can be sure she's tucked tight in the mayor's pocket. We can sell direct to the townsfolk. On the down-low. Now, let's go get ourselves a boat."

"You mean, let's go get *Wanda's* boat."

Cael doesn't say anything.

"This is insane. You know that?"

"It'll be fine," he says, unconvinced.

"My face feels like a hot pumpkin," Rigo says.

"Heck-a-damn, shut up, Rigo," Lane grumbles. "Let's get on with it, then."

• • •

All around the house stand the shadows of dead trees just visible behind the wisps and whorls of pollen. Each is like a darkened hand stripped of flesh, the finger bones reaching upward for something they'll never grasp.

The Mecklins used to make a living tending to the fruit trees—apples, pears, peaches—with the other orchard families, but then the Empyrean decided that the only crop worth growing was corn. And so they sent some men down here with tanks of an oily fluid, dark and turbid like the runoff from a motorvator's busted radiator, and they hosed down all the trees. Within days the leaves dropped, the bark blackened, and all the fruit shriveled to hard peach-pit nubs. Only a few trees produce fruit now, and that fruit ends up getting thrown at the likes of Pally Varrin. Or it gets left for the bees.

Once the Empyrean made its proclamation, Artie and Janine Mecklin went to work with the corn like most everybody else. They don't let Wanda work, though. Wanda stays home and tends to the farm.

Now Cael, Rigo, and Lane stand on the porch of that farm. They're mostly protected from the pollen by the porch roof above their heads, but it's gusted in, made the porch slippery. Rigo almost goes ass up not once but twice.

Biting the inside of his cheek, Cael knocks on the door.

They hear a flurry of hoarse barks rise up inside. It must be the infamous Mecklin mutt, a dog whose existence betrays all common sense and biology, a dog who should have died years ago. What's his name? Cael can't remember, but it's something to do with fruit.

The door flings open and out trundles the dog, a midheight mix-breed with a sausage body and thin little matchstick legs. His one eye is a winking asterisk. (He tangled with a plasto-vator, one of the robots that lays the plasto-sheen on the roads.) His tail is a vibrating stump. (He got it caught in a door.) And one half of his body shows caved-in ribs. (He thought it would be fun to go toe-to-toe with a fell-deer buck with one good antler.) Everyone jokes that the dog is still alive only because he's too stupid to know any better.

He comes out, sputtering and wheezing, and instantly runs to Cael and begins to lick his hand.

Then he growls at Rigo and Lane.

"The dog hates us but likes you," Rigo says, stepping back. "It's almost like you're—"

"Shut it."

"Family."

"Wanda and I aren't—"

Wanda is suddenly in the doorway, face lit up like a

sparkler, and she's throwing her long arms around Cael's neck. For a moment he thinks, *How many elbows does this girl have?* Because it seems as if she's got an extra couple joints in those gangly grabbers.

"You came to make sure I got home okay," she says.

"Uh-huh" is all Cael can muster. It occurs to him suddenly: if she were just a year younger, she would make a great bride for Rodrigo.

"Come on, Hazelnut," Wanda says, grabbing the lumpy mutt by the collar to usher him inside. "Leave Cael and his friends alone. Shoo! Shoo, now, shoo."

The dog gurgles assent and waddles through the doorway.

It just gives Wanda more room to hug Cael.

"Hello, my husband-to-be," she says, and he almost wonders if she's going to cry.

"Uh. Hey."

"Hi, guys!" she chirps over Cael's shoulder.

Rigo, still as bloated as a boiled blood sausage, waves. Lane just stands there looking guilty.

"Hurry inside," she says. "Gosh, it's *so* nice of you to think of me and my family here during the storm."

She grabs his hands and pulls Cael inside.

Lane gives him a look. "Hear that, Cael? How *nice* we are?"

"Shut it," Cael hisses.

• • •

Dogs sometimes look like their owners, and Hazelnut shares a look with the Mecklin patriarch, Artie. Artie's got the same long, thin limbs, the same fat-barreled body. Minimal neck. Lots of head.

Big smile, too. Because he loves Cael. Couldn't be happier that his daughter is Obligated to Cael. (Cael thinks sourly that he's probably just happy Wanda's betrothed at all.)

Artie hugs Cael as hard as Wanda did, and as he's being hugged, Cael looks over Artie's shoulder to the the photos hanging on the wall beneath the stairs. Most of the photos are crooked, but one of them isn't. It's a snapshot of Cael from just hours before, Wanda's arm around him. In the photo, Cael looks as if he's trying not to stand too close to a musky goat.

Artie beams. "Congratulations, my boy. Welcome to the family."

"Not yet," Cael says. "Uh, soon, though." *Not if I can help it.*

"Don't be silly. Obligated is Obligated. Family's family." The man sizes him up. "You came all this way. In a pollen drift."

"I did. We did. It's late, I know, and I'm sorry—"

"Late? It's early for us. You boys need some breakfast."

"What? No, I—"

Artie claps Cael on the shoulder. "Shush, now. We have—What do we have, Wanda?"

From behind Wanda comes a little girl's voice. "Mommy's got some day-old biscuits. And some shotgun gravy."

Rigo's eyes light up. "I love shotgun gravy."

"Rigo!" Cael whispers.

Wanda turns, and Cael sees it's her little sister, Zelda. She's got big hands, ears, and feet, but is skinny and small otherwise. Cael thinks she's eight, maybe nine years old.

Wanda shoos her. "Go on back to bed, little peach."

"Bye-bye," says the little girl. Then she totters upstairs.

Artie turns back to the boys. "Don't feel like you're imposing. You boys come in. Take a load off. Rodrigo, we can fix you some tea, get those histamines down."

"I don't know what that means," Rigo says, "but okay!"

Cael shoots him a look. But now they're in it, like boots stuck in mud.

Shotgun gravy. Cael's not sure why it earned the name. Maybe because it's such a mess, like something you'd blast with a shotgun. (Not that he's seen a shotgun—Empyrean law does not permit Heartlanders firearms.) It's like a gut-shot of everything but the kitchen sink: roast some bones, brown some old meat, make a flour roux with water, hope for the best. If Cael's nose is right, the meat today is . . . goat? Got that rich, gamy smell.

Rigo is salivating. So's the dog, who has his jowly, slobbery, one-eyed head lying on Cael's knee, a whiny noise like the sound of a bad motorvator fan belt coming from the back of the beast's throat.

Janine, who looks like an older facsimile of her daughter except with black hair done up in a ponytail, slides two platters in front of the boys. The biscuits look like clods of clay, but Cael is thankful to have them. The gravy softens them up a little, even if it does taste a hair past its prime. He about chokes on a wad of food, though, as Wanda's hand finds his thigh under the table.

Artie hands him a ragged cloth napkin. "You okay, son?"

Son. That word about makes him choke again; but he nods, swallows, and offers a strained smile. "Just fine. Sir." If this man thinks Cael's going to call him Daddy, he's baked his noodle.

"Is it Wanda?" The man winks. "She tickling you under the table?"

Rigo's eyes go as wide as moons, his cheeks bulging, midchew. Cael can only imagine what his own face reveals. Lane doesn't even bother hiding it: he snorts and almost chokes on his food.

Wanda giggles, too.

"What? Wait. No. No!" Cael cries. "It's fine. It's *fine*. It's not that. I'm just; it's—"

He's trying to find something to say, but his mouth is so dry. He could really use a glass of milk, but the Mecklins aren't lucky enough to have their own goat like Pop does. And then Artie laughs a big belly laugh, which makes it all the creepier.

"Son," Artie says, "Janine and I had Wanda when we were your age. It's okay to be . . . *sexually* expressive. This town could use a little romance. Ain't that right, Janine?"

Another giggle, this time from Wanda's mother. Cael's half expecting them to drag him up to Wanda's room and throw him down on her bed. *Have at 'er, boy.*

Artie leans across the table, clutching his chest as though he's having a perfectly happy heart attack. "Son, I *want* you two to be a little closer. That warms my soul."

Wanda's hand tightens on Cael's thigh. Moves northward. Cael can't contain himself.

"We want your boat!" he blurts. Voice too loud, too forceful. Everyone seems to retreat a few inches. Wanda's hand loosens, slides down to his knee.

"Our boat," Artie says. "Our *boat*? The pinnace? Why the heck would you need the pinnace?"

Cael knows that not everyone is fortunate enough to have

a hover-boat. They don't come cheap, and they're hard to maintain. A few folks have motorized carts and four-wheelers that need corn-diesel to run, but that's expensive, too.

The Mecklins have a pretty nice boat. It's not new, but a pinnace has two hover-rails beneath it. It moves faster than most, and the lean, pointed tip cuts through the wind and reduces resistance. It's a holdover from the days when the orchard was crazy productive, supercharged with high octane fertilizers and bug-juice. The days of Mecklin prosperity are long gone, but the boat remains.

Cael knows they're not going to lend him the boat. They'd be idiots to do that.

"What you need her for?" Artie asks again.

"Ah. Well." Cael's mouth is dry from the biscuit, and he can't think of a good lie. He can't tell the Mecklins he wants to harvest a secret garden in the hopes of striking it rich and changing his whole life. All before someone else, like that thick-skulled mayor's son, finds it.

Lane handles it. "Nancy the goat got out. Cael's family needs that goat, and with his father's hip . . . It's a tragedy to lose their one good animal. Delicious milk, that animal. I'm sure any family of Cael's could happily partake in said milk—"

"And the boat," Cael says, filling in the blanks, "ah, will

help us get a better vantage point above the corn. Let us move faster, too. Our boat got wrecked on a scavenge yesterday. We could use a boat in the interim until we get her fixed up and . . ." His voice trails off. This isn't going to go over well.

"That's awful," Artie says, clucking his tongue. It's clear to Cael, though, that this is a statement easily followed by the word *but*. As in *That's awful, but I can't just let you take our one and only land-boat, boy*. Except Artie says, "Heckadang, sure thing, Cael. *Doris* is all yours."

Cael blinks. "Wait. Seriously? Are you nuts?"

Rigo elbows him.

"I just mean—"

Artie cuts him off. "I know what you mean, son. But as of tonight you're the closest thing to family. We trust you to take good care of her. Of course we heard you busted up your cat-maran yesterday. It true you had that thing loaded for bear with some off-the-books hover-pads?"

How the hell did he hear that? Cael thinks.

But it's as if Wanda's father can read his mind, or at least his face, because he explains, "Boyland is going around telling everyone. Uh, Junior, not Senior. Not that I expect the mayor to be any kinder, of course."

Godsdamn Boyland.

Cael manages a strained smile. "It's true, we broke our boat. Now we need to find our goat." He's speaking the words of a children's rhyme.

"Then she's all yours."

These people, Cael thinks, *are too nice to live in the Heartland.*

"I want to go," Wanda blurts out. "I want to be on your crew."

Eyes turn to her. Is she serious?

"The piss-blizzard—erm, the pollen storm—is bad, real bad," Cael says.

"Horrible," Rigo adds, sipping a tea made from grape seed and butterbur. "Oh, uh, not the tea." Though by his puckered lips, Cael can tell that it is. "I mean, just look at my face."

Wanda shakes her head. "I don't care. I'm not allergic. I want to go. I want to be with my Obligated. Something happens to him, it needs to happen to me, too."

"Jeezum Crow," Artie says. "Janine, what do you think?"

Janine's got tears in her eyes. She takes her daughter's hands in hers. "I think that's the sweetest thing I ever did hear, Arthur."

"So it is. Wanda, you go ahead. Cael, I'll expect you to

take good care of her." He wags a fatherly finger, but his stern voice does nothing to hide his cheerful face.

Cael wishes Artie were talking about the boat, but he's not.

"Fine," Cael says, jaw tight. "That sounds . . . fine."

Wanda kisses him on the cheek. He tries not to wince. He winces anyway.

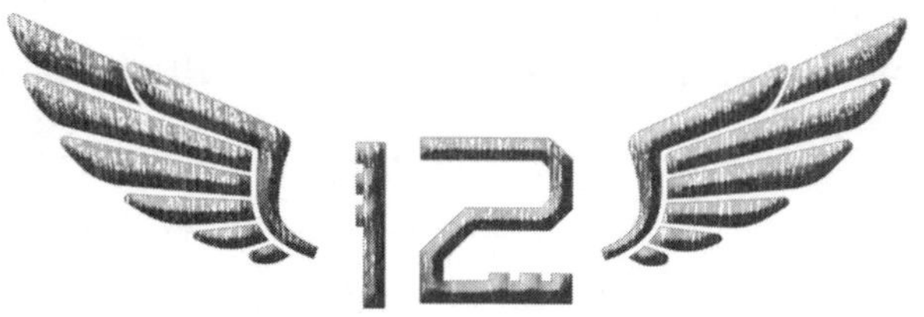

THE GARDEN TRAIL

AT A DISTANCE, the pinnace is a real beaut. Her shape calls to mind a lean fillet knife. Across the side is the boat's name painted up in fancy cursive: *Doris*. ("A goddess of the sea," Wanda yells over the wind and pollen.)

Up close, though, Cael starts to see some flaws. Dings and scratches. Hull scrapes. A splintering mast. He hopes they're just cosmetic.

Artie gets them set up with the boat—helps them unmoor it and power up the hover-rails—and off they go. But once they get her out in the storm, Cael starts to see that *Doris* has other problems. Real problems.

First up: the sail. It's got a big vertical slash down the middle. The wind just howls through the vent, the fabric

fluttering but failing to catch the air. Wanda, who's in one of her father's barn jackets, a blanket pulled up over her head like a hood, says she doesn't know how that happened. Says they use oar-poles to push the boat along.

Second problem: the hover-rails on the bottom are on the fritz. They're each like a lightbulb in a wobbly socket; they *buzz* and *sizzle*, flickering and sputtering. The boat can barely stay aloft. It keeps dipping sickeningly toward the ground, into the corn.

With the wind howling and the pollen raining down upon them, the boat only goes where the wind shoves it. The boat knocks around as if it's being struck by invisible hands, and everyone's sick and miserable and wants to go home. But Cael won't call it off. *Can't* call it off. The garden's out there. If they don't find it, someone else will. That's what he tells himself. Someone else will steal the vegetables, or the pollen from the piss-blizzard will ruin them. He invents a hundred other reasons why they need to get to the garden *tonight*, in the middle of the worst pollen drift Boxelder's seen in years.

But inside is that nagging voice, the one that tells him Gwennie never would have let this foolishness happen—she took risks sometimes, but she was always the brains of the operation, always the one with the *plan*, the one who never let Cael get away with his nonsense. Her job as first mate was to balance out Cael. And now that balance is gone, leaving him all kinds of off-kilter. *And don't forget that you're not gonna get to kiss her anymore, either.*

We don't need her, Cael thinks. *She held you back. That's why your crew was always second to Boyland's. Let her be first mate on his boat. Let her drag* him *down.*

Cael has the others fetch the oar-poles from the side of the boat, holding the poles and thrusting them down against the earth, the four of them walking the boat along and trying like hell to stop the wind from knocking them over into the corn.

"I miss *Betsy*!" Lane yells over the buffeting mistrals and seething, hissing pollen.

"We're lost," Rigo yells.

"We're not!" Cael says. It's a lie. Everything looks the same. Blowing pollen. Corn beneath them. Corn sky and horizon swallowed in dust. No roads. No farms. Even the boat's spotlight doesn't help. He's pretty sure they're going south? Now he's not so sure.

Suddenly Wanda hurries up behind him and tugs on his sleeve, talking right into his ear. "I'm so sorry again about the sails, sorry, sorry, so sorry—"

He waves her away.

"Wait, though, I thought you should know something."

He squints, wishing he had his goggles. "What?"

"We're going south."

"I know that," he lies.

"Your house is north of mine." She says it as if she finds that odd. Because it is.

"Ah." *Shit*. "Yeah. Wanda, we're not looking for the goat."

"What . . . what *are* we doing?"

He points and scowls. "I need you working that oar, Wanda. Go. Go!"

Chastened, she heads back.

But still the boat crawls. Every time the pollen blows, they lose sight of one another and then it's easy to get out of rhythm. The boat lists—the corn grabbing at the bottom, tugging at the oar-poles.

Cael tries to coordinate them, yelling, "Lift! *Push*. Lift! *Push*." With *lift*, the oar-poles rise, and with *push* they all bring the poles against the dry earth—moving the boat five feet, maybe ten, with each stroke. It's not great. But it's *something*.

Lane's manning the console, and even here in the pollen drift his face can be seen cast in an eerie green glow. His eyes go wide. "We're coming up on the beacon."

"Beacon?" Wanda asks. "What beacon?"

(*The beacon we left for the garden*, he thinks but does not say.)

Cael can't see anything. The wind kicks up a washout of

pollen so bright and complete he can't see his own hand in front of his face. But then the gale dies down and he *does* see: gauzy lights off to starboard—the lights of Boxelder.

That means it won't be far now. At least, he hopes. With the garden being way out in the corn like that, it's easy to lose your bearings. The corn distorts the sense of where you are and how to get back. Made doubly worse when it's night and *triply* worse when the sky is raining down golden dust into your eyes and mouth and nose.

Still. They have to push on. *Have to.*

He yells louder. "Lift! Push! Lift! Push!"

Cael sees Wanda's face. Hers is the visage of worry. She knows something's up. She just doesn't know what. He hates that soon she's going to find out.

Then Lane yells, "We're just about on top of it!"

The garden.

They ease the pinnace forward until all forward momentum ceases, though the wind still rocks it back and forth like a cup caught in a river's grip.

Cael slides the oar-pole back in its socket and goes to the edge of the boat. "Stay here," he yells. "I'm going to take a look."

"Wait!" Wanda says, grabbing hold of his arms. Her expression is pleading. "Where are you going? Please let me come."

Cael doesn't say anything. Instead, he gives Lane and Rigo his own pleading look. The two of them come from behind her and—gently, oh so gently—pry her off him.

He leaps over the edge of the boat and drops ten feet into the corn. Stalks crash under his feet, the greenery thrashing beneath him. When he rolls off, the damaged stalks quickly spring back up, shuddering. Again the corn reaches for him, the filaments of corn silk squirming like tentacles in the storm.

"Spotlight!" he yells.

A cone of bleary yellow light—jaundiced like the pollen drift and a stone's throw from being totally worthless—illuminates Cael. For a moment he thinks, *This can't be it.* He doesn't see the garden. No clearing. No plants. Nothing.

But then he catches sight of a red pepper hanging plump and lusty—a pepper where none dangled yesterday. *It really is aggressive. More aggressive than the corn.*

Cael plucks the pepper, hands it up.

It's Wanda who takes it.

"Is this what I think it is?" she hollers over the storm.

Cael says nothing. He eases forward, flagging them to nudge the boat alongside him. Rigo uses the spotlight to highlight the trail of vegetables. As they drift forward, the wind keening, the pollen stinging, Cael stoops again and again, fetching vegetable after vegetable. A tomato here. A pepper there. A scooped shirt full of pea pods. A bundle of some crinkly leafed green that smells crisp and clean when Cael gives it a twist and wrenches it up out of the earth. All the while the corn reaches for him—pulling a leaf along his skin, drawing a bead of blood—but none of that matters. It's here. The garden. The garden means ace notes. The ace notes mean buying a proper future for him and his family and his crew. He thinks of the flash in Gwennie's eyes when she told him she stole that chicha beer and suddenly wishes like hell he could see that same flash right now. *Damnit, Cael.*

He kicks the stalks aside and keeps moving.

It isn't long before he comes upon a small trail of strawberries. Lush, each as big as a baby's fist. He can't help it—he kneels down, pokes through the strawberries until he finds one mostly shielded from the pleach of corn leaves. He dusts off the pollen and pops it in his mouth.

He damn near faints. It's *that* good.

He hands everything else he grabs up to Wanda.

They've gone a hundred yards when Lane yells down, "Cael, you need to see this."

"Not now!" Cael yells.

"Yes. *Now*."

Muttering, Cael clambers back up into the boat.

Lane is pointing off the bow.

At first Cael doesn't see it. But then the wind eases and the cloud of pollen parts—Cael sees something out there, glinting. Then it's again swallowed by the drift. Cael scowls. "The hell am I looking at?"

"Martha's Bend."

Martha's Bend was a town like Boxelder once upon a time. Before Cael and them were even born. Now it's a dead town like so many others. For reasons that run the gamut of rumors—Blight! Hobos! Treachery by the Sleeping Dogs!—the Empyrean swooped in and quarantined it. All the people disappeared, and the Empyrean sealed up the town beneath a giant plasto-sheen bubble, the plastic fabric pinned not just to the ground but deep below it. (*As though to prevent roots from growing* is the thought that suddenly strikes Cael.)

A town like Martha's Bend is a scavenger's bread and butter—that is, after about fifty years pass and the Empyrean "opens" it, lancing the plastic blister and letting scavengers in to pick the bones. Martha's Bend has more time on its clock, though—the town's been concealed for almost thirty years now. Which means it's a long way from being opened back up to the likes of them.

"How'd we miss that earlier?" Cael asks.

Lane shrugs. "We were in the corn. Can't see squat from down there."

The glimmer Cael sees is a shaft of moonlight reflected off the metallic sheen of the bubble. "The trail," Cael says. "It leads to Martha's Bend."

"Coincidence?"

Cael grips the deck rail, looks out from the boat. It's then he feels something in his hand. A slight vibration. A vibration that's getting stronger.

He grabs Lane's hand, presses it against the railing. "You feel that?"

"Listen," Lane says. There, beneath the vibration, beneath the whisper of pollen and the rasp of cornstalk against cornstalk, is another, deeper sound. A rumble.

Like from a machine. Like from a motorvator.

Cael holds his hands over his eyes, trying to block the flying pollen. Sure enough, in the distance off to starboard, a pair of lights.

Coming right for them.

"Pull the boat back!" Cael says. "We've got a visitor."

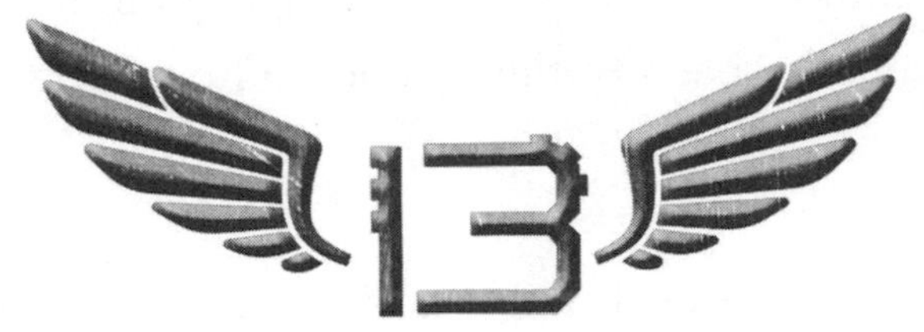

OF BLIGHT AND BOUNTY

THE RUMBLE GROWS louder. Headlights in the pollen grow brighter.

Soon the shape begins to resolve: It's a motorvator, all right. An old harvester by the look of it. The pollen whispers against the machine's metal side as it trudges through the corn, the thresher bar silent, stalks crushed underneath instead of sucked up and processed. Cael thinks it looks like a trundling beast: mouth open, teeth forward, haunches high in the air.

Lane keeps the pinnace off to the side as Rigo and Wanda stabilize the boat with the oar-poles. The harvester churns slowly forward, perpendicular to them. Before too long it'll cross over the garden trail, crushing the plants beneath.

"Spotlight," Cael says.

The spotlight flicks to life. Lane points it at the motorvator, letting the weak circle of light drift over the whole robot.

Cael had figured this was another harvester gone off the grid—prime pickings or, if it belongs to someone from Boxelder, something for Poltroon to fix. But in the light Cael sees this old harvester is looking pretty cleaned up already. No grime stains. Fresh paint job, red as a barn door. It's an older Thresher-Bot model, a 2400 series, but upgraded by hand.

"Take us over there," Cael says.

Lane hops over to an oar-pole, and Cael picks up one himself. They push with the oar-poles so that *Doris* will intersect with the harvester's path. As soon as they get close enough, Lane grabs a towrope and loops it around the Thresher-Bot's antenna box.

It begins to pull the pinnace along.

Cael yells, "Steady the boat. I'm gonna go over."

Wanda clutches at him, but he shakes her free.

"You sure?" Lane asks. "This isn't why we're out here."

Cael shrugs. "*You* want to turn down the ace notes?" The look on Lane's face answers that question. "Me neither. Besides, this might belong to someone from town." If so, the paperwork inside the cabin—which is generally unmanned, but still a place a field shepherd could sit if he wanted to ride along—should tell them.

They use the oar-poles to nudge the pinnace closer. Cael's about to take the leap across when Rigo mans the light and again shines the beam—

Something moves inside the motorvator.

A shadow passes by the window. And then it's gone.

Cael is so startled he almost tumbles over the side. Wanda grabs at his arm, stopping him from teetering over into the corn below. His eyes dart back to the motorvator. Nothing moves.

"Maybe it's a shuck rat," Rigo says.

Lane shakes his head. "Too big for a rat."

Cael's seen some damn big shuck rats. Almost the size of Wanda's mutt, Hazelnut. But Lane's right: the shadow within the harvester's cabin is too big.

Maybe they're just seeing things.

Or maybe there's someone in there.

"Give me the beatdown stick," Cael says, snapping his fingers at Rigo. The beatdown stick is an old baseball bat—from the days when the Empyrean still let them play that old game—studded with rusty nails, points sticking outward.

"This isn't *Betsy*," Rigo says. "No *Betsy*, no beatdown stick."

"Damn," Cael says. "Give me something, then. Wanda, what kind of weapons you have on board?"

Her blank stare answers the question.

"Seriously? No knives? No truncheons? Not even a damn mop handle?" He snatches up the oar-pole. To Rigo and Lane he says, "Stabilize the boat, will you?"

Then he uses the oar-pole to tap on the glass. *Thwack thwack thwack.*

"Hey!" Cael yells. "Someone in there? Show yourself!" He says to Lane: "You think there's a hobo in there?"

If there's a hobo in here, I hope like hell he's not one of the crazy, violent ones.

Cael yells over the motorvator engine: "Come on out, you damn hobo! I'll break that window!"

Nothing. Just wind and pollen and the rumbling of the harvester.

But then—

The window rattles. Everyone jumps.

Click! The glass frame unlatches. It slides open.

A face emerges.

Cael hears Wanda gasp.

"*Poltroon?*" Cael asks. Sure enough, staring back at him is the lean, haggard face of Earl Poltroon. He's got a few days' worth of beard stubble on his face, as white as salt on his otherwise dark skin. He blinks away a gust of pollen, wipes his nose across his forearm.

"You best get out of here, Cael McAvoy!" he yells. His

voice has a ragged edge to it, like a jagged-toothed saw running through hardwood. "You don't want any part of this."

Cael shares a What-the-hell? look with the others on the boat. Rigo mimes drinking from a bottle.

"Part of *what*?" Cael calls back.

"This! Me! All of it!" Poltroon snarls. "Go on. Get the hell gone."

"Poltroon, you look drunk as a skunk in a big blue funk. Why don't you come up on out of there? Come on over to the boat. We'll get you home so you can clean yourself up." *Plus, maybe he knows where the heck we are*, Cael thinks. He waves Poltroon forward.

Something moves behind Poltroon. Inside the cab.

Something long, lean, whip-like. Almost like Poltroon's got a tail.

Cael's blood goes cold. *Could it be . . . ?*

"I don't know how it happened," Poltroon says. His eyes lose focus, and he stares off at nothing as a blinding curtain of pollen separates them—Cael holds his forearm over his face, and when the drifting wind is gone, he can once more see Poltroon staring off at nothing. "I'm a good man. Always did right by my wife even though we never much liked each other. Did good by my kids. Tried to teach them what I can about these machines. And now . . ."

"Now what?" Lane asks. "What the hell are you talking about, old man?"

"Get out! Go away! Let me be at peace."

Lane snatches the oar-pole from Cael. He thrusts its tip toward Poltroon. "Hey! Poltroon! Grab the oar and we'll haul you over to the boat."

Another blinding sweep of pollen, and when they can see Poltroon again, he's staring at the pole with a baleful gaze. "Get that damn thing out of my face!"

Lane thrusts the oar-pole forward again, this time tapping Poltroon on the cheek.

A shadow whips in the cabin behind Poltroon.

Cael puts a hand on Lane's shoulder. "Lane, I don't know if that's a good—"

Poltroon cries out, bleating like a wounded animal—then his arm reaches out of the window and grabs hold of that oar-pole. But it's not a human hand that grabs it. Even in the pollen drift Cael can see the glistening darkness, the tangle of thick fibers—vines—dead-ending in something *resembling* a hand but with way too many fingers.

Those vine-fingers coil around the oar-pole.

The Blight, Cael thinks, his mind reeling in horror.

Cael's never seen someone Blight-afflicted this close. He feels woozy. Sick. Scared. Excited, too, though only Lord and Lady can say why that would be.

Poltroon comes climbing out the window, still holding tight to the oar-pole—Cael can see more of the arm now. It's a human elbow poking out of Poltroon's rolled-up shirtsleeve, but his forearm is thick and tuberous like a stalk of long-extinct sweetcane, the hand not a hand but a squid's beard of tightening vines.

"Take a *good, long look*!" Poltroon screams—not a scream of vengeance or anger but of fear and desperation. "Go on!"

Then, with one swift motion, he jerks the oar-pole with tremendous strength.

Lane lets go, but too late—he's already off-balance, and he starts to topple over the edge of the boat to the corn below.

But he doesn't.

Because Poltroon catches him. An impossible act, but there it is—Poltroon's vine-arm unbraids and unfurls, extending outward with eerie speed. Before Cael even knows what's happening, Poltroon's got Lane up on the hull of the motorvator. Vines wrapped tight around Lane's mouth, squirming tendrils forcing open his mouth and working their way inside.

Poltroon's going to kill Lane.

Cael has no choice now—he leaps across the boat and onto the motorvator.

"Earl, you're going to have to let go of Lane. That's my friend you have there. Let go of him, and we can figure this out." It's a lie; Poltroon has to know that it is. You get the Blight, you don't get a chance at *figuring it out*. You get quarantined. If you fight the quarantine, you die. If you go with it, then a battalion of Empyrean scientists in masks arrive suddenly, box you up like a rare antiquity, and then—you're gone. That's it. Never heard from again.

Lane struggles, his eyes bugging out.

"I can *hear* it," Poltroon blubbers. "The Blight. It talks to me. I can hear it inside my head. It hates us. Hates who we are. Like a child who hates its parents." Tears stream down his cheeks.

Lane's hands fumble uselessly at Poltroon's Blight-wracked arm.

"Hell with all this," Cael snarls, drawing the slingshot from his back pocket. Half a second later he's got a ball bearing in the pouch. He draws the pouch back.

He doesn't aim for the man.

He aims for the plant.

Cael opens his hand. The steel flies.

The ball bearing punches clean through the plant matter of Poltroon's arm with a spray of fluid. The vines open, then stiffen—and with a whip of Poltroon's Blighted arm, Lane's body comes flying past Cael, hurtling back onto *Doris* and crashing into the boxes of all the pilfered fruits and vegetables. The boat rocks. The boxes tumble over the edge of the boat into the corn.

Cael cries out for Lane—but inside he's mourning the loss of their garden bounty, too.

Wanda and Rigo hurry over to Lane as Poltroon stands, staring off at nothing, his chest rising and falling with great gulps of breath. Cael doesn't take his eyes off him.

Please, Lane, be okay.

Poltroon's gaze flicks toward Cael.

Cael slowly slides another metal ball into the slingshot pocket.

From the back of the pinnace, he hears Wanda yell, "He's all right."

"It's crying out," Poltroon says. His lips are trembling. "I hear it screaming."

Cael doesn't know what to do.

Poltroon mutters two words, the sound lost to the grumbling engine. Then he says them again, louder this time, shouting them:

"Kill me!"

"I can't," Cael says, horrified. "You're clear now. Step down. Come on, Poltroon. It doesn't have to be like this. Please. *Please*."

"You hurt it. But it's getting louder again. It's healing. Look." Earl holds up the arm. Little pea-shoot tendrils are braiding back together. "Do something. Kill me."

I can't kill him.

But he might make another move.

At Lane. At me. At any of us.

He's in pain. He's suffering.

Cael pinches another bearing, draws it back. Gets a bead on Earl's head.

His hand shakes.

I can't kill a person.

"You won't do it," Poltroon says. His vine-arm snakes toward the cabin, reaching in through the open window. "You tell my wife and kids that I love them and that my son Earl Jr. can take over the garage. Tell them that, McAvoy."

Suddenly, the thresher bar at the front comes to life—growling, grinding, stalks chewed up as the cobs are spit into the back bin. *Bang! Bang! Bang!*

Cael realizes what Poltroon's going to do. He screams out, but it's too late.

Poltroon pivots and takes a running leap toward the front of the harvester. His body hits the threshing teeth and is fast swallowed by the rotor bar. Cael can't see any of it from this vantage point, but the sound, the *sound* will forever remain with him: the ringing metal echo as Poltroon hits, the whirring teeth chewing fast through a human body, the sound of bones—not ears or cobs of corn but godsdamn *bones*—spit into the back carrier with a clanging clatter.

For a moment the yellow pollen in the air turns red.

And then it's over.

They sit huddled together on the pinnace, the pollen drift unrelenting. The rumbling of the motorvator is fading—the vibration on the boat now just a dull *thrum*.

"You good?" Cael asks Lane again.

He groans. Rubs his head. "I feel like I got stomped by a steer."

"But nothing's broken." Bone gets broken out here, no telling how well Doc will be able to mend it with what few supplies he gets from up above these days.

Lane moves his arms around, lets them swing loose like the arms of a puppet, shrugs. "Guess I'm all clear, doc."

"We did the right thing," Rigo says suddenly. "Didn't we?"

"We did," Cael answers, but he's not sure.

They let the motorvator go. Nobody will want to scavenge it for fear of the Blight.

Poltroon's dead. A bloody mess.

Dead with the Blight. A shame for his family.

Best to let the harvester keep on its path away from town—away, away, until it dies somewhere in the middle of the Heartland for some scavenger crew in some other town to find.

"We don't tell anybody about this," Cael says. He looks at Wanda when he says it. Something about her tells him she's the weakest link. Not a real member of the crew. Untested. He looks her dead in the eyes, sees the tears there. "They'll burn the boat if they think it was Blight-touched. They'll burn it and quarantine us."

"Okay," she says. Sniffling. Wiping her nose with the back of her hand.

"Okay?" he asks once more, his voice cold and insistent.

"I said *okay*."

"Good." He looks to Rigo and Lane. "We need to get those vegetables. The ones that fell off the boat."

But Lane shakes his head.

"No. Hell, no." Lane winces. "I hurt. Rigo's face looks like a pig bladder filled with phlegm. And her—" He just points to Wanda. "We're done here, Cael. We'll come back another day."

"But they could be gone another day."

Lane yells, "So let them be gone! They weren't going to do shit for us anyway, *Captain*. Who we gonna sell them to? The maven? The mayor? They'd string us up by our short and curlies. What would Gwennie say if she were here? If you hadn't—"

Lane's jaw tightens as if he's trying real hard not to let the words come out, and Cael's glad he doesn't say them.

He's not sure what he'd do. Agree? Punch Lane off the boat? Start crying like a little girl?

The pollen hisses against the side of the boat.

"I want to go home," Rigo says in a small voice.

Wanda nods.

Cael rubs his eyes and growls. "Fine. *Fine*. We go home. But we come *back*. You hear? We get this boat in better shape, and we come the hell back."

PART THREE
THE GARDEN

They've taen a weapon, long and sharp,
And cut him by the knee;
They ty'd him fast upon a cart,
Like a rogue for forgerie.

They laid him down upon his back,
And cudgell'd him full sore.
They hung him up before the storm,
And turn'd him o'er and o'er.

They wasted o'er a scorching flame
The marrow of his bones;
But a miller us'd him worst of all,
For he crush'd him between two stones.

John Barleycorn was a hero bold,
Of noble enterprise;
For if you do but taste his blood,
'Twill make your courage rise.

—*"John Barleycorn,"* Robert Burns

THIS LITTLE SQUEALER WENT TO MARKET

THE DREAM COMES again. Cael flying. Higher, higher, always higher. Toward the flotillas. Above the corn. Then something strikes him. And he falls. And the corn reaches for him.

And this time the corn tears him apart, his blood soaking into the earth.

Feeding Hiram's Golden Prolific.

It's been a week since the piss-blizzard came and went, but even still, everything's covered in a greasy film of golden pollen—the corn's seed spread far and wide.

The morning light filters through the smeared pollen veneer on Cael's window, soaking the room in a gauzy golden light. Outside, he can see the early sun casting a bright white line against the corn, the light pushing back a sky of spilled wine.

He can no longer detect the scent of Gwennie's hair on his pillow.

He wonders if Boyland has that smell on his pillow now. That thought is like a knife jammed in the space between his heart and his guts. Cael almost breaks out into a sweat just picturing it.

He runs his fingers through his hair. *Don't think about that.*

Think about the bounty. Think about the ace notes. From there a fantasy unfurls its wings and takes flight: the Big Sky Scavengers get stacks and decks of ace notes, they become the heroes of the town for bringing fresh vegetables and fruits back into the world, someone like Pop figures out how to grow new plants from the seeds, the orchards reopen, the school reopens, Lane fixes up his farm, Rigo gets his father free and clear of the fixy demon inside him, Pop becomes mayor, the pair of Boylands get thrown out on their asses, Gwennie comes back to him, and once again Cael can breathe her scent clinging to his pillow. . . .

It always comes back to Gwennie.

Never mind that.

Today there are things to do.

First, he goes to his mother. Dampens her brow. Feeds her water and a food slurry. Medicates her chapped tumors. This was once Merelda's morning job, but now it's his all the time.

Afterward, Cael milks the goat. Nancy's in a mood. Stomps and head-butts him as the meager squirts of milk hiss against the bottom of the tin pail.

Then inside. Pop's not gone yet—though a lot of mornings he disappears early and gets back later and later. They must be running him hard at the plant.

Pop leans against the counter, wincing and rubbing his hip. Cael knows what the processing facilities are like. He was in one of them once. Bright. Sterile. Steel everything. The people there are like parts of a machine. You stand for ten hours in one spot, sort through a fast-moving hoverbelt of corn, the yellow kernels shooting down the line in a gravity-defying stream. Those who work the line have to move fast to pull the tainted product—black fungal corn, kernels sprouting strange growths, shriveled bits—before it goes into processing.

People are always getting hurt on the line. Or dying. Dangers aplenty no matter how careful you are. The lights are so bright they're blinding. Picking corn for ten hours leaves your fingers numb. One of the pulverizing machines hanging above your head might bust a bolt and come down. Or spray hot fructose. Or catch fire. Just moving through the facility reveals a host of dangers: crushing machines and slick floors and chemical baths.

Pop applied to be in the field—one of the men who stands and watches the motorvators work the grid, makes sure nothing has gone sideways. But the mayor denied the application. Said Pop wasn't fast enough on his feet.

And he's not. Not really. The growth on his hip makes sure of that.

Pop—nostrils flaring, eyes wide—lifts up his shirt and pulls down the waist of his trousers on the right side. What resides there is the growth that plagues him—not a tumor like the ones suffocating Cael's mother but rather a cluster of bone spurs sticking up out of the dry, puckered skin. Cael hasn't seen the nodule in a while, and it's grown. It's as big as the fat end of a man's thumb, and it looks like a small formation of osseous crystals.

"Hurts?" Cael asks.

Pop nods. "Mm. Today it does. Not every day."

"You on shift soon?"

"Shift?" Pop asks. Then he says, "Oh, at the facility. Ayup. Heading there soon, as a matter of fact. So, two days till the Lottery. Excited?"

"I'm going to make my own Lottery."

"Are you, now?"

"Mm-hmm," Cael says. "We're gonna be rolling in the ace notes, Pop." A new seed is planted in the fertile seedbed of Cael's mind—not only will Pop stop working the line, but they'll get some of those fancy Empyrean unguents to apply to his hip. Ease the pain. Maybe even shrink the bone spurs a little bit.

"It's good to have fantasies, Cael. Just don't get too carried away."

Cael's mouth forms a straight, angry line. "It's not a fantasy."

"Don't start, Cael."

"Start what? I'm going to take care of this family if you're not."

Pop launches forward, shoves his finger in Cael's face. Red roses of anger bloom on the man's cheeks. "You think I like this? You think I don't want to reach up into the sky and pull down the Empyrean ships with my bare hands? I do! This isn't our fault. We didn't ask for any of this. But it is what it is. I made a choice. So did your mother. That choice was to settle down and have two kids, and by the Lord and Lady, that's what we did. And now our job is to play it smart and play it safe, you understand? Bad enough we have to protect you from the world outside our doorstep, but here it turns out we have to protect you two from yourselves. You think that makes me a coward? So be it. Call me a coward. But what I do, I do to keep this family together."

He goes silent. Rubbing his hip. Leans back against the counter.

"Go on," Pop says, voice soft. All the anger's gone out of it. Cael feels oddly disappointed. "Get out of here. Your crew's outside looking for you." Pop thumbs toward the cracked glass of the kitchen window.

Cael says nothing as he leaves.

"*Doris* sucks," Cael says. Sitting there in the barn on a mat of straw and dried corn husks is the Mecklin family's pinnace. "Ain't no good way around that."

Rigo kicks a stone. "Lucky Wanda's not here to hear you say that."

"That's why I didn't invite her."

"She cries at everything," Lane says, blowing twin plumes of ditchweed smoke from his nose. Inside the collar of his shirt is the expansive bruise—now fading to a pale eggplant hue—from where Poltroon threw him against the boxes. "It's actually pretty weird. *She's* weird."

Cael bucks at that—to his own surprise. "Shut your mouth. In a year she'll be my wife."

Wanda hasn't poked her head around much. Not after the night in the piss-blizzard. Not after Poltroon died. Cael hopes that's what it is. That she's just traumatized over what she saw that night. *And not traumatized over what she saw in* you *that night?* asks that nagging voice again.

Cael changes the subject. "Can't go get the rest of that garden with *Doris*, not in her condition. We need to do some repair work. First, the tear in that sail has to get mended. We'll use the tarp from on board; and, Lane, you're pretty good with a needle and thread, right?"

Lane narrows his eyes. "What are you trying to say?"

"I'm not saying anything, Jeezum Crow. I'm just saying you're good with it."

"That's woman's work."

"Oh, hell, it is not. You've done sail mends before. You, not Gwennie."

"Gwennie wouldn't have us working on this shit-wagon of a boat. She'd think this whole thing was harebrained, just another Cael McAvoy special. Gwennie would—"

"Gwennie's not here!" *Lord and Lady*, Cael thinks, *what crawled up Lane's hind-end, laid eggs, and died?* "I am. And we're doing this. Can you fix the godsdamn sail or not?"

". . . I can."

"Good. Then fix it! Rigo, I'll get you a clamp from Pop's workshop inside the stable. I'll need you to tighten up that mast. She's splintering bad in a few spots, and a clamp will keep her from breaking like a toothpick. Any problems with that?"

"Yes. I mean, no. I mean, yes, I have no problems with that."

"Whatever, Rigo. I'll get you the clamp."

Pop's got a workbench set up in the old stable. Spare parts and hunks of scrap lie everywhere—it looks like junk; but Cael's got an eye for what each thing is, what it does, and how much it sells for at the Mercado. It's an eye he inherited from his father and Pop's own love of stuff like this. Over there is a star-socket driver-wrench. Hanging on the pinboard are telescoping spray nozzles—same nozzles Pop uses on his weed-killer tanks. Pop's got artifacts from the old world, too: baseball cards once worth a lot of money but now not worth the paper they're printed on, a jar of buttons and copper-zinc coins, disks for those ancient computers that predate anything the Empyean uses.

Under the workbench Cael finds an old cardboard box. He roots around with a clang and clamor, finally finds what he's looking for: an old iron clamp that'll fit nice and snug around the worn mast of the Mecklin family's pinnace. He tucks it under his arm.

But then, just as he's about to shove the box under the desk, he hears something at the far end of the stable. A scuff. Like hay under a boot.

Couldn't be Nancy. She's in her pen in the other direction. Unless she got out . . .

Just then Nancy bleats. From the proper end of the stable.

Pop, maybe . . .

It's dark in here—the stable doesn't get much light—and so Cael eases around the workbench, works his way along the rusty milking stalls that have long fallen to disuse. He rounds the end of the stalls and sees someone standing there, digging through a big pile of hay and corn husks.

It's a hobo.

Cael's hand drifts to his back pocket, feels for his slingshot. The hobo—a pot-bellied fellow with thin lips and small, pebble-like teeth—turns and sees Cael. He holds up both hands. The moth-eaten rags around his arms sway, and bits of straw fall from what pass for his sleeves. He quickly pulls the ratty red cap off his head—again, more straw taking flight—and holds the hat between them.

"I don't want any trouble," the hobo says.

"What *do* you want, hobo?"

The hobo shoots a suspicious look toward the hay. Then back to Cael. A pink tongue slides along his dirty mouth—Cael can hear it rasp against the unshorn stubble of his chin. "Just a . . . uh, looking for a place to sleep is all. Hard to find a comfortable bed. Don't want to sleep in the corn."

"Your type ain't welcome around here."

"My type."

"We don't truck with vagrants."

"Vagrants." The hobo chuckles. "You don't get it, kid."

Cael eases the slingshot out of his back pocket. "Oh, I get it. You're here looking to take something that isn't yours. Place to sleep. Maybe our goat. It won't happen. You best get gone."

"I'll leave. But you better believe me, kid; you and every other dumb sum-bitch out here in the Heartland is a hair's breadth away from being me. We're all rats in the corn."

"We *work* for a living." Cael feels a sudden spike of anger. "If we're the rats, then what are you? Fleas and ticks on our backs is what."

Cael moves fast. Draws the slingshot, tucks a pebble in the pocket. The hobo sees what's happening and tries to duck out the back door of the stable, but Cael's faster. He lets fly, and the pebble clips the vagrant right in the ear. The man yowls in pain and busts out into the sunlight. Cael hurries after with another pebble loaded to fire.

But the wanderer is already bolting toward the corn, one hand cupped to his stung ear.

Having heard the commotion, Lane and Rigo come hurrying up and catch sight of the hobo just as he ducks into the carnivorous corn.

"The hell was that?" Lane asks.

"Damn hobo rooting around our stable. Looking for another free lunch."

"Don't you feel bad for them?" Rigo asks.

"Hell, no. I work. We all work. They can work, too."

"But they got other problems—Remittance Orders and no families and—"

Lane interrupts, says to Cael, "Isn't your sister basically a hobo?"

"Jeezum Crow, what the hell is your problem today? You having your period or something?"

Lane rolls his eyes. "You think I'm some girl?" He balls up his fists. "You want to have a go, McAvoy? I'll make you swallow your teeth, pretty boy."

Cael's about to step up, but Rigo gets between them.

"Hold on, let's get back to what really matters," Rigo says.

They give him a quizzical look.

"The bounty?" he reminds them.

"What of it?" Cael asks.

"What are we gonna do with it once we have it?" Rigo shifts his gaze from Lane to Cael. "Vegetables and fruits rot. We can't go selling it to the maven."

With a scowl Lane says, "It's a good question, Captain."

Cael shoots a glance sideways, makes sure Pop is still inside and the hobo is nowhere around. "It's not the veggies that matter. It's their *seeds*. Don't you get it? The produce we'll just eat. The important thing is, the Empyrean doesn't let anybody have proper seeds anymore—what few seeds they do parcel out are good for one planting and one planting only." Terminator seeds, they're called. Because the genetic heritage of the plant is terminated from the get-go. "But we've got the real deal. We can sit on those till we find the right buyer. Someone from another town, maybe. From another mercado—someone whose nose isn't brown with the mayor's stink."

"So." Lane leans in. "We're sticking it to the Empyrean."

"Yep. And we're sticking it to the mayor. And anybody else who ever tried to put their boots on our necks." Cael smiles. "Thought that might get your attention."

Lane chuckles, and the mood shifts.

"Still," Cael says, "we're not sticking it to anyone right now except ourselves as long as we've got the Mecklins' boat in such a state." He points over to the stable door, where just inside lies the clamp from when he pulled the slingshot. "Rigo—there's the clamp. We still need one more hover-rail to balance out the other one." He rubs his eyes. He's been dreading this, but it seems like they don't have any other way to do it. "Means I best hit the Mercado."

• • •

The maven of the Mercado is Pesha Cartwright. She's built like a spinning top: thin and narrow up top, hamhock hips flared out wide and broad, and then stubby legs with ankles so thick they look like you could cut rashers of bacon off them.

She moves likes a spinning top, too: always frittering about, whirling from one rickety metal shelf to another, rearranging rusted items on a wooden table, moving a cabinet three inches to the right, then four inches to the left. She can't stop moving. Can't stop touching things. It's as if she's got an image in her head as to how things must look, but that image changes every five minutes.

The Mercado—tucked in a pocket of corn on an old farmstead at the northernmost point in Boxelder—is a crazy person's flea market, a hoarder's paradise. Rust. Glass. Electronics. Plastics. Weird fluids in old jars. As Cael enters the market, he brushes past a set of wind chimes somebody's made out of a dozen forks and spoons.

"Mr. McAvoy," Pesha says, her voice wet and guttural, the sound of a knife sliding kernels of corn off the cob. The way she says it creeps him out: *Missssster McAvooooy*. "How's the life of a scavenger?"

She's well aware of the score. She's just needling him.

"You know how it's going," he says. His elbow clips some kind of rickety birdcage. Who around here has birds for pets? That seems like an Empyrean thing. Then again, the Heartland is the dumping ground for the oldest and weirdest Empyrean trash, and that trash often finds its way to the Mercado.

He steps over a cardboard box of wires and conduits. "I'm using a temporary boat. Bet you thought I didn't have a boat at all. But I do. The Mecklins' boat."

Her eyes, pressed between folds of skin that look like pinching fingers, twinkle. "A fine boat for a fine captain." She's messing with him. She probably knows it's a piece of shit.

"I need something for it."

"Sorry, Mr. McAvoy, I do not have any . . . *off-the-books* hover-panels for sale."

Truth is, Pesha Cartwright doesn't just deal in stuff. She deals in information. But *that* always comes with a price too high to pay.

"No, Maven, I need a single hover-rail, if you please." He can feel the tendons in his neck pulled tight as he strains to be polite. But it behooves you to remember your manners with the maven, because it's amazing what she can perceive as a slight. And she's one to hold grudges till the world's end. "Regulation is fine. If not a strip, then maybe a cage-prop. Something for the back of the boat."

"I may be able to help you," she says, clucking her tongue.

She waves him toward the back door.

Outside, the junk does not merely continue but explodes forth like the bowels from a gutted possum. The messy tangle of debris is piled high into walls that form a labyrinth. In the center of the maze stands the skeleton of an old silo. Cael has never been to the center of this junkyard, but he assumes the rumors are true: the maven keeps the very best stuff there.

She waves him along as she totters forth, her fingers forever working as though she's playing some kind of invisible harp. Cael can see all manner of things—nearly every bit of it worthless to him—packed into these walls. Corrugated tin, motorvator wheels, hand-plows pocked with corrosion. They turn a corner, and he sees a skinny cat dart under a tire. They turn another corner, and he sees a different cat—this one dead, mummified on an old harvester door as though the cat were sunbathing one day and died the next.

They walk like this for what feels like an eternity. The maven doesn't talk. She mumbles to herself, then fritters over to a loose cable or picks up a piece of broken glass and stares at it. Cael's about to say something, about to give up and bail on this whole expedition; but then they round one of the junkyard corners, and there it is:

A trio of hover-rails lying against one another like a bundle of sticks.

None of them is worth writing home about. Hell, they

don't match the one on *Doris*'s undercarriage, which means she'll always have a funky lean, but any one of those three will do. With Rigo on the mast and Lane on the sail, they might be able to pick up the rest of that garden by the end of the day. Tomorrow at the latest. Cael's starting to feel as if his luck is really turning.

But then the maven moves past the hover-panels.

He clears his throat. "Uh. Maven? Hey. Excuse me."

She turns, an eyebrow cocked. Her eyes flash with irritation.

"Look," he says. "Any of these here will do. I mean, unless you have something better?"

She shrugs. "I don't see what you're talking about, Mr. McAvoy."

"Here. These hover-rails."

"I see no such thing."

Cael laughs, even though this isn't funny. Surely this is some kind of joke. Or maybe she's crazier than he imagined. He steps forward, jangles the strips against one another. "See?"

"Oh." She nods and slides closer, squinting. "*Those*."

"Right. I'll take one. I should have the ace notes. . . ." He scrounged the last of their pile and has a few Spades and one Heart. He starts to pull them out of the deck he keeps in his pocket.

"They're not for sale."

"Not . . . wh . . . how are they not for sale?"

She shrugs. "They are already claimed."

"By who?"

"By *whom*," she says. "The way we speak is important, Mr. McAvoy. I do not remember who has claimed these devices, only that they are claimed."

Cael doesn't understand, not until he takes a good look at her face. Then he catches a glimpse of a smile trying to form on her lips, as if someone is tugging on the corners of her mouth with fishhooks and string.

"This is a game," he says. His palms are slick. "You're just messing with me, aren't you? You're not going to sell me these. You're not selling me jack or shit. Not if I had a red wagon of ace notes pulled behind me. Ain't that right?"

She shrugs. "You sound very paranoid. Your father raised you to be suspicious."

"For good reason! Godsdamnit. That's great. That's just godsdamn great."

"My apologies, Mr. McAvoy. I'll have to ask you to leave." Another lie of a smile. "Have a wonderful day."

He tells her she should say "hi" to Boyland One and Boyland Two for him. He's about to tell her to go to hell, that he hopes Old Scratch steals her eyes so she'll never be able to look upon her glorious piles of junk again, but he bites the side of his cheek to shut up.

As he storms out, he tastes blood.

Cael's mad. Spent too damn long at the Mercado. Boat's in the barn with a stitched sail and a straightened mast—his friends did their part, but he didn't do his. Without a second hover-rail the boat will remain shakier than a drunken vagrant, which means they could lose their haul again if it tilts too far to one side. Damnit.

As Cael crosses his broken driveway, his feet crunching on the shattered macadam while the faint odor of lavender tickles his nostrils, he sees the provisionist unloading his rusty hover-cart by their front step. Bhuja is his name. He's got some kind of palsy where half of his face looks as if it's lost all muscle cohesion. It droops like a puppet with its strings cut. Just the same, he's a nice enough sort—not an unpleasant face to see. He waves as he sees Cael approach.

"Cael!" he says. "Hello, hello."

"Bhuja." Cael nods. "Provision time, I take it."

"And then some," he says.

"Huh?"

"I have more than your provisions, young man."

That's odd. Few people send or receive anything

anymore. You need reams of Empyrean permits to send anything between towns, and it's not worth paying the fees to send materials within Boxelder when you can just walk it over to your neighbor.

Half of Bhuja's mouth twists into a sympathetic smile. "Appears as though you're having a dark day. If the look on your face is any indication."

Cael shrugs.

Bhuja sighs. "Then we'll see how this affects your day."

He hands Cael a slip. It's a Tally slip, and it shows the McAvoys haven't been giving enough back to the Empyrean. For a long while everyone tithed part of their income, so no matter what you made, you gave a percentage. Now, though, the Empyrean requires you to pay a base fee. They said it would increase productivity, but mostly it just puts families in the hole—and once you fall into that dark place, the penalty fees make it hard to climb out.

"Shit," Cael says with a sigh. "Bleeding us for everything we have." *But that's life in the Heartland.* Then he thinks: *The garden. The garden will save us.*

Bhuja offers a pained half smile but then holds up a finger. "Ah. Well. I have something else. Something . . . very interesting."

"Go on."

"This is for your family." Bhuja holds up a box. As he

hands it over, Cael sees it's bound tight with red ribbon, and that ribbon must have a metallic sheen or be woven through with little glittery bits, because it's sparkling in the sun. The box catches the light and twinkles like stars in the sky.

"What . . . is it? I've never seen anything like it."

"It's Empyrean. Beyond that, who can say?" Bhuja pats Cael on the shoulder. "Tell your father hello for me."

Cael nods. He doesn't say anything.

It must be some kind of mistake.

This box is too nice for them. Too nice for anybody here in the Heartland except maybe the mayor, who probably gets plenty of nice packages for sucking so hard at the Empyrean teat.

As Bhuja pilots his little cart away—wobbling as he goes—Cael remembers to yell after him to say hello to his wife.

The package isn't big. About as big as a hatbox, Cael figures. The box itself is the color of Nancy's milk. But it's that red, glittery ribbon that draws the eye. In the center of the ribbon—which culminates in a box-top bow with poufed, presumptuous loops—sits a tag.

On the tag is the fanciest handwriting Cael has ever seen. Black ink. As loopy and indulgent as the bow atop the box. The text reads:

For the McAvoy family.

It *is* for them.

Cael can't wait for his father. He has to open it now. Thing is, he's not really sure how to undo the ribbon. Its arrangement is intricate, with knotting that looks as if it might confound the mightiest sails man. He reaches down and barely touches it with one tentative finger—

But that's all it takes.

Cael yanks back his hand as the ribbon unfolds like a swiftly blooming flower, the fabric slithering backward through its own knot.

The sides of the box fall down one at a time, clockwise.

The bottom of the box rises up, as though by its own mechanism.

Cael stares in wonderment. At the back of the rising platform, Cael sees a toy no taller than his two fists stacked one upon the other. The toy has the head and neck of a giraffe and is clad in a white plastic tuxedo. Its lower jaw begins to move up and down, and tinny music begins to play from a small speaker in its back. Cael hears a peppy high hat, a warbling set of horns, and a crooning voice that sounds smoother than butter melting in a hot skillet.

The toy presides over three items:

A round fruit or vegetable, smaller than a pigskin

football, with smooth skin that's green on one side but then transitions into a pink ripeness.

A small, ornate jar with a metal screw top and a glass handle decorated with crystal butterflies. Contained within is a dark, creamy substance.

A rough-textured envelope of handmade paper.

It's the envelope Cael grabs first. In it he hopes to find answers.

And he does. They're just not the answers he expects.

Inside the envelope, Cael discovers a wad of ace notes. He doesn't count them, not yet, but he guesses there are fifty or more. That's a week's worth of family income. A *good* week.

And behind those a letter. Written not in the same froofy calligraphy as the box's tag but in handwriting Cael knows all too well.

Mer's handwriting.

Cael holds up the letter in the bold, bright light of the afternoon sun. But as he starts to read it, he feels a blue light scan across his vision. And then, the strangest thing yet, his sister's handwriting glows blue, too.

Above the letter, her face appears. A three-dimensional image—diaphanous, digital gossamer threads come together to form his sister.

She speaks, reading the words of her own letter aloud.

"Hey, Pop, Mom, Cael. I know you all are probably mad

at me, and I don't blame you. I just wanted you to know that I'm safe. I . . . had a plan this time, not like the other times when I went off half-cocked, but a real plan. I followed the train tracks to the Provisional Depot. You probably know this, but the scows come and bring down provisions from above, and the last time I ran away I met somebody in the Provisionist's Office. . . ."

Her face looks sad then for a moment.

"*Well. Whatever. Point is, he helped me hitch a ride, and now I'm up on one of the flotillas. And, no, I won't tell you which one. I don't want you coming after me. No good can come of that.*

"*I've gone and sent you a package. I hope you like it. I'll send one every few weeks as long as I am able. See, Cael? I told you I'd hold up my end of the bargain.*

"*I love you all. Please do not come and find me. I'm . . . happy here.*

"*Love, Merelda.*"

Cael blinks.

"Well, I'll be a possum's mama," he says, shaking his head.

She did it. Mer really did it. She ran away, and she's not coming back.

The taste in his mouth is like nothing he's ever experienced. Cael's had chocolate before—it's been some years now, but back in day-school, once a year they'd get these little buttons of chocolate with caramel centers. They were his favorite thing in the whole world.

But this? The stuff in the glass jar with the butterfly handle?

This is his *new* favorite thing in the world. It's thick but light. It's creamy but silky, too. This must be what it's like to take a big bite out of the nighttime sky. Dark, rich, sweet. And a little tingly bite of salt, too, which only seems to bring out all the other flavors.

He licks the back of the spoon. "What's this stuff called again? Pot of cream?"

"*Pot de crème*," Pop says. Way he pronounces it is "poh-de-crem." "It's a custard."

Cael doesn't know what a custard is, but he believes a jar of this per household would make all the hardships of the Heartland worth it.

He hands the jar back to his father, who takes a spoonful and slides it into Mom's mouth. She groans, her jaw working just enough so Cael can see it. The groan doesn't sound like one of pleasure, but it's the only sound she can really make. He hopes she's enjoying it.

It's nice sitting here like a family.

Outside, night has fallen, and for a moment Cael feels as though everything is as it should be. Odd how a taste of good food or drink can make you feel like all the world is in order.

His father puts an old book in his lap, uses the cover as a cutting board, and draws the knife twice down the center of the swollen fruit Mer sent them. He pulls out the middle and cuts around it, exposing and removing a fat, flat pit—itself as big as a Heartland peach (which are admittedly sad, wrinkled little things). The other half he scores with the knife and reverses so that the skin pops inward, the fruit's golden flesh thrust outward.

Pop cuts a cube, leaves it on the end of the knife, and extends it to Cael.

A sweet explosion with a sour kick fills Cael's mouth, and now he thinks *this* might be the best thing he's ever eaten. He feels chills on the back of his neck.

"Mango," Pop says.

Cael presses the fruit against the roof of his mouth with his tongue. He doesn't really need to *chew* it: It's so soft, it practically evaporates. "Oh, Lord and Lady, this is so fantastic. I didn't think tastes like this *existed*. Am I dead? Am I at the gates of the Lord and Lady's mansion? I am, aren't I?"

Pop laughs. It feels good to see him laugh. "No, Cael. You have not died. Or, if you have, I came along with you." He flicks a mango cube into his mouth. The pleasure on his face isn't as plain as on Cael's, but the way he draws a deep breath is telling.

"How'd you know it's a mango?" Cael says, taking another cube and sliding it between his mother's lips. "I've never even heard of one of these before."

His father shrugs, says, "I read books. That's all." But the way he says it, Cael's not so sure. Pop doesn't give him a chance to ask. "So. Your sister. She's on one of the flotillas."

Cael barks a laugh. "I almost don't believe it. But I guess that explains the treats."

"I know you've never seen anything like this in the Heartland." Pop pulls out the giraffe-headed toy, turns it around. Rubs his finger on the back of the toy's faux tuxedo, across the eight little speaker holes back there. "These are Empyrean goods, all right. These are the spoils of a good life."

Those words echo in Cael's mind. *Spoils of a good life.* He likes that idea just fine.

"Thanks to Mer," Cael says.

"To Mer."

Cael waits. Decides to say it. "She's not coming back, Pop. Not this time."

"No. I don't think she is." For a moment his father looks sad. Finally he forces a smile. "Well. It is what it is. Mer has her own path now, and it's not ours to interrupt."

"Least she's not a hobo."

"If she were, we'd still love her."

"Her leaving is going to come back to us, isn't it?" Cael already knows the answer. Nobody's allowed to leave her hometown, not without special dispensation, without a whole passel of permits, and without a handful of bribes few can afford. It's bad enough they have the shame of everyone thinking Merelda is wandering around like some vagrant. But a crime committed by one member of a family is punishable against all members of the family. "What if the proctor finds out?"

Pop shrugs. "She won't. Harvest Home is done and so we dodged that charging bull. She doesn't have much reason to come down here until the next quarterly tally. She lives on one of the flotillas, and her gaze is not that far-reaching. She cares little about us. We're too small."

"But—"

"It'll be okay," Pop says. He claps Cael on the shoulder. "Let's just enjoy this strange and wonderful family meal, huh?"

Cael tries. Tries to focus on this, on the Lottery, on the garden they will soon harvest. But dark clouds continue to shadow these bright moments. Merelda. Gwennie. Boyland.

"Sure, Pop," he says, forcing a smile.

• • •

"The mango was so syrupy—"

"'You couldn't stop licking your finger for days,'" mocks Lane. The three of them are walking down Main Street.

"Well, not days," Cael says. "Hours, at least."

"Thanks for sharing it with me and Rigo." Lane elbows Cael in the ribs. "We, your *bestest friends* in the whole hell of the Heartland."

Rigo makes a sad face. "Yeah, Cael. What gives?"

"Come on, don't bust my nuts on this," Cael says. "It was nice to just sit there with Mom and Pop for a while. Eating some Empyrean treats."

"The Empyrean." Lane snorts, then spits in the dirt. "Your sister's one of *them* now."

Cael shrugs. "She'll never be one of them."

"She's up there. Drinking chocolate. Eating weird fruits. Draping herself in their sparkly ribbons and dancing with robots." Lane does a quick dance forward and stomps on a corn shoot pushing up through the earth. "She's basically a traitor to the Heartland, you know."

"That's a bit melodramatic."

"And you're a traitor, too. For not sharing with your buddies." Lane gives Cael a hard elbow in the ribs, and Cael's not sure if he's joking or half serious or all-the-way serious. "You've changed, Captain. Grown cold in your pursuit of fame and fortune."

"Now you're just making stuff up."

"It's all right. I'm going to be a traitor, too, someday." Lane stomps on another corn shoot. "One day the Sleeping Dogs are going to come through here and I'm gone."

Cael rolls his eyes. "This again."

"Yeah. *This* again. You have your dreams. I have mine, pal." Lane pops his knuckles. "The raiders are real."

"I know they're real. They're just not as noble as you think. You think they're armed, Empyrean-hating mutineers hiding out in the Heartland, working for the common man, trying to change things by bringing down the heavens. They raid towns, Lane. *Our* towns. Don't be naive."

Lane shrugs. "Some of our towns need raiding."

"What kind of name is that anyway?" Cael asks. "Sleeping Dogs. Who's afraid of a bunch of sleeping dogs anyway? You ever watch a dog sleep? Wanda's mutt just lies on his back, snoring, slobbering, and passing gas so bad it could strip the plasto-sheen off a long road."

"It's a saying. Let sleeping dogs lie."

"It's a dumb saying, then. You ask me, you should wake them the hell up. Maybe you wake a dog up—" Cael's about to say more on the subject, but it's then they arrive at their destination.

Poltroon's garage.

They all stop and stare. Inside they see Poltroon's son,

also Earl, sharpening a spiral of harvester blades. Sparks rain down around him as he stomps a pedal to spin the whetting wheel. The embers reflect back in Earl Jr.'s dark goggles.

"I don't want to go in there," Rigo says.

"We got to," Cael answers.

"We know things," Lane says. He doesn't need to explain what things. Town's been abuzz with what happened to Poltroon. Most assume he went on a bender and took his motorvator out. Some have whispered that the Empyrean thought he was too good at his job and whisked him away in the middle of the night—either to put him to work for them or to slit his throat, depending on the teller of the tale.

Cael grabs the other two, drags them in. "C'mon, we need to do this."

Earl Jr. sees them approaching. He stops sharpening the blade and lifts the goggles from his eyes—around his eyes are deep pink impressions where the specs bit into his skin.

"Boys," Earl says. He's a few years older than they are. He looks them over with narrow eyes. "Now, I know you don't need any motorvator parts. What's up?"

Cael looks around the garage at all the motorvator parts hanging off the walls on pinboards and dangling from chains: control boards and rasp bars and wheel-treads. "I figure you don't deal much with boats, but we need a new hover-rail for *Doris*—ah, the pinnace we're borrowing."

Earl Jr. stands. Bites at the fingers of his gloves to pull the gloves off. "Yeah. Heard you wrecked yours. That's tough stuff. Life in the Heartland, right?"

"Life in the Heartland," the boys intone together.

"Sorry," Earl says, shaking his head. "Had something, but Boyland came in, bought it."

"Godsdamnit!" Cael mutters. *Figures.*

"I'll keep my ear to the ground, though. If anything turns up, it's yours."

Cael offers a hand. "Thanks just the same, Earl Jr."

Earl shakes it. His grip lingers. It's as if he's searching Cael's eyes. Which is insane; no way he could know anything about what they saw. It looks like he's about to ask something—Cael can feel the sweat on his hands and brow go suddenly cold. But then Earl nods, pulls away.

"See you, Cael."

"See you, Earl."

They hurry out of there. As they step outside, Rigo says, "I feel like he knows."

"He doesn't know," Lane says. "Don't be an ass."

"We should tell him."

"We should tell him his daddy was a Blighter? That'll go over well. Word gets out, people will be throwing him in the jail, locking the door, and calling the proctor."

The two of them continue to argue, but Cael barely

hears them. Because the wind turns, and a smell reaches his nose: a familiar soap scent coupled with a deeper, fancier fragrance.

Rose hips.

Vanilla.

Gwennie.

Cael turns, sees her standing about ten feet away. She gives him a small wave.

"Cael," she calls to him. "I need to speak with you."

"Stay here," he hisses to the others before he heads over.

She looks different. She's got on a little makeup, for one: a bit of blush, a pink shine to her lips. But her clothes have gotten an upgrade, too. Good denim. Red crosshatch shirt with some frills on it.

"Hey," she says, shifting nervously.

"Don't you look nice." Way he says it, though, doesn't sound nice at all.

"New clothes."

"And makeup."

"That, too." She stares him up and down. "What's your damage, Cael?"

"I'm just saying, nice clothing. Boyland has good tastes."

She rolls her eyes. "Are we doing this already?"

"You thought we'd exchange pleasantries?"

"You don't have to like it, Cael McAvoy, but Boyland is

my Obligated. We are to be married in one year's time. And I am now an official crew member of the Boxelder Butchers."

Cael's nostrils flare. His head feels hot, his palms slick. "Question isn't whether I like it, *Gwendolyn Shawcatch*; it's whether *you* like it. And I bet you do."

She doesn't offer any answer to that. Which galls him all the more.

"Listen," she says, "I've come to fetch you."

"Fetch me. Like a dog looking for a bone."

"Boyland's back at your house."

Cael's jaw tightens. "My house. Why is that bastard at my house?"

"That's his business, not mine. My business is fetching you."

"Fine. Tell him I'll be along."

She shakes her head. "I brought the yacht. We can hop in and take it—"

"I *said*, I'll be along. I'm not riding with you. You go on ahead. I'll get there when I get there."

"Fine."

"*Fine*."

"You've changed, Cael."

"Really? Because I'm not the one in whore's paint and a frilly shirt."

Her jaw drops. She heaves back, gives him a hard slap

that reddens his cheek and makes his molars bite into the inside of his mouth. And then she storms away.

His friends ease up behind him.

"You have a real way with women," Lane says.

"Come on," Cael snarls. "I've got an ass to kick."

Marching back home, Cael stops to reach into the field, ignoring the way the leaves lacerate his arm, and wrenches an ear of corn right off the stalk. The corn squeals in pain, a sound just loud enough to be heard up close.

As he walks, he shucks the corn, leaving a trail of silk and husk.

Rigo and Lane walk on either side of him. They're doing all the talking.

"He's the mayor's son," Lane says.

"And he's built like two motorvators stacked on top of each other," Rigo adds.

"I don't know what you're planning on doing—"

"Cael, you better think about this."

"—but I don't like the look in your eye."

"Maybe take a breath!"

"Cool down a little."

"Let's stop walking for a minute."

Cael hasn't said a damn thing this whole time. But

now he stops and gives them both a look—a look so toxic it could probably kill a ten-foot radius of corn with just a sweep of his gaze.

"This ends *here*." His jaw tightens, and his eyes narrow. "It's time Boyland Barnes Jr. gets what's coming to him."

And then he continues walking.

Rigo and Lane don't say anything after that.

Cael comes up from the side of the house; but before he does, he stops, unzips his fly, and coats the corncob with his own piss, taking care to avoid splash-back. Not that it really matters: It's his piss no matter how you cut it. Then he rolls the corncob in the dust with his foot, picks it back up, and tucks the whole ear into the pocket of his slingshot.

Boyland's up by the front door. The shovelhead's got a little wax candy bottle in his hand, and he's pinching the last of some colored corn syrup into his wide mouth.

Boyland turns and notices Cael, but it's too late.

The dirty, piss-soaked corncob pirouettes through the air and nails the dumb bastard right across the bridge of his nose. He blinks away dust and urine, crying out, and that's all the opportunity Cael needs.

Cael runs at a full clip and jumps like a dog trying to catch a stick. He tackles Boyland right in the midsection, knocking the mayor's son off the front step and into the dead shrubs that ring the old farmhouse.

"You godsdamn dirt-monkey!" Boyland yells just before Cael elbows him under the chin.

The two tussle on the ground, rolling out of the shrubs, covered in broken branches and dry leaves. Cael thinks he's got the upper hand—after all, he has got his knee in Boyland's chest, his arm across his foe's throat—but both of Boyland's hamhock hands remain unaccounted for. Rigo yells for Cael to "watch out!" but it's too late. One fist clubs Cael on the side of the head; the other comes in from the opposite direction and does the same.

Cael's ears ring. It's like that day when they crashed the cat-maran, just a high-pitched whine echoing in his head. Boyland picks up Cael and throws him to the ground. The mayor's son casts a long shadow over Cael as he stands tall. Boyland grabs Cael again, but Cael's not done yet, not by a long shot. Even though his vision is blurry and his ears are going *eeeeeeeEEEEeeee*, he still has enough wherewithal to slam his head forward into Boyland's mouth. *Boom*.

It hurts like a sonofabitch, what with Boyland's teeth cutting into Cael's forehead like that. But even still, it does the job—Boyland recoils, dropping Cael against the steps. Blood dribbles from Boyland's split lip, his teeth smeared

red. Both of them are bleeding: one across the forehead, the other from his mouth.

Cael can't help but laugh—this is what he's wanted to do since forever, to make that buckethead *bleed*. It's not as if he hasn't fought back before, but then it was always a shove here, a scuffle there. But this, *this* is how it should be. This, he thinks, is not how children fight but how men do. With fists and blood.

This moment is like the eye of the storm. But just before the mighty winds can crash together once more, the front door opens.

Pop steps out.

And so does Mayor Boyland Barnes.

"Uh-oh," Lane says. Which just about covers it.

The mayor smiles, licks his teeth. "Why don't you boys come on inside?"

A PROPOSITION, THICK AND FOUL

MAYOR BARNES IS sauced. Not fall-on-his-face drunk; he never is. The elder Boyland always walks the razor-thin bridge between clear-headed sobriety and full-on dipsomania. Even now he sits there in the kitchen of the farmhouse with the pewter mug he carries with him most times. Cael can smell the sour beer within. The mayor swirls his mug, takes a deep breath by sticking his nose in it, and then satisfies himself with a long, indulgent slurp. As if it's his morning coffee.

The mayor and his bloody-lipped son are now the focal point of the room. Barnes Sr. sits at their small table alone. Barnes Jr. stands behind him, arms crossed, chest puffed out like a strutting rooster, a smug look on his face that shows he knows what's coming next. Cael, his friends, and Pop stand at the other end of the room.

Pop leans his body so it's tilted away from his bad hip. It must be hurting.

But something else is bothering him, too.

Cael thinks Pop is afraid. He can't suss out why, but there it is.

"Boys," the mayor says, winking and dipping his chin in a friendly nod. The man tucks a thumb under one of his red suspenders, draws it out like a bowstring. "I'm to understand you're having some difficulty with your operation."

Cael sees the flash of satisfaction across Junior's face.

"Now, that's a right shame," the mayor continues. "Your crew always did . . . nice work. Forever number two, hot on the heels of Junior's operation. Scavenging, as you know, is useful—perhaps even critical—to our town's survival. The Empyrean, Lord and Lady bless them and favor them, have instituted a stiff policy of self-reliance, which is a wonderful thing. We Heartlanders take to self-reliance the way a squealer takes to mud: we like to get all up in it."

Lane bristles.

"Scavenging prevents us from seeking handouts from our friends in the heavens. It lets us embrace that self-reliance. Whether you find a crate of canned peas or a binary carburetor for an old model Straw-Walker, well, that's just one more thing we do ourselves. Ain't that right?"

Cael and his crew share bitter glances. Grudgingly, they nod.

"You might think I was happy to hear of your predicament, what with that limiting competition for my son's crew and thus increasing his potential compensation." Mayor Barnes leans in, smacking his lips, his jowls trembling. "But that could not be further from the truth, boys. The loss of one of your crew is a detriment to Boxelder's continued survival."

Cael can't help it; he speaks up. "We didn't lose a crewmate; she was *stolen*, and we're not in a predicament! We got a boat now, and we're getting her up to speed. It'll just be a day or three—"

"Fixing up that boat means buying parts, but last I checked, those parts seemed woefully unavailable." Did Cael just see the two Boylands share a conspiratorial look? *Of course they're unavailable, you sonsabitches.* "Your farm's already behind. You're just not bringing in the ace notes. Maybe you want to dip into your savings?"

The mayor waits. Cael's sparking mad now, and it takes everything he's got not to say something that will only sink him in deeper.

The elder Barnes *mmm-hmm*s and nods. "Don't have savings? Lord and Lady, who could blame you? People's piggy banks ain't full of fatback—hell, the only thing sitting in most of those banks is the squeal of the pig. Times are tough for all of us."

"Tough for you," Pop says, sucking air between his teeth. "Nice yacht. Big house. A cut of all the ace notes that get kicked upstairs. Sounds hardscrabble, Mr. Mayor."

Barnes shoots Pop a sly look—his mouth is smiling, but his eyes flash with sudden irritation. Then the mayor stifles a quiet burp, thumps his diaphragm with the side of his fist. He turns back to Cael, ignoring Pop. "What I'm saying, boys, is that you're just not bringing in the money. You're all getting older, so it seems a good time to let another, younger crew come up—I hear the Shustacks got a strong captain candidate in their son Lucas."

"Lucas is only twelve!" Rigo blurts.

Cael steadies himself against the table with both hands. He leans in to the mayor and feels his shoulders slump with the burden of what he's about to say. "Sir, Mr. Mayor, please. We're a good crew. This is just one bad kernel in a good cob—we're strong scavengers, each of us has another year in us, easy. We'll be getting back on our feet in no time at all."

If they put us on the processing line, we'll lose the boat and won't have a spare hour to spend harvesting that garden.

Mayor Barnes chews on this. It almost looks as though

he's rolling the idea around his mouth with a drunken tongue. "Well. You're right that you're good scavengers. And you do have some more time on that clock—now, I've gone ahead and set you up with other jobs already at the processing facility, but I might could hit the brakes on that if you were willing to . . . dissolve your own crew and join up with the Butchers."

"Wh . . ." Rigo can't even finish the word. "Whuh?"

But it seems Boyland Jr. feels the same way. His jaw near falls off his stunned face. "Dad. Daddy. Come on, you can't be serious. Don't mess around, now. They aren't Butchers material, and you damn well know it!"

Suddenly, the room erupts as everyone talks over everyone else. Lane gets all up in Boyland Jr.'s face, telling the mayor's son to keep his mouth shut. Rigo's babbling about what his father's going to think. Cael's going back and forth between the elder Barnes and his own father, trying to get one of them to inject a little sanity into this kitchen table meeting.

It's over when the mayor stands up suddenly, the chair behind him grinding on the floor and almost toppling over. He slugs back the rest of his beer and then clips the mug to a carabiner on his belt. He reaches out with a meaty paw, shakes everybody's hands from Pop on down.

"I'll be looking for your answer . . ." The elder Barnes

stops and thinks. "Well, Lottery's tomorrow night, so guess we could hold out on the very rare chance one of you wins a free ticket to the life in the big sky above. Let's call it morning after next, then."

"Barnes," Pop starts, but the mayor stops him with a silencing finger.

"Arthur. Boys. One more tiny little thing I may have forgotten to mention. A caviling grackle landed on my shoulder the other day and told me a secret, a secret I'm sure couldn't be true. That little birdy said that not only had your daughter run away again, Arthur, but that she is sending you packages that could've come from nowhere else but upstairs." The mayor's presence suddenly looms large, and Pop looks small. "Now, I'm sure that's not true. You're an upstanding man with a good family, and the shame of your daughter being a vagrant is enough for you to bear. But I'd hate to have to alert Proctor Agrasanto to all of this ugly business." He shrugs. "Why not stay still? Why struggle? Lie back and dream of better days."

"Pop—" Cael starts, but Pop silences him with a sound that could silence a hound.

"Go on, Mayor," Pop says, forcing a mirthless smile. "You won't find any trouble here."

"Good to hear." The elder Barnes looks to his son. "Come on, boy. Your momma's probably cooking up some stew." He gives a sideways glance to Arthur. "We managed to get a quarter cow. You believe that? A quarter cow." The message is implicit: *You'll never get hold of a quarter cow, will you?*

And then the Boxelder mayor chuckles and pushes past the boys toward the door. Boyland Jr. follows after but pauses to linger in front of Cael. He sets his jaw and offers his own looming presence. "McAvoy, don't you even think of joining the Butchers. You do, and I'll make you wish your daddy never pissed you out into your momma's—"

Pop shoulders hard into Junior from behind, shoving him forward toward the door. Cael's father holds up both hands, feigning an accident. "Sorry. This hip makes me clumsier than a drunken moon-cat." Junior just growls and follows after his father.

Cael watches them mount up into the yacht outside. He sees Mole turning the sail, Felicity giving Gwennie a hard elbow on the way to the rudder wheel. *So she's not exactly one of the crew*, Cael thinks, but he doesn't let that thought linger. He can't be feeling bad for her right now. He's got his own problems. Not like she's hurting, either, what with her standing there in a rugged new outfit, her face plastered with makeup.

Gwennie gives Cael a look. A sadness lives there on her face. She doesn't wave, doesn't mouth any words. She just stands there and gives him a small, defeated shrug.

She looks pretty, Cael thinks, and for a moment he wants to yell that out to her.

But then the wind catches the sails, the hover-rails thrum to life, and the prop-fans whirr. The yacht is already pivoting and heading back down the drive, lifting up above the corn tassels.

And then they're gone.

She's gone.

As soon as they're out of sight, Cael storms over to a tin pail sitting by the front stoop and kicks it as hard as he can. It sails toward the edge of their property, hits the ground, and rolls into the corn with a rustle.

"Shit!" he yells. "Sonofabitch!"

He kicks a clod of dirt with some dry grass sticking out of it like a bad haircut.

Rigo sits on the front steps, his face drooping. Lane paces like a worried barn cat.

"Cael," Pop says. "Calm down and we'll talk this through."

"Godsdamn, Pop," Cael says. "Seriously? Talk it *through*? Talk what through? That we just got bent over a barrel *again*, but this time by our own fellow Heartlanders instead of the damn Empyrean? No matter what we do, we can't catch a break."

"We'll figure it out."

"No, *we* won't figure anything out. I'll figure it out. You just keep doing what you do best, which is get punched in the face and smile like someone just fed you a bite of pie."

But Pop's pencil-thin eyebrows kink up like two caterpillars inching down the branch of his brow. "I understand, Cael. Maybe you're right." Pop stands there for a second, breathing deep through his nose, looking up at the sky. "Well. I . . . I better get ready. Shift starts soon. I'm going to have to leave early tomorrow, too. Bessie will watch your mother if you've got . . . things to do."

"We've got things to do all right," Cael says, his words like spit hitting hard earth. "So you go on. Do whatever."

And Pop does. He gives the boys a spiritless nod and heads off to the house.

Cael tilts his head back, stares up at the wide expanse of sky, so blue it might as well be the sea. Wonders for a moment what his father sees up there: the limitless wonder of the sky or invisible chains connecting those drifting flotillas to the soul of every Heartlander living and dead.

"That was harsh," Rigo finally says.

Lane moves over to a nearby barrel, starts rolling up a cigarette on the crooked wood. "Rigo's right. Your pops is a pretty good dude. Rigo's dad is a mean drunk. Mine is dead because he was dumber than a sack of donkey apples—and never mind the fact my mother is a traitor to everything

I could possibly believe in. Yours taught us everything we know. He's nice. Doesn't whup on you. Smart, too. You can't expect him to be the one man single-handedly sticking his thumb in the eye of Barnes and Agrasanto and everybody else in the Empyrean who thought to shit in our mouths from above."

Cael knows Lane's right. But knowing something and feeling something are two different things, and Cael just can't get past it. He's mad at his father. He's been mad at him for a long time, and the anger's only getting stronger. He says, "You really don't think one man could make a difference?"

Lane shrugs. "Maybe. But you ask me, you need a group—like the Sleeping Dogs—to change things." He licks the twisted ends of the ditchweed cig, pinches it between his lips as he lights a match, and takes a few puffs before coughing. "I'm just saying to lay off your pops is all."

"I don't want to talk about that anymore," Cael says. "Because I got a plan."

Rigo's eyes light up. "Ooh."

Lane just frowns and rotates his finger. "Let's hear it."

Cael tells them the plan, and the others seem reluctant. But Cael doesn't want to hear it. "We meet back here tomorrow morning."

"But tomorrow's the Lottery," Rigo says.

Cael cocks an eyebrow. "Fuck the Lottery. We make our own fate."

"Ballsy," Lane says. "But hell, I like ballsy. See you tomorrow, Captain."

That night, with the camel crickets chirping outside, the wind whispering through the corn, Cael slides open his window and crawls out onto the roof.

In the sky, the moon is fat and round. Not yet full but almost. The pregnant moon, they call it. Pregnant with what, Cael never understood. Possibility. Tragedy. Little moon-babies.

A shadow passes in front of the moon. One of the flotillas.

Cael wonders what it must be like for Merelda up there.

The sweet treats and the high society parties. He can't even imagine how it feels being that high up in the sky. When flying that high, why look down? The Heartland will soon be nothing but a dream to her, Cael knows. He hopes she'll keep sending care packages.

He wonders when they'll see her again. Could be never. Not unless they end up on the flotilla, and what are the chances of that? Part of him thinks, *Maybe that's what we need to do. Run away. Catch a ride up to the sky.*

But how much money would that take?
How much of the hidden garden must they harvest?
All of it depends on what secrets Martha's Bend holds.
Because that's where they're going in the morning.

LANCING THE BLISTER

THE DAY IS hot, and they're scared. Excited, too. Because way off in the distance sits the sealed-away town of Martha's Bend.

And it's taking them forever to get there.

The sail's repaired and the mast is straight, but the air is still, refusing to give them even a moment's worth of wind to blow them toward their destination. So once again the boat floats wobbly on its single hover-rail as they use the oar-poles to push themselves forward.

"By this rate we won't get there until noon," Lane growls through gritted teeth.

"I'm hungry," Rigo says.

"Here." Cael fishes through his satchel, finds some

hardtack biscuits. He breaks off a couple of porous chunks and tosses one to Rigo, one to Lane. Then Cael bites into the remaining third, wincing. Feels and tastes as if he's biting into a brick of salty clay.

Rigo pushes forward on the oar-pole and then bites into his hardtack. "*Thish shucks.*"

Lane rests his cheek against the oar-pole as he lifts, drops, and pushes. "If you believe Cael here, we're about to walk into the Lord and Lady's very own garden; ain't that right, Captain?"

"That's what I believe, yeah."

"Soon as we cross the garden trail," Lane says, "we'll stop and pick up some lunch. Couple strawberries, a big fat tomato, a handful of snap peas."

"We're not crossing the trail today," Cael says.

"What?"

"Doesn't make any sense to. We're already hamstrung with *Doris* here. We're going to come up to Martha's Bend from the south. Other way's the long way."

"The other way's the we-get-to-eat-strawberries way."

Cael shrugs. "Sorry, guys. Garden trail leads to Martha's Bend. I want to grab the head of the beast, not wrestle with its tail."

Rigo says suddenly, "Maybe we shouldn't do this. Maybe we should turn back around. Or just go harvest more of the garden. This is a bad idea. I can feel it in my gut. We don't know what's in Martha's Bend. They must've closed it off for a reason. Could be Blight there. Or maybe some kind of real bad weed killer that'll creep into your bones and turn them to pudding. What if it's an Empyrean outpost? Or what if the Maize Witch is there!"

"The Maize Witch isn't a real thing," Lane says. "What are you, four?"

"I'm just saying, this is a bad idea. I want to turn back around."

Cael shakes his head, bites into the hardtack again. *Crunch crunch crunch*. He tastes blood from where it bites into the roof of his mouth. "We're not turning around."

And then Lane points. "Damn right we're not. Look."

There it is.

Martha's Bend.

Plastic bubble, bright white in the sun.

Behind the plastic, the fuzzy shadows of distant buildings.

They're still a ways away. But for the next hour, nobody says anything. They just push the boat forward, ten feet at a time, the corn whispering underneath.

As they get closer, the corn starts to die off. It doesn't go all dead, not at first. Instead, about a half mile out the corn begins to darken, the leaves mottled with rusty flecks and black patches. The stalks curl in on themselves. Before long they stop seeing ears of corn hanging. The corn here still grows, but each stalk is as dead as a coffin nail. The ground looks different, too: white and dry, as if covered with a rime of hoarfrost or a dusting of milled flour.

Cael's seen this before—a phenomenon common to all the dead towns.

Then the wind shifts against them. And with the wind comes a faint smell, an acrid, chemical tang that smells like a high-test version of Queeny's Quietdown. The smell crawls up inside Cael's nose like a sick possum and dies there.

All of this—the smell, the ground, the corn—is from what the Empyrean did to this town way back when. The real question is, *Why?* Why do that? What were they trying to kill? Just what the hell are Cael and his friends going to *find* here in town?

Poison air? A deep crater? A pit to nowhere? A menace of hobos? A cult of Blighters? The Maize Witch? Cael's mind starts running away with an unholy menu of terrifying possibilities.

No turning back now.

This is my shot, Cael thinks. *Lord and Lady bless us and keep an eye over our endeavors, because it's the only shot we're gonna get.*

• • •

They come up from the south. Rigo anchors *Doris* with a cinder block, and they all hop out.

Here they see the plastic blister up close—it's the same plasto-sheen they pour over the roads, except thinner. Thin enough, at least, that when the wind kicks up, the bubble shifts and rustles. All along the perimeter, the Empyrean have put up signs—old signs, the edges eaten by bloody rust: NO TRESPASSING. TOXICITY AT FATAL LEVELS. INTERLOPERS WILL BE PUNISHED.

Rigo swallows hard, points to them as if to say, *See?*

But Cael ignores him. He just puts out his hand and says to Lane, "Knife."

Lane puts a saw-knife with a serrated blade in Cael's palm.

Time to cut an entrance.

Cael stabs the knife into the plastic. It's hard going—the plastic won't puncture at first, so he has to push the flat of his hand against the hilt of the knife and stab forward again and again until finally it pokes through with a rupturing *pop*.

Then Cael grits his teeth and starts sawing.

In five minutes he's gotten maybe three inches and his face is covered in a lather of sweat. The sun is like corn roots, sucking all the juice clean out of him the way it dries up the earth. Panting, he hands the knife to Lane, letting him take over. Lane gets another few inches. Then it's

Rigo's turn, and he doesn't get more than an inch before he collapses on his butt.

They go like this for a while. Sawing, sweating, taking sips of water from the canteen before going back to more sawing and more sweating.

Finally, they cut a vent. A ragged line from head height to the barren earth.

It's enough. One by one, they slip through.

Rigo doesn't feel so good. This whole situation makes him nervous. His palms are slick with sweat, and his stomach has gone as sour as a cup of vinegar. *This is a bad idea*, he thinks. Cael should have let well enough alone—eventually they were going to have to buckle down and get real jobs anyway. Can't hold off fate forever. So why not just give in? Why go messing with the Empyrean's things? The Empyrean doesn't want them here.

It's a high-pressure situation.

And Rigo doesn't like pressure. Pressure makes him want to throw up.

But he forgets all that as they step through the vent into the forbidden town of Martha's Bend.

Martha's Bend was probably three times the size of Boxelder, Rigo thinks. Some of the buildings around them go up to two, even three, stories. And they don't look as if they'd blow over in a stiff wind, either—a good number of them are made of brick, limestone, even marble, with roofs of slate and asbestos shingle. The bank building stands tall, looking to Rigo like some kind of temple built for the Lord and Lady, what with the pair of bulbous columns standing out front. Across the street sits a department store—an ace note emporium called Dewberry's Variety. Even from the outside, Rigo can see through the shattered storefront windows that Dewberry's Variety makes Boxelder's provisional store look like a hobo's lean-to.

Hell, all of Martha's Bend—even dead—makes Boxelder look like some kind of vagabond's shantytown.

For a moment Rigo wonders what it would have been like to live here. Go down to the candy store for some rock candy or maybe a cream soda. Hit Dewberry's and buy a new hat. Fly a kite down Main Street.

Wasn't Martha's Bend a horse town? Rigo knows he might be making that up, but that's all right; he's making all this up. He's thinking how a nice town like this might have made things different. Maybe his father wouldn't be drunk. Maybe his mother would care what happens to him. Suddenly Cael's little pipe dream doesn't feel so faraway. Maybe there's something to it.

But then it all hits him. He sees how the town is given

over to a creepy, watery pallor from the way the sun shines down through the plastic above. *This is a dead place.* Whatever prosperity was here is gone. The people are *gone*. Taken away to Lord and Lady know where. Maybe the people of Martha's Bend had the same dream Cael had. Maybe they pushed too hard, too far.

Maybe the Empyrean pushed back.

What's worse, Rigo doesn't see any sign of any garden. They're only here at the one side of town but so far, no apple trees, no berry bushes, no fat lettuce mounds or plumes of spinach. It's all concrete and dirt and brick—nary even a corn shoot pushing up through shattered earth.

And that's when Rigo's dream dies on the vine—a cold chill sweeps up his spine, and his hands go clammy. Martha's Bend isn't here anymore, and it hasn't been here for a long time.

Cael comes up next to him, and Rigo says, "I think I might throw up."

"You'll be fine."

"We're doing something real bad here." Rigo rubs his hands together. "I don't see any garden, either. Cael, we should go."

Cael keeps his voice low. "Look, even if we don't find the garden, we still have a whole town here to scavenge. The Butchers aren't here. We are. This is opportunity.

And I'm not willing to pass it by. Are you?"

"I think so."

"You are not. Stop talking like that. Look at it this way: Does your father have the balls to take risks like this?" Rigo says nothing. "Well, does he?"

"No." *He barely has the balls to get up off the chair to get himself a new drink*, Rigo thinks.

"Well, there you go. You do. You're a better man than him by a Heartland mile, Rodrigo. Now, quit your caviling and let's go make ourselves rich, yeah?"

Above their heads, the plastic bubble shifts and burbles as the wind pushes on it from the outside. Lane saunters over, twirling the saw-knife. "I hear we're getting rich. What's the plan, ladies?"

"I figure we split up," Cael says. "Cover more ground that way. Keep an eye out for anything—we're looking for the source of the garden, yeah, but we can take anything that isn't nailed down. You don't need to grab it now, but make a list in your head or on your hand—we'll need to start hauling stuff out of here before dark." He takes a look up and down the street. "Lane, you head east. Rigo, go west. I'm going to cut through that alley over there. I assume there's a street parallel I can scope out."

• • •

Lane heads in the direction Cael points him.

As he walks, it occurs to him suddenly: he doesn't really believe in Cael's dream. He wants to. Really. It's just that he's not that naive. Lane knows the truth. The truth is, the game is rigged.

Always has been. Always will be.

The system . . . that's where Cael's dream falls down. The Empyrean has created a feedback loop wherein power stays in the hands of the powerful and everybody else falls into a pecking order ranging from *a little bit screwed* to *a whole lot fucked.*

Lane knows that the Big Sky Scavengers are better than the Boxelder Butchers. That's never been in contention. What's also not been in contention—at least for Lane—is that it just doesn't matter. Skill? Talent? Hell with 'em. Meaningless! Even if the three of them are lucky enough to find something, somehow Boyland Barnes Jr. and his cronies will come out on top. Because he's the mayor's son, and the mayor has a direct line to the top.

The privileged are like cats: they always land on their feet, even when knocked out of a tree.

Cael thinks a pile of money is going to buy their way to the top. Lane knows differently. The Empyrean will come along and invent some new tax. Or they'll make ace notes worth less all of a sudden. Or they'll just send a pack of soldiers to come in and wipe Boxelder clean, seal it up in a big plastic bubble. Hell, maybe that's what happened to Martha's Bend. Maybe they got too rich. *Too uppity*. Needed to be swept under the rug before they started to believe their delusions of grandeur.

It is what it is. If they find something here today, good. Maybe it'll afford them some small comfort in the coming days. Maybe it'll be enough to stop Mayor Barnes from disbanding the crew.

Lane loves his friends. He may not show it well all the time, but that's because . . .

Well. He has to be a little standoffish. He doesn't want them to know the real Lane Moreau.

So, that's his mission here: keep the crew together. At any cost. Rigo and Cael are his family, and even though they don't know everything about him, they know more than anybody else.

Lane sees the Dewberry ace note emporium and suspects that's as good a place as any to start.

He ducks inside the door, ready to hunt and pick.

First thing Rigo does is run over to the MOM: the Monetary Offset Machine by the bank. Folks would walk up and put cash into the machine, and it would spit out a number of ace notes based on the current (and probably crappy) exchange rate. Rigo remembers when they used to have one at the Boxelder bank. He also remembers when they came and tore out the machine. And later, when they repurposed the bank as the Tallyman's office. What was it the Empyrean had said? Something like, "The Empyrean is best equipped to handle the financial accounts of those strong and stalwart citizens of the Heartland, citizens who shouldn't have to worry about such petty and paltry details."

The MOM is stylized, showing off the art deco earmarks of Empyrean design: vertical chrome, now rotten with rust, culminating in hard-angled edges; the celadon buttons—once polished Bakelite, now cracked and chipped; the faceplate where the Empyrean sigil—the winged horse known as the pegasus—still sits. (The old Empyrean logo plates are worth quite a few ace notes, not only for the eyes of jade and ruby but because Empyrean citizens are frequently collectors.) But what troubles Rigo is the bent metal opposite the hinges.

Somebody had already jacked open this thing. And stolen all the ace notes inside.

Curious.

The Empyrean, probably. Cleaning out the banks before closing off the town.

Just the same, Rigo reminds himself to come back here and pry off that pegasus seal.

For now he moves on. Across the street, he sees an old liquor store—it's called Busser's Booze, which makes him wonder if there's any relation to the Boxelder Busser. Both being in the booze business can't be a coincidence, can it?

Rigo pushes his way inside.

Cael cuts through the alley, metal chain-link fence rattling as he runs his hands along it. He steps out onto a second, smaller street—and there, right across from him, is an old hologram theater, the marquis leaning hard to the right, crooked letters still announcing the holo-flicks they were playing the day the Empyrean came in and shut down the town: *Nightshaders* and *The Day of the Dark Sun* and *Asmo's Road*. Cael's too young to have ever seen a holo-flick; but when he was little, Pop would tell him about them, often at bedtime. His father would paint such a picture, he could imagine the holograms playing out in front of him as they once had for Pop.

At first he thinks to bypass it. Much as he wants to go inside, see the old candy cases and the theater-in-the-round where the hologram played out onstage, he knows there won't be anything worth much in there.

But then something catches Cael's eagle eye.

The *N* in *Nightshaders* is poking out. Just slightly. Casting a shadow.

And behind it is a curl of green. A shoot or tendril. Showing off a few little leaves.

Maybe the theater *is* a good place to start.

Dewberry's appears entirely untouched.

Lane can't believe it.

Jeans folded up on shelves. Dresses on racks. Dapper white suits displayed on the wall. On the other side are dishes and pots and mugs and silverware. Beyond that, fishing poles, skinner knives, tents. Anything a Heartlander could want is here, and suddenly Lane regrets that Boxelder is too small to ever sport an ace note emporium like this.

All of it is covered in dust and spiderwebs. Motes of pollen float in beams of light.

This is heaven. Lane truly feels as if he's been swept up in the Lord and Lady's embrace, held between them and carried aloft to their mountain manor house in the sky.

With joy in his heart, he goes flipping through racks of clothing.

A seersucker with leather elbow pads.

A pair of black trousers with red suspenders.

A cable-knit sweater. A gingham blouse. Blue socks. White fedoras.

It's just too much. He's got to try on something. Something here has to fit him. He's heard girls call him "willowy," which isn't really a compliment, but he'll take it. Not that he needs girls to compliment him. And Francine . . . well. He doesn't want to think about her. Or any girls. The Heartland doesn't understand certain things, after all, and he just doesn't want to open that door.

Lane starts slipping out of his pants, his shirt. He wipes his hands and brow, as he doesn't want to sully these clothes or get dust stuck all over his skin.

He skips a new shirt and goes right for the seersucker jacket—it's a white suit with lavender pads and faint gray vertical stripes. He slips it on, bare chested.

But then, pulling back the jacket, something is revealed—

A little curl of pale green snaking up the center chrome of the rack.

Lane drops down to one knee and follows the coiled vine—as thin as a carburetor wire—down to the floor where it has poked up through the carpet.

"Strong little guy," he says. Like the rest of the garden.

He hears a scuff behind him: a footstep.

Lane wheels, expecting to see Cael or Rigo standing there.

But all he sees is a white cloth and a black-gloved hand descending toward his face.

His mind goes sideways. Everything fuzzes at the margins. He wills his knee to move, but all it does it give out beneath him.

Rigo ducks behind the counter of Busser's Booze, looking out over the empty crates and collapsed shelving. He thinks suddenly of his own drunken father ("I drink because you make me," he can hear his old man say) but puts that out of his mind. *Don't be scared. Stay in the moment. Let's get rich.*

Most of the booze is gone. Broken brown and green glass is everywhere. An old metal icebox sits in the corner, rust eaten but in pretty good shape. The floor beneath it is scratched up—ruts and furrows dug out of the wood. A light fixture above has a shattered bulb now home to a family of long-limbed cellar spiders.

If Father were here he'd be sniffing along the shelves for a taste.

There he goes again, thinking about him. Hard not to in a place like this.

Rigo wonders suddenly: How long has his father been a drunk? At first Rigo thinks, *Forever, he's been a drunk since the day I was born*; but he suspects that's not really true. The memories are few and far between—they're gauzy and uncertain, as if Rigo is staring through the greasy bottom of an old drinking glass—but he recalls his father being clean shaven, bright eyed, even smiling. Before the booze nibbled away at his soul, one drink at a time.

He used to hide it from Rigo. Successfully at first, but over time he got sloppier. He had a little cubbyhole behind the pellet stove in the root cellar, a space carved right out of the rock and dirt and concealed behind an old, moldy dartboard. Always a bottle or two back there. And a pair of glasses, as though someday he might be drinking with somebody instead of drinking alone.

Then one day his father just stopped hiding it.

Hiding it.

Rigo has an idea.

He totters to the back of the liquor store, brushing aside cobwebs. He heads to the icebox—but it's not the icebox he's interested in. It's the marks on the floor. Those furrows in the wood lead out from the base of the box. As if it's been moved. As if it's been moved many times over the course of months, even years.

Rigo sucks in a breath, wraps his arms around the box, and begins to groan and croak as he shimmies the box away from the wall.

An opening in the wall is revealed.

"Holy moly," Rigo says. Then crawls through the hole.

The entire theater is a garden.

The plants have pushed up from underneath, tearing through floorboards and shredding carpet. Tomato plants grow up through a shattered candy case. Grape vines hang from the ceiling beams like a giant's beard. Cael races through the double doors, sees that row after row of theater seats are torn asunder, springs exposed and made a part of various garden plants—again he spies glimpses of green beans and long, tapered red peppers and other leafy vegetables he can't identify.

In the center, the round stage with its glass plate—on which the holo-flicks were once projected from above—sits shattered, and up through the center grows a narrow-trunked tree.

From its boughs hang fat-bottomed pears.

Dozens of them.

A hundred maybe.

Cael has to have a taste. *Has* to.

He runs to the stage, hungry to taste the first pear he's eaten in almost a decade.

He doesn't notice that someone has come into the theater behind him.

• • •

Micky Finn's Botanical Gin.

Boxes upon boxes of it.

Rigo squats, hunkering down and squeezing his way through the small opening he discovered behind the icebox, and peers into a secret stash of spirits.

He does a quick count: thirteen boxes. An unlucky number any other time, but now, Rigo thinks, the number's run of bad mojo has petered out and flipped to the other side.

Rigo's sour feeling is gone; the snakes inside his stomach turn to butterflies, and they loosen a giggle that bubbles up and out of his throat. Cael is right. They're going to be rich.

Even better—

Cael didn't find this.

It's not that Rigo wants to take anything away from his friend, his captain. This whole endeavor was Cael's idea. But Cael's *always* the one who finds the good stuff. It's as if he has an eye that won't quit. Meanwhile, Rigo's always left looking for scraps.

Not this time.

He pumps his arm and does an awkward two-step victory dance.

The boxes, then.

The Micky Finn Botanical Gin logo shows a dapper

shark wearing a center-crease trilby hat on his head, with a sprig of blue juniper berries clutched in the broad, needle-toothed grin. The shark is winking, not so much as if he knows something you don't but rather as if you and he know something the rest of the world does not. The brand's motto is Micky Finn's: The Toothiest Gin.

Rigo pops the top off one of those crates and sees nine cork-tops staring back at him, each sealed to the glass with blue wax. The bottles themselves are a pale blue—the color of the shark, the color of juniper berries, the color of the sky just after a rain.

He takes out one of the bottles. The gin within sloshes about.

Rigo's forgotten all his anxiety. These are old spirits. The old boozers at Busser's Tavern are always going on about the brands they used to drink back in the day: Spalding & Wolboch's Vodka, Corazon Brandy, Jack Kenney Whiskey, something called Kin's Tucky Bourbon. All Heartland-made but popular enough on the Empyrean flotillas to keep the on-the-ground distilleries in business. Of course, someone up there figured out how to make this stuff in a lab, which means they don't need the Heartlander brands anymore. Rigo remembers being a kid when they made selling booze illegal. You can still make it; you just can't sell it. These days, it's all cheap fixy and chicha.

These bottles are prime stuff. Maven Cartwright will have no choice but to recognize their skills and pay out a few decks of ace notes. He tries to imagine the look on his own father's face—"See, Father? I brought you something, something you really want." For a moment, Rigo is lost in his reverie. What will everyone say? "Oh, did you hear? The Cozido kid found a stash of Micky Finn gin. That's right. Haven't seen Micky Finn's in a dog's age. No, no, you heard me right. Little Rodrigo was the one who found it. The Big Sky Scavengers, sure, sure. I bet Mayor Barnes is none too happy about that. Makes his son look bad, don't it? Hell, three cheers for Rodrigo Cozido! I hear even his father was proud. . . ."

But wait.

There's more.

The dust patterns on the floor—these boxes have been moved.

Recently.

The pried-open bank machine. The furrows by the icebox. And now this disturbed dust.

Rigo hunkers down low, gets his shoulders behind the boxes. They don't move easily; but while he's not strong, he's got some bulk (Father calls him a "fat little tamale"), and he's able to push several boxes at one time. He runs his fingers along the floor—

Along the edge of a door. A trapdoor.

A rope knot sits recessed into the wood. Rigo works his stubby fingers around the knot, pulls it up—and the trapdoor opens.

A tunnel awaits. Dirt walled. But lit—bathed in the sodium glow of lights strung up along the side. And in the middle of the tunnel: a set of iron tracks. Like train tracks, fixed to cross tie slats buried in the hard-packed earth.

Rigo dangles his head upside down through the hole. He sees the tunnel go about fifty feet one direction, then turn. He grunts, shifting his body so he can look in the other direction—

And ends up face-to-face with a strange man.

The man is jowly. Fat cheeks lined with ill-shorn beard bristle.

From his nose grows a thin spiral curl of a vine.

"Lord and Lady!" Rigo gasps, the blood rushing to his head, making him dizzy. He struggles to lift himself out of the hole; but the man growls, grabs Rigo's head in the crook of his arm, and presses a dirty red handkerchief laced with stinking chemicals against Rigo's nose and mouth.

Rigo feels his whole body sliding through the trapdoor like so much dead meat.

And then it's lights-out for Rigo.

• • •

The juice runs down Cael's elbow. Floods his mouth. The pear skin has bite, but the creamy flesh is so soft and smooth it melts in his mouth like lard in a hot skillet.

For a moment it's enough to wash everything else away.

He doesn't think about Gwennie and Boyland.

He doesn't think about his fight with Pop.

He doesn't think about Mayor Barnes disbanding the crew or the Empyrean flotillas or the rest of his life with weird little Wanda. Or even his dream of striking it rich here in Martha's Bend.

He doesn't *think* at all.

He just enjoys.

The moment is regrettably short-lived.

He hears a footstep behind him—the glass projector stage shifts and crackles—and instantly Cael is whipping around with the half-eaten pear and chucking it like a baseball. The fruit whacks off the head of a filthy, rag-swaddled vagrant.

As the pear rebounds, spraying juice and spinning away, Cael realizes he's seen this vagrant before. The pot belly, the teeth like white stones. The raggedy red cap on his dirty head.

This is the one Cael caught snooping through their stable.

Something isn't right. The realization has set him off-kilter—a keen frequency of dread runs through his every pore and follicle.

"You," Cael says.

The hobo's got something in his hand: a white cloth, like a table napkin. Soaked in something. Cael's nose catches a scent hanging in the air: an astringent odor—harsh, biting.

"Kid, don't make this tougher than it—" But suddenly the hobo leans in, squints. "It's you."

"The one with the slingshot," Cael says, whipping that very thing out of his back pocket.

"Wait!"

He lets fly with a ball bearing—no pebble this time—and the vagrant staggers back, flinging up his arm defensively. The ball bearing cracks hard against the hobo's wrist, drawing blood, probably chipping bone. The man staggers backward and tumbles off the stage.

Cael takes a running leap over the hobo—*Run!*—but between the man's yowls of pain he hears the hobo call after him.

"We have your friends!"

Cael skids to a stop. Breathes deep. *Rigo. Lane.*

He pauses. Breathing deep again. The slingshot heavy in his hand.

Cael turns and marches back to the vagrant, who lies

on the floor cradling his wrist and wincing in pain. The chemical-soaked cloth lies off to the side like a fallen dove.

Cael straddles the man, draws back the pocket of his slingshot as far as it'll go, a ball bearing pinched between his thumb and forefinger. He draws a bead between the man's eyes.

"I'll kill you if you hurt them," Cael says.

"They're all right."

"Prove it. Take me to them. Unless you want this metal marble buried in the meat of your brain."

"No, no, I'll show you. I swear. Don't kill me."

Cael nods. "Then show me."

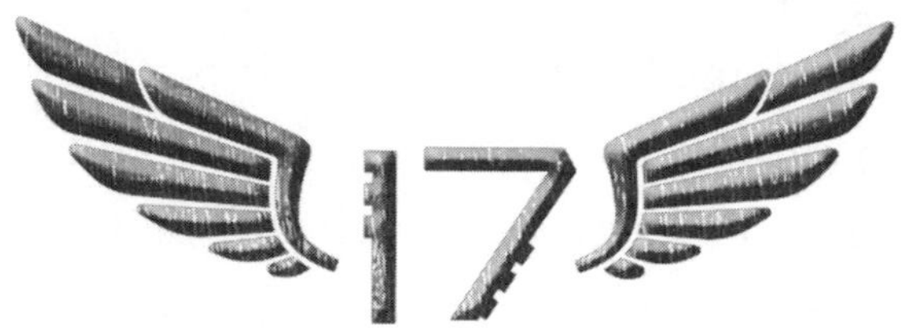

THE BURROW

THE SLINGSHOT POINTS right to the base of the vagrant's brain as he walks forward. Cael makes it clear that if he lets fly, the ball bearing will kill the stranger lickety-split—it will sever the brain from the spinal cord, and the curtain will close for this hobo's one-man show. Cael doesn't know if that's true, but it sure sounds good, and he's angry enough to be convincing.

The vagrant leads Cael down another alley, this one between a motorvator garage bay and a little old café with a half-collapsed awning. Halfway down, the hobo stops.

"Here," he says, nudging a ratty blanket with his ragged boot.

"Go on, then."

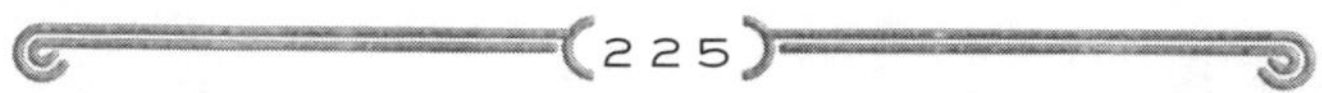

The vagrant stoops over with a grunt and, with his good arm, pulls back the blanket; beneath it is a corrugated tin door like you might find leading into a farmhouse root cellar. He gets his dirty, callused hands under it and lifts while Cael stands back, one eye aiming over the pinched slingshot pocket.

A doorway—dark and breathy with the scent of fresh earth—leads down.

"You better not be leading me into some sort of trap," Cael says.

"No," the hobo says. "Though once you see what's down here, I don't rightly know what happens next."

They descend into the earthen tunnel. It starts to slope further, and someone has dug out part of the ground and buried flat-level stones, creating a set of makeshift steps so you don't slip and go tumbling down. It gets darker and darker, but soon the light appears: buzzing sodium bulbs strung up in the distance.

They cross over a set of rails. Like for a train but smaller. *A mine cart maybe*, Cael thinks.

The tunnel bends.

They go with it. And there, ahead, is another vagrant.

This one is a woman. Her dirty red hair is braided in a crown above her head, her cheeks made orange by smudges of dirt. She's got on a dress, a rich-lady's dress like you might see on a mayor's wife; but it's been modified—the skirt torn at the knees, the sleeves shredded, bands of leather wrapped around the wrists. The dress was once pretty, Cael imagines, but now it's ruined—like everything the hobos touch. The woman stands there, writing on a chalkboard hanging on the wall, marking off *X*s and question marks and other symbols Cael doesn't know on a big, taped-off grid—he sees words at the top and along the side of the grid such as *yield* and *f1* and *f2*. She doesn't see Cael there yet.

"Hey, Jed," she says, marking off another *X* and comparing it to a paper in her hand. "Heard we found some kids messing around up above. Got two of them, but did you find the—"

"Marlene," the hobo says, and clears his throat once, then again more loudly.

She looks up. Eyes go wide. "Oh."

"Ma'am," Cael says, figuring that, hobo or no, a lady still deserves a modicum of respect. *After all, your sister's a vagrant, isn't she?*

The one called Jed swallows hard. "You're, ah, you're gonna want to get the boss for this."

"The boss," she says, spaced-out. Staring at Cael's slingshot. Then she snaps back to it. "The boss. Right."

She drops the chalk and runs off.

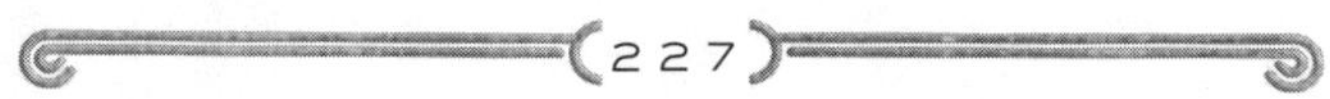

"Jed, huh," Cael says. "Well, lead on, Jed. Let's find my friends."

Cots. Tents. Tables.

Vagrants everywhere. Cael does a quick count—two dozen. Maybe more. Two are milling around an old brass coffeepot with a circle of blue flame flickering underneath. Another handful are lugging bags of something dark and earthy—could be soil, Cael thinks, but the color's off. Another sweeps the floor. All of them dressed in the telltale rags and repurposed clothing that separates a hobo from every other Heartlander. *It's like they* want *to look different*, Cael thinks. *Like they're proud of it.*

The lights bathe everything in a muddy yellow glow. Cael glances around and sees several other tunnels shooting off from this room. *These people are like groundhogs*, he thinks. *Or ants. They've dug a burrow, and now they live here. Hiding away from everyone else.*

Someone finally notices Jed and Cael.

A big hobo—skin as black as night, body built like a grain silo—cries out in alarm and draws a small sonic shooter from a holster at his hip.

"No, no, no!" Jed yells, waving his hands. "Don't shoot, Homer, don't shoot."

Cael's pulse is kicking now like a cranky horse, and the adrenalin shoots through him in a cold saline rush. He draws the ball bearing back farther, the tubing on his slingshot tightening with a creak. "You shoot me, I shoot him. I just came for my friends."

"Jeezum Crow, Jed," Homer mutters, shaking his head. "Asked you to do one thing, and you bring this to our door."

"Just go get the kid's friends, okay?"

Homer doesn't holster the sonic shooter, but he backs around a table and winds through a cluster of cots, disappearing down one of the side tunnels.

"What the hell are you people doing down here?" Cael asks.

"You'll see," Jed says, "*if* the boss wants you to see."

Someone moves off to Cael's left. Another woman. Matronly. But tough, too. Broad hips *and* broad shoulders. Skin weathered like saddle leather. She's got something behind her back.

A small hand-shovel.

Cael shoots her a look. Nods toward his slingshot. "Drop the shovel, ma'am."

The woman rolls her eyes and then shows the shovel and lets it clatter to the ground. But the shovel isn't the problem. Not anymore.

It's her hand.

Or what passes for a hand.

It's like Poltroon all over again. Her fingers are vines, though her thumb is human. Her vine-fingers—leafy, green, whispering against one another—drift and twitch.

Oh, Lord and Lady, no.

"The Blight," Cael whispers. Suddenly he feels sick and dizzy and scared. He hears Rigo's voice in the hollow of his mind: *Told you this was a bad idea, Captain.*

"We're good people," Jed says.

"You're Blighters. You're sick."

"Not all of us. We're not bad people."

Cael remembers the things Poltroon said: *The Blight. It talks to me. I can hear it inside my head. It hates us. Hates who we are. Like a child who hates its parents.*

Suddenly, a distant squeaking fast approaching. Homer emerges from the same side tunnel, this time pushing a rusty wheelbarrow with a half-flat front wheel. Piled into the wheelbarrow are two bodies: Lane and Rigo.

They're dead.

Cael can't breathe. He feels the adrenalin turn to poison panic—a high-pitched whine in his ears, a sense of vertigo threatening to knock him to the ground.

But then Rigo moans and his arm flops over the side, hitting the metal wheelbarrow bucket with a dull bang.

What should he do? Cael can't think. His friends are . . .

unconscious. Maybe hurt. Trapped in an underground lair full of contaminated Blighters and homeless wretches.

The big hobo shrugs impatiently. “Well? You said you wanted your friends. Here they are, boy. It’s like dinnertime, *ding-ding-ding*. Come and get ’em.”

Cael steps out from behind Jed. His hands are shaking. He repoints the slingshot at Homer as he steps forward into the middle of the room. He can feel all eyes on him. He spies another Blighter off to the side: a man whose whole neck is green, veiny, textured like the underside of a leaf.

“Step back,” Cael says to Homer, gesturing with the slingshot. “Go on. Move away.”

Homer holds up both hands and shakes his head. “You’re asking for trouble, kid.”

They won’t let us leave here, Cael thinks. *They know we could spill the beans. Bring the Empyrean down on their heads. Shit!*

Cael lifts up a knee, nudges Rigo’s hand. “Rigo. *Rigo*.”

“Muh,” Rigo mutters. “Muh grub whuh wee.”

“Wake up.”

“Fuh. Nuh now.”

Damnit.

Cael starts formulating a plan: he’ll point the slingshot at Jed again, make Jed push the wheelbarrow back down the tunnel and up through the cellar doors. By then, Lord and Lady willing, Rigo and Lane will finally have stirred.

But he never gets to enact that brilliant plan.

Because the boss is here.

Cael hears someone call his name.

"*Cael?*"

He looks over his shoulder.

And there stands Pop.

THE LORD AND LADY'S GARDEN

"THEY SAID THEY saw some kids up in town, but I had no idea," Pop says. "Though I should've figured it was you."

Cael's not sure what to say.

"You . . . have some questions," Pop says, sitting at a small table made of a board lashed to a couple of old barrels. Cael sits on a chair that's really just a barrel cut in half.

"Pop, I feel like I'm dreaming. But I'm just not sure yet if it's a good dream or a bad one."

Pop says nothing, just pushes a tin cup of coffee toward Cael.

Cael takes it. It's cool down here in the burrow, and the steam from the coffee rises like ghosts from a fresh-dug grave.

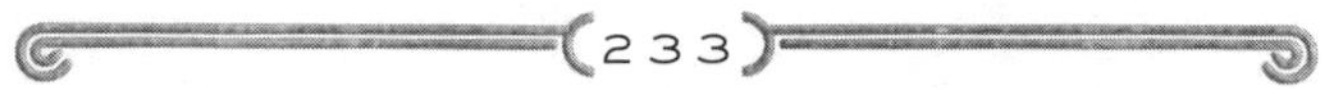

"Pop, there're hobos down here." Cael lowers his voice. "*And Blighters*."

"I know, son."

"That ain't right."

Pop forces a smile. "It's okay, son. They're nothing to be scared of."

"I didn't say I was scared—"

"I know, I know, but these are people just like us. Given a bad turn of the worm, any Heartlander at any time could become one of them. The Empyrean doesn't like our tax bill or we get three strikes against our Tally, and we get booted out of town on a Remittance Order, too. You know a Remittance Order used to pay?" Pop takes his own cup of coffee, sips from it. "It's true. They used to pay you a small stipend—a remittance—to get out of town. That practice is long gone, but the name stuck, I guess. Anyway. Point is, you get a raw deal from the Empyrean—or worse, you wake up one morning and find a scaly patch of plant fiber or a leaf growing up out of your chin whiskers—and that's it. It's not your fault. It's piss luck is all."

Like Poltroon, Cael thinks. *He didn't ask for what happened to him.*

Cael tells his father everything. It comes spilling out of him like water from an overturned bucket. He tells Pop how he'd been seeing Gwennie, how they found the garden and then went out in the piss-blizzard to collect more of the harvest. He tells Pop about Poltroon, too. About what he was. What he said. And how he ended up ground up in his own machine—suicide by harvester.

Pop listens the whole time, nodding, making all the right sounds. When he hears about Poltroon, it seems to strike him deeply. "We could've offered him a place here."

"Pop, the Blight . . . if what he said was true, you can't trust these people."

"What he said *is* true, son. The Blight is a sickness; don't mistake what I'm telling you. But we've found a way to stave off its worst effects, to halt its march toward taking over the victim's body." Pop takes another slow, delicate sip of coffee, almost as if he's drinking it as part of an Empyrean tea service rather than here at a barrel table in an underground bunker full of hobos and vine-heads. "Besides, the Blight victims have a very special gift that comes with their curse."

"Gift?"

Pop nods. "Come on; I'll show you."

"Welcome to the garden."

Splayed out before them is a massive underground chamber. Cael figures it's easily as big as the acreage of their own homestead. Everything is bright: humming ultraviolet lights hang from above, bathing everything in a warm glow. Row after row of tables line the room, and on these tables are wooden boxes cut into grids—each square about a foot on every side and filled with soil. The boxes are planters, and Cael spies tomatoes and beans and peppers. A red flash of strawberry. An orange butternut squash shaped like a dog's head.

The front half of the room is the model of scientific order. Everything in neat boxes, everything kept to the grids.

But toward the back half of the room the garden descends into chaos. Wildness has taken hold. The boxes are bulging; some are broken outright. Roots dangle from beneath the tables. The plants are thick, robust stalks—the tomatoes that hang are bigger than a baby's head. The peppers are thick, swollen with asymmetrical lumps and curves. At the far side of the room, the plants have left the boxes entirely—they're climbing up and growing *out of* the walls. They ascend toward the ceiling and push through the earth, clearly seeking proper sunlight.

Two Blighted women—one with a tail-like vine emerging from the waistband of her trousers, another with an ear that looks like a knob of cauliflower—tend to the plants, misting them with water, tying stalks to stakes, stroking the leaves with gentle caresses.

Pop goes out, stoops down to whisper to one of the kneeling women. She hands him something wrapped in a cloth, and he returns to Cael with a handful of strawberries so big they could be small apples.

"Here," Pop says. "Taste."

Syrupy sweet. A rush of pink juices. The smell is intoxicating: a sharp, earthy sweetness. It stains Cael's hands red.

Cael hears a footstep behind him, followed by a "Whoa."

He turns to see Rigo and Lane—both looking groggy, like the morning after Rigo's father pickles himself with fixy—flanked by the big hobo.

"Thanks, Homer."

"You got it, Pop," Homer says with a deferential nod.

Cael's not sure he likes other people calling his father Pop, but he doesn't have time to worry about that right now.

"You okay?" Cael asks his two friends.

"Feels like I've got shuck rats fighting over a corncob inside my skull," Lane says. "But yeah."

Rigo nods, too, but in a barely-paying-attention way. Instead, he steps up next to Pop, eyes goggled out, staring at the garden of order descending into chaos, of sanity tumbling toward wild, unfettered growth. "Holy smokes."

Pop hands Rigo a strawberry. Lane, too. They both bite in, and Cael wonders if that's what he looked like: eyes rolling backward, head lolling about on the neck. And the sounds: *nngh*, *mmmph*, *ohhhhhguhhh*.

"What you see here," Pop says, "you can't tell anyone. Not Gwennie, not Maven Cartwright, not a single soul up in Boxelder. Not yet."

Cael stares out over the garden. He sees brown roots—like roots from a pear tree—and realizes they're beneath the holo-flick theater. "What *do* I see here, Pop?"

Before Pop can answer, Lane pushes to the front. "It's the future. Isn't it, Mr. McAvoy?"

Pop nods. "I think so."

"Your dad's sticking it to the man." Lane laughs and pops his knuckles. "Bad. Ass."

"We thought we'd provide a safe haven for hobos and Blight victims," Pop says, "and in the process grow some proper food. Start putting it out to those families in the Heartland we know need a boost—not to sell, but to eat."

"But you could be rich," Cael says. "*We* could be rich."

"Being rich doesn't mean squat out here, son. Sure, maybe we'd make enough ace notes to climb to the top of the manure heap, but it'd still be us sitting on dung. Things need to change. And food is where that change starts. That's how the Empyrean controls everything. We're not allowed to grow real crops. We're forced to grow an invasive corn species that isn't even supposed to be eaten. The amount of corn it takes to make a single tank of fuel or sugar syrup for the Empyrean flotillas could have been enough corn—were it properly edible—to feed a single person for the better part of a year. And it's killing the soil. Ten more years of Hiram's Golden Prolific and our land won't be able to support anything but the corn—*if* that. But they"—Pop stabs a finger upward—"don't give a shuck rat's right foot about us down here. They shut the schools. Killed off the livestock farms. We're just slaves down here. Horseshoes for their pretty pegasus." Pop takes a deep breath. "Besides, this is illegal. We start selling these plants, the flotillas will send down squadron after squadron of soldiers to clean house."

"See?" Lane says, poking Cael in the ribs. "This is what I've been talking about, man. The rich don't want us getting all think-for-yourselfy down here."

Cael ignores his friend. "So, you can't sell it. Now what?"

"Turns out we have a secret weapon."

Lane grins. "I like the sound of that."

Pop says, "We thought we'd tend a nice little garden, have some yield, sneak it to the Heartlanders, and at least make sure people were eating healthy. But this stuff . . ." He spreads his arms out so they can behold the chaotic majesty of the garden. "This garden will not be denied. The plants don't need much sunlight. Or water. Or anything. They're like Hiram's Golden Prolific: These plants are aggressive.

They'll grow anywhere. They're real competitors." Pop points to the ceiling. "And they're spreading. They've come up through the floorboards and carpets. Give it another year and this whole town will be a jungle of fresh fruits and vegetables. And as you know, it's already left Martha's Bend."

"The garden trail," Rigo says.

"Mmm-hmm. Heading toward Boxelder. And we've found other plants growing in other directions. The roots and tendrils have pierced the plastic blister. They won't be stopped. Before long we won't have to do anything at all—if we can keep this place hidden for long enough, the Empyrean won't be able to stop the garden. It'll be like Eden all over again."

Eden: the garden where the Lord and Lady were born from the womb of the mother earth, from the bosom of the Heartland itself.

Just an old story, Cael thinks. *But maybe not anymore.*

"Where'd you get the seeds to grow this stuff?" Cael asks.

Suddenly his father pulls back. Cagey. Licks his lips. "Well, son. I have a . . . contact. . . ."

Lane blurts out, "It's someone in the Sleeping Dogs, isn't it?"

"An Empyrean double agent?" Rigo asks, still goggle-eyed.

Footsteps behind them. In a hurry. Homer and the

woman from earlier, Marlene, appear in a worried panic.

"Pop," Marlene says. "We have more uninvited guests up top."

"More kids," Homer says, shooting Cael an accusing look.

"What?" Cael asks. "We didn't tell anybody!"

"Come on," Pop says. "I better take a look myself this time."

Pop leads them to a backroom in the burrow, and Cael is surprised to see projected on the floor a series of changing three-dimensional holographic images, each revealing a location from the town up above. Outside the motorvator garage. Inside the Dewberry emporium. Looking out from the MOM bank machine. No wonder the hobos knew Cael and his crew were in town. They were on camera the whole time.

Pop explains, "Martha's Bend is—er, was—a more prosperous town than Boxelder. Got a bigger hunk of the Empyrean dole, too. That means Empyrean agents were watching. But they cut the feed long ago after they wiped the town clean. We just hooked the cameras back up and used the holo-flick projector to give us access."

It occurs to Cael that his father is far smarter than he ever gave him credit for.

"What the heck happened to Martha's Bend?" Lane asks.

Cael sees his father's brow knit, same as it does whenever he doesn't want to admit an unpleasant truth. But Lane doesn't have a chance to press him, because as the holographic surveillance flicks through image after image, one registers real trouble:

Boyland Barnes Jr.

His buckethead comes roving into view, trailed by the rest of his crew: Mole, Felicity, and Gwennie.

Gwennie.

Cael's palms go sweaty.

Pop tenses. "That's not good."

Homer leans in. The sonic shooter is back in his hand. "You want us to handle it?"

"We'll fix it," Cael blurts.

Rigo and Lane give him a quizzical look.

"Son—"

"If they're here, they're here because of us. I don't know why or how, but they are. This is our mess, and we'll run them off."

Pop claps Cael on the shoulder. "I trust you. Go do what you have to do. And above all else, *don't* let them find out what we have going on here."

UNEXPECTED GUESTS

BOYLAND'S CALLING HIS NAME.

"McAvoy! I know you're here."

The words echo through the dead town of Martha's Bend.

Cael and his friends come up through the trapdoor behind the icebox inside Busser's Booze. Out the greasy, dust-caked window they spy the Boxelder Butchers walking down the street. Felicity's got a corn sickle. Mole's dragging a comically large chain behind him. Gwennie's hanging back, arms crossed, looking none too pleased about any of this.

"They're itching for a fight," Lane says. "That's not good. Rigo, why don't you go kick all their asses while me and Cael here sip some Micky Finn's gin."

Rigo bugs out. "I'm not going out there!"

"Hey. *You* said you were a tough guy. Always talking about putting the beatdown on the Butchers. Here's your chance, stud."

Cael gives them both a scowl. "Hush up. We're all going out there."

He sucks in a breath, puffs out his chest, and exits the store.

Boyland and the others have already passed by—but Mole hears the door and turns his squirrelly little head toward the sound. "Whistle-pig at the hole!"

The Butchers turn and face Cael just as Lane pushes Rigo out the door and follows after.

"Hey, McAvoy," Boyland says, laughing. "Funny seeing you here. I don't remember the Empyrean opening up Martha's Bend yet. Did you get a special dispensation from Proctor Agrasanto? Did he, Mole?"

"I don't think so!" Mole says, cackling, the chain rattling behind him.

"I don't think so, either. What gives, McAvoy? Lottery's not till tonight. Did you think you won early? Did you think you'd bust your way in here, get first pick on the scavenge, and make off like a magpie with money in his beak?"

Cael shrugs. "Guess that's exactly what I figured."

Boyland walks forward, closing the distance between them. He tilts his head left and right—the bones in his neck pop and grind. "That's not gonna happen."

"You could've just told your daddy. Begged and whined and had him put in a call to Agrasanto." Cael watches Boyland's lip twitch. "Why didn't you?"

"Maybe I like to handle things myself."

"That ain't it. You think you're gonna get first pick instead of us. You just couldn't stand it. Just the *thought* of us coming out number one really burns your hide, doesn't it? How'd you know we were here anyway?"

"Field shepherd saw you heading this direction. I grabbed the yacht, and we took a ride. Followed your stench all the way here."

That corn sickle of Felicity's is rusty but sharp. Cael can see the edge whetted to a steel gleam. Mole might not do much with that chain of his; but if Felicity wants to, she'll cut them all up pretty good. And out here in the middle of nowhere, too.

The slingshot feels heavy in his back pocket.

Cael's fast. Real fast. But can he draw a bead on her before she puts that blade to Lane's neck? Or sticks it in Rigo's stomach? He wouldn't put it past her. She's crazy, that one. Always was a bully. Cael's pretty sure she has a thing for Boyland, too. Can't be happy about Gwennie being on his arm and with them now.

Gwennie's watching the whole thing, not saying a word.

"What do you want to do here, Junior? We gonna throw down? Is that the plan?"

"Might be, McAvoy. I still owe you for sucker punching me back at that turd-box you call a farm. We all know I can take you."

Cael sneers. "I wouldn't be so quick on the stick with that one." A little voice inside his head is screaming: *You're supposed to be getting rid of them, not getting caught up in a pissing match*. But here? Now? In front of Gwennie? With his father watching on camera? Cael wants to tussle. He wants to make this thick-necked dope eat a whole fistful of ball bearings.

"Wait!" Rigo says, stepping between them. "*Wait*. We'll give you what we found."

"*Rigo*," Cael hisses.

"What'd you find?" Boyland asks.

"Buncha cases of Micky Finn gin," Rigo says. "Good stuff. *Old* stuff. Worth a ton of ace notes. Get you all the recognition you want. Heck, with a find like that, they'll be carrying you around on their shoulders for a week."

Their drunken shoulders, Cael thinks. *Hope they drop you on your head.*

"Micky Finn, huh," Boyland says. "What else?"

"That's . . . that's it," Rigo says.

"Rest is picked over," Cael lies.

Boyland shoves Rigo out of the way, thrusts his face up in Cael's. "You think I'm mule kicked?"

"I do," Cael says.

A fist pistons into Cael's stomach. Pain radiates up into his chest and down into his balls. Boyland doesn't let him fall, though. He hauls Cael to his feet. "I know the drill, dirtbag. You give me the Micky Finn, and meanwhile you're sitting on something here that's a hundred times bigger. I come home thinking I'm the champion and then you roll into town like Jeezum Crow himself. No way." The mayor's son reaches down, grabs Cael's wrist, turns the hand over. "And what's with the pink hands, anyway? You smell like a girl."

Cael, still hurting, can't help himself. "I was with your mother last night."

Pow. Another gut-punch. Cael doubles over. Feels a string of drool creep out over his bottom lip and dangle there.

"You're dead, McAvoy. All of you are—"

"Put him down, Boyland." Gwennie steps in next to the mayor's son.

"What?"

"I said, put him down."

Boyland drops Cael, whose legs barely manage to keep him standing.

"Now," Gwennie says, "we're going to take their deal and

go. We shouldn't even be here. You really think a mayor's son should get caught in a place like this? You really want your father to pay for what you did here today?"

Boyland's thinking about it, his eyes roving. The thought bouncing back and forth around the inside of his skull like a rubber ball whipped against the wall. "Hell with all that. I want what they found." Boyland points at Cael. "And I want *his* head on the end of my boot." He practically barks it as he says it, lips wet with a shining froth.

It's then that Gwennie gets real close to Boyland.

"You like the things we do together, Boyland? You like kissing me? Getting your hand up under my shirt? Or inside my pants?" She says it loud enough for only Cael and Boyland to hear. Those words cut Cael to the heart—he's not sure whether she's trying to help him or hurt him.

But then he sees that it cuts to the heart of another as well: Felicity's knuckles go white around the handle of her sickle. So she heard, too. Gwennie keeps talking. "You want those things to keep on keeping on, then I suggest you leave this alone and we all say our good-byes. Otherwise, you and me will have a problem."

It takes a moment, but Boyland nods. "Fine." He steps back and points to Rigo. "Go start bringing out the gin, you little piece of crap."

"Boyland!" Felicity snarls. "You're just gonna bend over like that?"

"Felicity, leave it."

"For that cooze?"

"She's my Obligated, Felicity; you keep your damn—"

It all happens so fast.

Cael tracks Felicity's gaze. Sees how it falls on Gwennie. Sees how it burns with a kind of hatred he doesn't even see when Boyland looks at him.

Felicity pushes past Boyland.

The sickle knife is in her hand.

Gwennie's facing the other way.

Lane cries out. Boyland, too.

The knife rises—the watery sunlight glints off the edge.

Then: a sharp crack.

The bones in Felicity's hand snap like firecrackers going off.

The ball bearing—the one that just flew from Cael's slingshot—falls to the dirt.

Alongside the corn sickle.

Lane swoops in and snatches up the knife. Boyland pulls Gwennie aside in a protective hug—a movement that burns Cael deep. Felicity drops to her side and rolls in the dirt like a shot dog, cradling her shattered hand, howling, sobbing. Somewhere in those bleats of pain, Cael hears her trying to scream Boyland's name.

Mole runs away. He drops the chain into the dust and hightails it.

"Get out of here," Lane hisses, gesturing with the sickle. "Go on! Go home. Tell your daddy if you want. Take this moon-cat with you." He nudges Felicity with his shoe, spurs her to scramble to her feet and come up alongside Boyland—who pulls away from her.

To Cael's surprise, they do as Lane says.

Boyland holds Gwennie close. And she holds him right back. Felicity flags behind, sobbing, begging for him to wait. The Big Sky Scavengers watch as the Boxelder Butchers retreat from the streets of Martha's Bend, chastened, defeated.

The victory tastes of dust and bitter fruit.

GAMES OF CHANCE

HE SHOULD FEEL good right now, but he doesn't. Cael instead feels as if he's got a nest of snakes balling up in his gut. His heart won't stop pounding in his chest. He's already gnawed his thumbnail down to the bloody quick. The scene replays out again and again. Boyland. Gwennie. Felicity. The breaking of bones. The knife in the dust.

This should be a good day. But it's not. Not anymore.

"Go home," Pop says. "It's going to be dark before long."

"Pop, that went sideways, and it's all my fault."

"You stood up for yourself." Pop musses his hair. "You saved Gwennie."

"I shot a girl."

"Felicity Jenkins is barely a girl. She's more like a wolverine in a dress."

Cael feels as if he should laugh, but he can't find the humor right now. "What if Boyland tells the mayor?"

"So he tells him. He tells him he caught you here. Or maybe he doesn't say anything because he doesn't want to admit he went sticking his hands in the honey jar. It'll be okay." That last sentence is a lie. Cael can feel it. *It's not going to be okay.*

"I think I love Gwennie."

"I know you do."

"But I can't have her. She's Obligated to *him*."

Pop smiles a soft, sad smile. "I'll tell you a funny story sometime. But all I'll say right now is, don't count your ace notes till the deal is done. In the meantime, we need to get you out of here. Just in case Barnes comes poking around our farm looking to confirm what his son tells him. Least that way we don't get you in trouble."

"Shoot, Pop, don't even bother. Wanda's boat ain't any faster than a donkey with both his back legs broken. We won't get home before dark. We'll be lucky to get home before *morning* the way that piece of crap boat drags along." Cael presses his face into his hands and moans.

"That's why you'll leave the boat here. Take the rail-raft."

"The what-now?"

"Come on, I'll show you."

The twin rails dead-end against a backstop made of logs and railroad ties. Homer comes up behind them with Marlene, the two of them carrying a raft made of wooden planks lashed together.

Pop twirls his finger, asks them to turn it over.

"Look here," Pop says, pointing out the four metal caltrops—one bolted to each corner of the raft. To Cael they look like a child's jacks. But he knows what they are—he's scavenged a couple dozen over the years.

"Magna-cruxes."

They're all gleaming steel and hard edges. A magna-crux is a simple-enough device—a person could make his or her own given time and materials. They're just big magnets shaped into three-dimensional *X*s. Cael's never seen them in action before, and when Homer flips over the raft—one-handed—he places it on the tracks. The magna-cruxes fit over the rails, letting the raft hover.

"A raft-rail," Cael says. "Genius."

Rigo and Lane show up with a couple of bags full of fruit and veggies.

"For the trip," Lane says, biting into a pepper.

Pop puts his foot on the raft, moving it back and forth. "The raft is frictionless. She'll go pretty fast if you want her to. We've cut a few short oar-poles; all you need to do is give it a few good pushes, and you'll be zipping along at a fast clip."

"Where's it go?"

"Underneath our stable."

Of course. "That's why I saw the vagr—er, Jed there."

Pop nods. "He was coming to fetch me with the raft. Now, you boys go home. Get some sleep. It's been a challenging day. I'll try to come home later tonight. Oh, hey, the Lottery's on tonight." He winks. "Maybe we can forget all this garden nonsense if we win."

"Yeah, yeah, yeah." Cael steps up to his father, gives him a sudden hug.

"I love you, Cael."

"Love you, too, Pop."

"Give a kiss to your mother for me. Tell her I'll be home soon."

Cael pulls away and steps onto the raft. Rigo follows, waves. "Later, Mr. McAvoy."

Before Lane steps on, he looks to Pop. "You really are a badass, you know that? I wish you were my dad. Then I could be proud."

Pop shakes Lane's hand. "We're family, Lane. Don't

ever think we're not. Now, go! Go!"

The rail-raft starts to drift even before they use the oar-poles. They climb on board and Lane and Rigo man the oars, thrusting them downward and giving a good push—and the raft zips along like a greased-up piglet down a metal chute.

The back of the mayor's hand cracks hard against Boyland Jr.'s face. Junior's head snaps back, the cheek reddened, his teeth biting the inside of his mouth. He immediately tastes blood.

"You dumb shit," the mayor says.

"You're drunk," Junior mumbles.

"Better than dumb!" The elder Barnes rounds his desk and plops down into the chair behind it, slouching as he does so. With a thumb, he spins the cap off a bottle of Jack Kenney whiskey, takes a pull right from the bottle. "Martha's Bend. Martha's Godsdamn Bend? You want to get me fired? Maybe you don't like this house? Perhaps you don't enjoy the *comforts* that my *position* affords—"

Junior's mother pokes her head into the office. "Everything okay in here? Lottery's on the Marconi in fifteen minutes. Just in case you want to listen."

"Woman, get the hell out of here," the mayor slurs.

He waves his hands dismissively, still holding the whiskey bottle. The booze sloshes up inside the bottle, almost spills. She leaves, and when she does, Junior feels the heat of his father's gaze. "You're as bad as she is. I see her in you."

Boyland Jr.'s face still stings with the strike. He licks away a drop of blood trickling toward the inside corner of his mouth. He hates it when his father gets like this. Which is all too often these days. And it's not just him. Half the town is drunk and pissed off anymore. It's like they don't appreciate what they have.

Savages. All of them. He won't be like them.

He cinches up his wounded pride and says, "Sorry, Daddy."

"Damn right you're sorry." The mayor tilts the bottle toward his son. "You want?"

"Nah, I'm . . . I'm okay."

"For your face. Your cheek. It'll numb it."

"I'm all right."

The elder Barnes narrows his eyes. "When a Heartlander offers you a drink, you don't say no. That's just good manners."

Junior nods gamely, reaches for the bottle, takes a swig. It tastes like hot, scorched sugar. He coughs. His eyes water. He hands back the bottle.

"Smooth, isn't it?"

"Real smooth," Junior lies, his throat feeling as if he just swallowed a bunch of angry yellow jackets. He turns to go. "I'm gonna go grab something to eat before the Lottery."

"Hold up. What happened out there anyway? What'd you find at Martha's Bend, boy? I remember going there as a kid. When the road there was still open and not grown over with all that damn corn."

"Nothing," Boyland lies. Images flash before him: Cael's defiance, Gwennie talking him down, Felicity going at her with a sickle. With a damn sickle! She can't be on the crew anymore. Not after that. Damnit. *Damnit*. He shakes it off. "Place was, uh, already long picked over. The Empyrean, probably. You know how it is."

"But you saw the McAvoy boy there."

"Yessir." He thinks to add, "And we beat his ass real good."

"*He* didn't find anything, either?"

"Not by the looks of it." This isn't a lie, but Boyland suspects Cael found something.

"But you don't know for sure."

"No. I don't—I'm not sure." Junior just wants to leave. He doesn't want to be in this room anymore with his stinking skunk-of-a-drunk father. "He had pink hands."

"What?"

"His hands were pink. Sweet smelling, too."

"Like perfume."

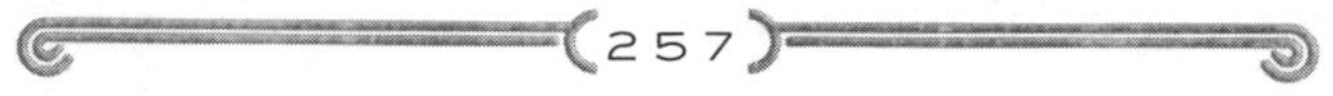

"Yeah. Like perfume. Strawberry perfume."

Mayor Barnes leans back in his chair. The furrows in his forehead are so deep you could tuck a few ace notes in there and they'd stand up straight. The man takes another deep swig of whiskey. "Strawberries. Shit. *Shit*." He sets down the bottle and recaps it. "That's it. Lord and Lady, come and kiss my bum-cheeks; *that's it*."

The elder Barnes stands up, knocking over his chair. He steadies himself on the desk, blinks a few times as though to make the room stop spinning, and then marches over to his son and pats him on the cheek. "You did good, boy."

"Thanks, Dad," Junior says, not sure what he just did.

From the other room, Junior's mother calls, "Lottery's on!"

A big, goofy grin spreads across the mayor's face like a pool of spilled pancake syrup. His eyes light up, and he licks his lips. "Hell with that Lottery. I just won a Lottery all my own, boy. I have to go make a call to a Proctor Agrasanto. If you'll excuse me now."

Giggling like a madman, Mayor Barnes pushes past his son and saunters out of the room, happy as a squealer knee-deep in his own shit.

• • •

The string of lights are lit only so far.

The cable ends, and with it the light. The rail-raft glides into darkness.

It's a strange sensation, Cael thinks. It's like floating. Or flying.

Riding the rail-raft isn't that different from piloting one of the land-boats, but those still give you some sense of being connected to the ground: the corn tickling the underside of the boat, the horizon line separating ground and sky, the wind running its fingers through your hair. This is a frictionless, soundless slide through a black tunnel.

The boys don't talk much along the way. Not about Martha's Bend. Or Pop and his garden. Or Gwennie and Boyland.

Eventually, way down the tunnel, they see a winking orb—a faint, golden light that gets closer and closer as the string of lamp-bulbs appear once more.

Cael's almost home. It's hard to think they left just this morning. The day at Martha's Bend feels as though it stretched on into forever like a wad of taffy pulled thinner and thinner.

They come up fast on the backstop. Suddenly it's a race to jam the oar-poles against the ground or the tunnel walls to slow the raft down. Rigo thrusts his out, and it hits a stone and snaps—his head pulls back, a line of blood trickling down his nose where the broken stick whips back and smacks him. Lane and Cael wince, gritting their teeth, the bottoms of the oar-poles juddering against the ground like flat stones bouncing across the surface of a pond.

They slam into the backstop and tumble forward, shouldering hard into the mound of dirt and railroad ties. Rigo piles on last—yelping like a puppy as he does. They end up in a heap on the still-bobbling rail-raft.

"I think my foot traveled up my ass," Lane says.

Rigo wipes his head. "I'm bleeding."

Cael grunts, untangling himself from the other two. He dusts himself off, then points to a ladder leading up. "Guess that's the way out." *A secret tunnel under our stable. Here the whole time, and I never knew it.* Again he feels a pang of pride at his own father's adventuresome exploits.

They all clamber up to the ladder. Ready to put this day behind them.

But the day has more in store.

They push open the hatch, displacing a big pile of straw. Motes of dust swirl in the air, capturing the fading light of day. Rigo sneezes. Lane punches his shoulder. All feels right with the world. The three of them exit the stable and head back toward the house.

"I better get home," Rigo says. "I'm sure I'm gonna

catch hell for being gone so long. Wish I thought to bring at least one bottle of that gin back for him."

Lane shrugs. "Don't you want to come inside, catch the Lottery?"

"Nah. None of us are gonna win." He lowers his voice. "Besides, who wants to end up on one of those crappy-ass floatillas, huh? The Empyrean can *suck* it."

He and Lane share a clumsy high five.

"You know what?" Lane says. "Rigo's right. Who cares? I don't want to win the Lottery, and I pity the fool who does. Suckers."

The front door opens, and Bessie comes out, wreathed in the medicinal smell of the bag-balm unguent she uses to moisturize the tumor that hangs off her shoulder. "Hiya, boys. You out here gabbing about the Lottery? Can you believe it?"

"Believe what?" Rigo asks.

Cael cocks an eyebrow. "Did we miss it?"

Bessie's face registers an emotion halfway between shock and confusion. "So you don't know?"

"Know what?"

"Gwendolyn Shawcatch and her family just won the Heartland Lottery."

• • •

Gwennie feels as if she's falling.

Her parents are dancing around the kitchen. Her father hooting. Her mother cackling like the Maize Witch. Her little brother—Richard Jr., but everyone calls him Scooter—is giggling so hard he might pass out right there on the floor.

We won the Lottery.

She got home, feeling hollowed out by the events at Martha's Bend. On the one hand, she felt as if she betrayed Cael just by being there with Boyland—and saying those things! On the other, she felt as if Cael had betrayed *her*. It was his fault she wasn't in the crew anymore. And then Boyland being Boyland . . . pretends he's all tough, but she suspects inside he's just a scared little boy. After Felicity came at her with that corn sickle, well—Boyland dumped Felicity off in the corn and wanted Gwennie to come home with him. One day soon Gwennie will have little choice in the matter, but they aren't married yet. She just wanted to come home to her family. Put the day out of her mind.

They gathered around the Marconi, tuning in to the one channel everyone gets—the Empyrean frequency—and listened for a while to the dead air crackle and whisper through the speaker.

Listening to the Lottery this way brought on a mix of disappointment and excitement. Disappointment because every year the Lottery was announced at the Harvest Home festival—it was a party, and all the people of Boxelder gathered together and shared in the drunken spirit of the thing, comforting one another when they all lost as one, spiting the town from where that year's winner hailed. But there was excitement because this was a new way of hearing it: intimate, just the family collected together around the radio. They announced the Lottery every year on the Marconi for those homesteads too far from a Harvest Home festival, but Gwennie had never heard it before.

Then came a chime—*ding!*—and the broadcast began. The announcer, a woman (who, Gwennie thought, did not sound precisely *human*, reminding her of stories that said the Empyrean had all manner of automatons capable of intricate movement and speech), came on and gave the standard pleasantries in a far more endearing manner than Mayor Barnes ever had.

She went on and on about the indomitable spirit of the Heartlanders and of their "mighty toil" that deserved "recompense." Gwennie's family knew it was all a bit of hullaballoo—well, everyone but ten-year-old Scooter, whose blissful ignorance clung to life like a drowning shuck rat.

The woman continued her speech. Father rolled his eyes. Mother made a goofy face.

And then they announced the winners.

The Shawcatch family.

Of Boxelder.

Gwennie's family stared at one another in stunned silence. It was Scooter who broke the spell, saying as innocent as a wayward lamb, "Who won?"

"We did," Gwennie's mother said.

And that began the celebration.

Gwennie now stands in the doorway to her kitchen, her whole world feeling as if it's spinning beneath her feet. She thinks about Cael. And Boyland. And all the Heartlanders she knows and loves—even those she knows and dislikes so much she'd like to slap them in the face.

Scooter runs to the window. "I see lights! I see lights!"

She walks—though it feels more like she drifts, detached from everything that's real—to the window and looks out, expecting him to be looking at a reflection from inside the house.

But he's right. Red running lights shine in the evening sky. A dark shape behind it: an Empyrean skiff. Coming this way.

"They're coming," she says to no one but herself. "They're coming to take us away."

The Marconi hits the wall and shatters. Speaker wire lies on the floor. The speaker plate itself spins on the floor before falling inert.

"Junior," Boyland's mother says in shock. "Sweetie, I—"

"They're taking her away," Boyland snarls. "They're taking my Gwennie."

"Hon, you'll just get a new Obligation next year. . . ."

Junior storms over to her. "I don't want a new Obligation. I want *her*; don't you get it?"

The mayor comes stomping into the room, a scowl plastered on his whiskey-sodden face. "Can't get a line to the godsdamn proctor. She better make time for me." He looks over. "What? They announce the Lottery?"

Boyland's mother says, "It's Gwendolyn. The Shawcatches won."

The mayor takes a few moments to process the information.

"That means Agrasanto's on her way to Boxelder. To the Shawcatch cabin. Perfect. *Perfect*." He starts gathering up his things.

Junior can't help it. He throws himself on his father's mercies.

"Dad, please." He hurries over, grabs at his father's shoulder, shakes the man. "You gotta tell them. Tell the proctor not to take Gwennie. Pick someone else. Anybody else. She's *mine*."

The mayor shoves his son back. "Get off me, boy. I've got business. I'm taking the yacht."

"What? No. You can't—"

"I can and will. Who pays for a nice boat like that? You? You're daft as a broom, boy. It's *me*. It's always me. That's my boat out there. I just let you borrow it."

"Then let me come with you."

"You stay here." Mayor Barnes moves to open the door but then he turns back around and sticks a finger in the younger Boyland's face. "Word of advice, son. Forget about that girl. She's just a damn Shawcatch. They're weak people. Got spit for blood. I never liked you being Obligated to that little urchin anyhow."

"Dad—"

The mayor grunts, dismisses his son with a hand, and flies out the door.

Leaving Junior behind. Seething.

Young Boyland marches around the room—orbiting his mother, who stands there looking afraid. *Good. Let her be scared*, Boyland thinks. *She should be. She doesn't understand.* Neither does his father.

He loves Gwennie.

And they're going to take her away from him.

No, he thinks. *This can't happen. This won't happen.*

I need to see her.

I need to go to her.

He throws open the door and runs outside. The yacht's

already hovering above the corn and starting to drift away. But that's fine. He can run if he has to.

I can run if I have to, Cael thinks.

"I have to go," he says to Lane and Rigo. He turns to Bessie. "You okay to watch my mom still?"

"I am, you know I am; but Cael, you can't go messing with things—"

Cael waves her away. Hops off the front stoop.

Lane steps in front of him. "She's right, Cael. Now's not the time. What are you doing?"

"I don't have a boat," Cael says. "Going to hoof it. To Gwennie's. I'm not letting them take her."

"Are you sure that's smart?" Rigo asks.

Cael throws up his hands. "I don't know! I don't know anything anymore. All I know is, after what I saw today, things are going to change. The winds are shifting for the Heartland, and the Lottery is . . . it's the next-door neighbor to kidnapping is what it is. Gwennie has a life down here, and for the love of the Lord and Lady, it's gonna be with *me*."

"Go," Lane says.

"Change?" Bessie asks. "What's changing? What are you going on about?"

Rigo shrugs. "Better hurry."

Cael breaks into a run.

It's not a skiff that lands but a ketch-boat. Gwennie's seen the Empyrean skiffs before: flat, small, with red sails on the sides as well as the top, calling to mind the fins of a fish. Skiffs are lean and utilitarian. But she's never seen a ketch-boat up close before.

The ketch descends out of the darkening sky, twin plumes of steam shaking the corn that is then crushed beneath the boat's hover-rails as it lands fifty yards out past the Shawcatch pole-barn. The bow is a gilded nose cone, intricate and ornate, looking like a peacock's feathers dipped in gold and then flattened against the front of the boat. The sails that thrust up from the sides and top are not at all like the fins of a fish but rather mime both the shape and pattern of a blue-and-black butterfly's wing.

A skiff carries a half dozen Empyrean agents uncomfortably—the ketch can carry four times that and still have room for more.

From beneath the ketch, a set of steps emerge—each ornamental step leveling out before another step unfolds from atop it, one by one by one until the last lands just outside the corn. Gwennie's family is smushed up against the window, Scooter's nose pressed upon the glass, as they see a trio of armed Empyrean soldiers with their plumed helmets and horse-like masks descend first, followed by Proctor Agrasanto.

"They're here for us?" Scooter says, disbelieving.

"They're here for us," Gwennie says.

Even before they're on the ground, Proctor Simone Agrasanto can feel the dirt between her toes. As the ketch drifted lower and lower, she kept feeling the grit building between her fingers, the pollen building up on the lenses of her cat's-eye spectacles, the soil in her boots that would take days—*weeks!*—to shake loose.

It disgusts her.

She exits the ketch behind three *evocati augusti*—a fancy name for guardsmen who have been lucky enough to join a rather cushy duty. Each is armed with a sonic rifle clipped into the brackets on his back and a coiled lash—a bog-standard thrum-whip—bound at his hip. The guardsmen are there *just in case*. Heartlanders can be an unpredictable lot. The winners never resist, of course. But jealousy is a mean thing, and any Heartland dog gazing long upon an Empyrean citizen has an unending checklist of reasons to be envious.

"Proctor," her attaché, Devon Miles, calls from behind her. "Did you want your tea?"

The response in her head sounds like *uck*, or perhaps *ggghhh*—the sound one makes when suffering through a mouthful of medicine. She does not vocalize this but instead says a short, sharp "No."

Miles approaches, uncapping a thermos. "But you had me make it?"

"I no longer want it." She scowls. "Unless there's brandy in there."

"There's . . . not," he says.

"I know."

"Oh." Miles twitches—a nervous tell she's noticed about him. It appears he doesn't know what to do: jump left, jump right, duck, run screaming for the hills. It's as though his body is trying to make a decision his mind hasn't yet agreed upon. He seems nervous down here.

He's weak, is what he is.

He's been her attendant for less than a month now. Her last attaché—Jacinda—had been with her for more than a year. A good girl, Jacinda. Knew her place, which was just to the left and rear of Proctor Simone Agrasanto, with visidex ever in hand. A single holographic screen beamed into existence onto any flat surface from two chip-sized lenses implanted in Jacinda's fingertips. Devon does not yet have such implants, and so he has a much older visidex in his trembling grip: a glass screen with plastic backing, a piece of antiquated technology the proctor does not find quaint. Devon's family, it seems, did not prepare him accordingly for this life.

If she decides to keep him, she'll have so many things to fix.

Since Jacinda went missing—with all signs pointing to those foul insurgents from the Sleeping Dogs, those contemptible vagrants—she's felt an emptiness inside. She was quite fond of that girl. Quite fond, indeed.

Jacinda did not need fixing.

Devon, however, needs it in heaps and hills.

She idly ponders throwing up. The only thing that stops the urge is the feel of the wind—the sweet, sweet wind. Indicative of the sky, the stars, the sun. Away from this brown, moribund clod of clay. The wind is the only reminder of home.

Life on the flotillas gives you the sense that nothing is stable, that the very ground beneath your feet could drop out from under you at any time. Because, theoretically, it could. That's not a bad thing, not as the proctor sees it. To her it means that she's flying free. That anything can happen. It's a wonderful, unburdening sensation—the feel of raw potential as big as the sky. The ground beneath her feet only heightens her queasiness.

Being here, on the ground, is disorienting. Like getting off a carnival ride and still feeling the motion inside. Truthfully, she doesn't know how the Heartlanders stomach it. Something in their breeding makes them tolerant to it, the way farm animals don't even notice when they're lounging around in mud. That's how she sees these people: They're all just livestock. As lunkheaded and docile as the average cow, as preprogrammed to duty and misery as a common motorvator.

Of course, they're not all docile, are they? Sometimes a motorvator goes off its program, a cow wanders free from its paddock with dreams of greener pastures and bovine independence. So too it is with the Heartlanders. Once in a while one gets an idea in his fool head and makes no end of trouble.

Hence the guards. Three ahead of her. Another six back in the ketch.

It's not they who emerge behind her now but the four concomitants. Helpers. Two men, two women. Here to facilitate whatever needs to happen to get this family on the boat as swiftly and painlessly as possible. Pack a small bag for each. Seal up the house. Package any small pets and execute any large ones. Brew tea to settle nerves. Whatever needs doing, the concomitants will do. And what they need to do right now is unfurl the golden runner.

"Ma'am," they say, allowing the proctor to step aside as two of them tiptoe forward, the golden plasto-sheen unrolling behind them—textured so that none will slip on it.

They roll the runner toward the house.

Better get on with it, then. Agrasanto steps onto the runner and snaps her fingers at Devon.

"What are their names?"

He stammers, "Wh-what?"

"The *names*. Of the Heartlanders with whom we are forced to play nice."

"Ah," Devon says, setting down the thermos of tea and drawing up the screen on his visidex. He flips through icons with the tip of his finger and then double-taps the glass. "The winners are: Richard Shawcatch; wife, Maevey; daughter, Gwendolyn; son, Richard Jr."

She snatches the screen from his hands. He pulls back his hands as though burned.

Proctor Simone Agrasanto takes the rudimentary visidex and scrolls through what few pages of information they have on this family. Minimal troubles. Father is a field shepherd. Mother a seamstress. Daughter a . . . well, that's interesting. Member of a scavenger crew and recently Obligated to the mayor's son. *I bet I'll hear about* that *one.* Mayor Barnes often has it in mind that he isn't *like* all these other people. Simply because he holds a position of dubious authority, he assumes that he's—*wink-wink*—one of the Empyrean.

Idiot.

Well, no time to worry about that now. "One foot in front of the other, dear," as her husband always said, sipping his tea, the servo-man reading from the day's news-roll. She'll soon have these Shawcatch fools bundled up and carried high into the sky where they think they'll become—

Over the corn, she sees headlamps in the distance. Hears the hum of a prop-engine.

Agrasanto whistles, and the *evocati augusti* form a three-pointed perimeter around her, sonic rifles popped free from their back-brackets and drawn. Already they dial up the power on their rifles—these won't just make the interloper fall to the ground sick. They'll cook his brains. Cause his internal organs to evacuate out whatever hole the viscera slurry can find. Turn the enemy into a bubbling skin-suit.

The elder male Lottery winner pokes his head out through the doorway. "Is something wrong?"

Simone waves him back inside, hissing, "*Close the door!*"

Whoever this is, they're going to wish they hadn't tangled with her today. Because the dirt between her toes—real or imagined—has made her very, *very* irritable.

• • •

Cael runs.

He runs hard and fast, his legs burning at the hips, his calf muscles feeling as though they'll soon snap like banjo strings. Gwendolyn's house is on the other side of town. Getting the boat would take too long—going back to Martha's Bend, fetching the pinnace, using the oar-poles to nudge that clunky brick *Doris* along at a rock-turtle's pace.

And so Cael runs.

He takes the road. The corn would be faster, but evening is upon him and will soon give way to night—and the last thing he needs now is to get lost in the stalks and lose any chance of stealing Gwennie away.

Because that is his plan.

He's going to find her. And he's going to rescue her.

From the clutches of the Barneses.

From the clutches of the Empyrean.

And with Pop's garden coming to fruition, from all the miseries the Heartland offers.

A little voice inside tells him: *She doesn't need rescuing, you thick-witted pony. She's always been smarter and tougher than you.* But he has no time for that kind of thinking, true or not.

Cael's feet clomp across the plasto-sheen roads.

As he bolts down the main thoroughfare of Boxelder,

passing all the town's sights—Poltroon's garage (poor Poltroon), the Tallyman's office (hell with the Tallyman!), Busser's Tavern (gonna need a drink after tonight, that's for damn sure)—he keeps his eyes focused foward, his heart pinned neatly to the dream of scooping up Gwennie in his arms and making her his bride.

He doesn't see the attack coming.

A two-by-four cracks him across the face. Blossoms of jagged light like electrical pulses bloom inside his skull.

He opens his eyes and realizes he's on his back. Staring up at the stars.

Tasting blood. He tries to breathe through his nose, but he can't.

"Guh," he says.

Boyland Barnes Jr. appears over him, blotting out the purple nighttime sky.

"I know what you're up to, McAvoy," Barnes growls. "She's mine."

Then he punches Cael in the face with a meaty, hamhock fist.

The first sonic blast from one of the guardsman's rifles warbles over the yacht's bow, and Mayor Barnes hits the deck, slamming his hip into a cooler and wincing. He hears

Agrasanto say something, but his eardrums are still pulsing from the sound of the rifle firing. The elder Barnes yells out, "It's me! It's Mayor Barnes!" His own voice sounds watery, full, distorted.

He waves his hand over the edge of the boat. Then he fumbles up to the console to dim the hover-rails so the yacht eases down to the ground.

Hands come up over the side. Grab at him. Throw him over the edge.

The proctor's guardsmen stand over him, their rifles pointed at his face and chest. Their black-lacquered horse-faced helmets stare dispassionately down.

Agrasanto eases them aside. "I should have figured it was you."

"This isn't the respect a mayor deserves," he stammers. The proctor has always been a brutish woman, but she's always afforded him a measure of mannerly—if grudging—regard.

"Get him up."

Two guards grab under his armpits, haul him to his feet.

"Respect," she mumbles. Agrasanto clears her throat, and her red-painted lips stretch into a false smile. "Mayor Barnes! *So* good to see you again. I see you've come to wish your fellow Boxelder citizens good luck as they depart on their journey to a better life in the bosom of the Empyrean flotillas. I'm sure they appreciate their town's most *estimable citizen* showing his—" And now the false face falls away like leaves off a tree. "Drunken, unshaven self. So, Mayor Barnes, before I have my *evocati augusti* punch a hole in your chest or lash you to the underside of our ketch with one of their whips, I suggest you mosey along."

That word, *mosey*. He can hear the mockery in her voice. Barnes waves her off. "It's not about *them*, Proctor." He leans in. Lowers his voice. "We have a terrorist in our midst."

"A terrorist."

He can see she doesn't believe him.

Behind her, two servants—one man, one woman, each in a red plasticky jumpsuit—appear. "Ma'am, may we begin the extraction?"

Agrasanto makes a dismissive gesture. "Yes. Go. Make it snappy." As they flitter off, she looks to Barnes. "They're going to try to take their sweet time. They always do. They want all their family photos, their favorite gingham skirts, some favorite dust ball behind the rickety wooden torture device they call a chair; but we have to hurry them along. They won't be needing any of that up above."

"About the terrorist—"

"Terrorist. Right. Go on."

He quickly tells her what he knows—which is,

admittedly, very little. His son. Martha's Bend. The McAvoy boy. *Strawberry hands*. He lets her know he's been seeing suspicious signs around town: the votary with an apple, a trash pile with melon rinds sticking out of the top, evidence of fruits and vegetables that are *plainly* forbidden. But still Agrasanto doesn't seem to care.

"Votaries of the Lord and Lady often find . . . fortune," she says. "Apples aren't illegal. Sometimes they show up in provisions, Mayor Barnes. As do melons. And all manner of foodstuffs."

"Not like this," he says. "This apple was as big as a fist. Red, too. Not a dark spot on it."

Her face, as impassive as a stone wall.

He kicks it up a notch. "I . . . saw it with my own eyes."

"You went to Martha's Bend. Illegally."

Risky play, he thinks, but—fingers crossed—worth it. He nods with faux reluctance. "I could not abide the thought that someone from my town was growing illicit plants and vegetables. I went to see with my own two eyes." He clears his throat. "Besides, there's something you ought to know about the family. The daughter's gone—gone hobo and hightailed it to Jeezum Crow knows where. And the father, Arthur McAvoy . . . he's the real terrorist."

There. He has her. A little snake tongue of curiosity flickering in the dark of her eye. He suspects she was moments away from hauling him off and leaving him to wander the corn, but now he has her interested.

"Go on," she says.

"When Arthur McAvoy—the boy's father—was younger, he took off. Ran away from Boxelder. I've heard rumors. About what he did during that time."

"So let me hear them."

He does. The mayor leans forward and whispers them in her ear.

She worries at a lip with her teeth. "Fine," she says finally. "I'll give you six of the *evocati augusti*. Lead them to Martha's Bend. Bring in McAvoy. If all is as you say it is, then there will be a bounty awaiting you. For your loyalty to the Empyrean."

But then she grabs him by the scruff of his beard, wrenching his head suddenly close to hers. He can smell her breath: mint and bergamot. Cold, too. Not warm and boozy like his.

"But if you're wrong—if no garden exists, if McAvoy is just another toothless Heartland dog—then I will have you strung up with thrum-whips and vibrated into a half dozen pieces. Are we clear, Mr. Mayor?"

He hopes suddenly that his lies and guesses add up to something. Is there really a garden? Could Arthur McAvoy be behind all this?

The mayor's voice is ragged like a burr: "We're . . . we're clear, Proctor."

"Good." Once again her fake smile. "Now, go! Go and catch this tiger by the toe."

"She's *mine*," Barnes snarls, grabbing Cael by the shirt and pitching him into a pair of barrels sitting out in front of Doc's place.

Cael's head is spinning. He scrambles to stand, plants a foot in the dirt, and throws a fist at Boyland. But it's a long, clumsy haymaker, the kind that takes ten minutes to get where it's going and sends off a postcard RSVP long before it arrives. The mayor's son has no problem leaning back as Cael's fist whiffs through open air. *Swing and a miss.*

Barnes responds by leaning in and pulling Cael close. Then he pumps his knee into Cael's gut once, twice, three times. Cael topples. Bloody. Breathless.

He rolls on his side, wheezing and gasping.

By now people have started to come out of Doc's and, across the street, Busser's. Nobody's looking to break anything up. Not yet. Fights like this tend to run their course, and unspoken Heartland etiquette says you don't go breaking up a fight unless someone's a stone's throw from dead. This is how the hard people of this place settle their business.

Barnes kneels down. Grabs Cael's face so he can talk right in his ear.

"Listen, punk. Gwennie's Obligated to me. You think I don't know that you're running to her right now? Lord and Lady only know what you think a lowland corn-weevil like yourself is going to be able to do. I'm the godsdamn mayor's son. I got pull. She's mine to get and yours to leave. You understand me, McAvoy?"

"I can't hear you," Cael mumbles, blood and saliva dribbling into the dirt.

Boyland gets even closer, bares his teeth, starts to say something—

Cael cocks his head hard to the right, smacking his skull straight into Boyland's teeth. It hurts Cael—the sum-bitch's teeth bite into his skin—but it hurts Boyland worse. The younger Barnes tumbles backward, howling and clutching his mouth.

Suddenly Cael's up again in a plume of dust. He's still as wobbly as a plate spinning on a stick, but there's no way he's letting this thick-necked child of privilege take home the love of *his* life.

Boyland launches himself at Cael, but this time Cael's ready—he steps aside, lets the bull stumble past, then pops a fist right into Boyland's ear. *Pow*.

Barnes staggers sideways and launches a punch—but it's a telegraphed attack. Cael ducks low, slams a boot right into Boyland's knee.

The big lug howls and falls over.

Cael steps in, draws the slingshot. A ball bearing is twisted up in the pocket, the sling drawn so far back he can feel the muscles in his arm burning for release.

"Back down," Cael says, a spit-bubble blowing and popping on his lips as he speaks. "We're done here. Gwennie's been mine, and she'll always be mine. I ever see you lay a hand on her, I'll put one of these into your mouth and down your fat throat. Now do *you* understand *me*, Bar—"

A warbling blast hits Cael from the side. The slingshot drops to the ground. The ball bearing rolls away. A foot steps out, kicks it away like it's a rattlesnake about to bite.

The sonic strike mixes up Cael's insides—he gets up on his hands and knees and barfs onto the street. Retching. Dry heaving. He looks up through watery eyes to see Boyland backing away.

Then a face stoops down in front of his own.

Pally Varrin.

"Hey, Cael," Pally says, twirling his sonic shooter. "Saw you trying to murder the mayor's son there. That's a no-no, in case you didn't realize." He gets closer. "I did enjoy it, though. Same as I'm sure you enjoyed dunking me at Harvest Home."

"Gwuh—"

Pally just puts a boot between Cael's shoulder blades and pushes him down. Holds him there while Cael hacks and sputters.

Pally waves off the onlookers. "Go on home, everyone. I got this taken care of. It's handled. It's handled! Go drink something, you skunks!" The Babysitter points to Boyland. "And you. Barnes. Shoo, we're done here. I didn't see nothing."

And that's that. Barnes shoots Cael one last look before hauling ass down the street. He goes to get Gwennie while Cael is left with nothing but arms and legs that feel like overcooked noodles and a stomach that's doing barrel rolls inside his torso.

Pally just laughs as Cael passes into darkness.

PART FOUR
THE NOOSE

In the Big Rock Candy Mountains
All the cops have wooden legs
And the bulldogs all have rubber teeth
And the hens lay soft-boiled eggs
The farmers' trees are full of fruit
And the barns are full of hay
Oh I'm bound to go
Where there ain't no snow
Where the rain don't fall
The winds don't blow
In the Big Rock Candy Mountains.

—*"The Big Rock Candy Mountains," Harry "Haywire Mac" McClintock*

THE LORD AND LADY BLESS US AND FREE US FROM OUR BONDS

CRUNCH.

Mayor Barnes bites into an apple. Juice runs into his beard.

The sodium lights buzz.

"It's a very good apple," he says.

Arthur McAvoy sits across from the mayor, trembling from what he's seen. For a while there he felt like a raw nerve, watching his fellow garden tenders falling to the sonic blasts and thrum-whips of the Empyrean guardsmen in their emotionless black horse masks. The thrum-whips coiled around arms and necks and feet, the whips vibrating

so fast and so completely they bit into the flesh and left the hobos screaming as their teeth ground against one another and the blood ran red. The sonic blasts knocked them to the earth, too, causing their bodies to seize up so bad some of them broke their arms or legs by going so dreadfully rigid.

The guardsmen dragged the others up to the surface of Martha's Bend. Pop heard them call in for an "extraction barge," which meant his people were going to be taken away. Snatched up out of the Heartland and taken up above. Marlene. Jed. Homer. All taken away.

Those who had the Blight . . .

They did not fare so well.

The Blighters' bodies have been dragged outside to be burned.

All while Barnes eats an apple.

Crunch crunch crunch.

"You want a drink?" Barnes asks while picking apple skin from his teeth.

"I do not," Arthur says through stiffened lips.

"How's your hip?"

"Hurts."

"I bet."

The mayor himself hit Arthur right in the bone spurs with a beatdown stick. Now the bone spurs are like a beacon drawing a loud frequency of radiating pain.

Just the same, Barnes pulls a flask of whiskey and two telescoping metal cups. He opens both little cups and holds them together with one hand as he pours with another.

"Go on now. Have a taste. Here I'm offering you two fingers of thirty-year whiskey. What kind of a man refuses an offer like that?"

Arthur takes the cup, runs a thumb along the rim, and then spills the contents on the ground.

"I don't drink anymore."

"Ah," Barnes says. "So you're *that* kind of man. Lots of things you don't do anymore." The mayor snorts. "Perfectly good whiskey. Well, whatever. Let's get down to it, then. We can each admit that I've got you bent over the barrel?"

Arthur tenses. "You do."

"The Empyrean's not going to be happy about all *this*." Barnes gestures to the underground burrow that they almost didn't discover. But once they found the holo-flick theater and saw the tree growing there in the center, it was all over. The guardsmen blasted a hole clean through the glass stage and came pouring in through the breach like fire-biters out of an anthill. A few of Pop's gardeners managed to escape on rail-rafts. But Pop and the others stayed behind to rescue what seeds they could and got caught or got dead because of it.

We all should have run. Let this one go.

Too late now.

"They might not be happy," says Barnes, "but me? I'm happy as a squirrel with a nut, old friend. This has been my dream for a long time. To catch you doing something . . . *sticky*. Something the McAvoy of old would have done. Shame about you, really. You were being groomed, smart fellow that you were. Science minded. Engineer—wasn't that it? Fast-tracked to the Big Sky. Maybe even make your own flotilla one day. Have your name on one of them floating behemoths. Whatever happened with that anyway?"

"You know full well what happened."

The Empyrean had pulled the rug out from under that program. Back then Heartlanders had a way off this rock and out of the fields—the truly gifted got a shot to apprentice on one of the flotillas, gain a life up above rather than down below. But at some point the Empyrean decided it just wasn't worth the time or the money. What was it that had come across the Marconi? *We regret to inform you at this time that, due to a superfluity of talent, we have temporarily shuttered our apprenticeship program. Please check back in six months.*

Translation: *We've got our own smart people now, and we don't need you.*

Temporarily. What a joke. That's what they said when they closed the schools, too.

"Oh, right. I do remember now. You know what else I remember? I remember you taking off like a shot." The mayor whistles low and slow, slaps his hands together. "Like a cat with chiggers biting his tail. And you went and took Filomena with you."

Filomena. His wife. Of course it would come back to this.

"You stole her from me," Barnes says.

So, there it is, then.

"She made her choice."

The tendons stand out in the mayor's neck as he leans across the table.

"It wasn't *about* choice," he spits. "We don't get choice in these matters. We don't follow our godsdamn hearts like a . . . a butterfly chasing flower petals on the wind, Arthur. She got the envelope. She got the letter. She was Obligated to *me*."

"And yet she chose *me*," Arthur says.

"You left. You left town. And don't think we don't know why you went, or where you went, or who you went with. You took her from me, off on your little adventure. You have any idea what that put me through? My Obligated bride, snatched away from me by some anarchist . . . some godsdamned anarchist punk?" He slams the metal cup down on the table, collapsing it with the flat of his hand. "You took her! You sonofabitch."

The mayor's nostrils flare like a bull's.

Which is what Filomena called Barnes, wasn't it? *A snorting bull.* She thought he was crass. Thick and dumb. Common in all the worst ways and none of the best. All reasons why she chose the mayor's opposite in Arthur.

"Your fault she's sick. Taking her out of town to the far-flung corners of the Heartland."

And beyond, Arthur thinks. His mouth forms a tight and bitter line. "That's all ancient history. Go and appreciate the wife you have."

"And what a wife she is! Got an ass like two hogs wrestling under a quilt. A sour face like she's always smelling an updraft of shit somewhere. My son's mother is not my wife. Legally, yes. In the eyes of the Empyrean, *yes*. But in my heart?" He angrily thumps his chest. Then he foregoes the cups, takes a long pull of whiskey straight from the flask, swallowing it with a growl. He wipes his mouth and says, "In my heart, it's Filomena."

For a little while the mayor just stares. First at Arthur, and his eyes drift as he looks off at an unfixed point in the distance.

Behind Mayor Barnes, two of the Empyrean soldiers come from separate corners and meet in the middle. They face away from the Heartlanders, but Arthur can still hear the taller of the two say after taking off his horse helmet that he found another Blighter hiding in the garden and pulsed her with the sonic rifle. He says they'll need to bring in something to "take care of" the garden. A flame-tosser, maybe. Or a couple of boom-cube explosives that'll collapse the whole burrow, bring down the town above with it.

Outside, someone yells.

A cry of alarm by the sound of it.

Barnes doesn't seem to notice. Just keeps staring. Licking and sucking his teeth as he does. The mayor mutters, "You had your shot, Arthur. Now I'm bringing you down."

Then Pop hears it: the sound of footsteps. Coming fast. The ground even shakes a little.

The two guards have just enough time to give each other a look before Homer—bruised, bloodied, the whites of his eyes gone entirely red—barrels into the room like a wild horse fresh from branding. The guards react—but they're too slow.

Homer snatches the sonic rifle off the back of one guard and pushes him forward with a hard knee. Then he takes aim and lets fly with a pair of sonic blasts—the one without the helmet takes it to the face. He cries out and gurgles at the fluids fast accumulating in his throat. The other drops to the ground, given over to a shuddering seizure.

The mayor spins, standing up so fast he almost falls

backward. From down the other hall, Arthur hears voices—more guards, alerted by the blasts.

Barnes is no fool. He shrieks like a barn owl and dives behind a cot as Homer raises the rifle.

"Go!" Homer yells to Arthur. "Run!"

Arthur hops up. He can't move fast—the spurs in his hip shoot a lightning bolt of misery all the way down to the tips of each toe—but he hobbles along toward the escape tunnel.

Voices rise behind him. A commotion. He throws a look over his shoulder and sees Homer kick over a table. The huge hobo staggers behind it and starts taking shots over the edge. Four more guards emerge from different tunnels. A thrum-whip catches the table and starts vibrating with the telltale high-pitched frequency and—*vzzzt!*—cuts the whole table in half.

No time now.

Arthur limps toward the tunnel opening.

Homer stands.

A thrum-whip catches the big vagrant around the middle. He screams. Pivots. Points the sonic rifle *at* Arthur, and for a moment Arthur doesn't understand—

But then a sonic blast hits the earthen frame of the tunnel gateway, collapsing it with a pulse of shrieking sound. Clods of dirt fall. Dust kicks up.

There, leaning against the wall, is a rail-raft.

Arthur, with a grunt, turns it over and places it upon the rails. The magna-cruxes buoy the raft, letting it bob atop the tracks.

As he throws himself on it, he hears Homer scream one last time and then—

Nothing.

Oh, Homer.

Arthur blinks back tears, snatches an oar-pole off the wall, and begins pushing the raft forward—left side, right side, left side, right side—until he's firing like a bullet down a barrel.

The Boxelder jail isn't much to look at. A square room, all cinder block and mud. Its one window is just above the too-small plywood door at the fore. The whole place sits at the south end of town down a footpath that leads up a small, dusty berm where the corn doesn't grow.

The jail has two cells separated by sheets of plastosheen, the plastic perforated by a series of little holes so the "guest" doesn't suffocate while waiting for justice to be delivered by the Empyrean. The plastic cells don't have doors, exactly—they have hatches at the bottom where you crawl in and out like a dog on his belly.

Because that's how it happens. A Heartlander does something wrong, gets tossed in here. Small offenses—and most of them are—get one a sentence of a few days or until the Babysitters grow tired of sitting in this hot box. Anything bigger than that gets reported upstairs. Then the proctor comes. And then the offender disappears.

Cael's never been in here before. Lane has. He got caught stealing some ditchweed from Doc's cabinet. Lane was in here less than a day before the Babysitters threw him back out with a proclamation that he was to pay Doc twice what was owed.

Which is bad news for Cael.

Pally roves into view. His face is distorted by the plasto-sheen. His breath fogs the plastic.

"Hey, McAvoy," Pally says. "How you doing in there?"

Cael doesn't say anything. Gwennie's name is still perched on the edge of his lips. If he could, he'd punch a pair of holes through the plastic, grab Pally by the neck, and choke Varrin till the sonofabitch passed out.

"You know, I'm gonna leave you dangling out by your heel on this one. The Empyrean doesn't like little wannabe murderers. Who knows what they'll do to you? March you up to one of them flotillas. Maybe experiment on you. Or you know what I hear? Sometimes they make you walk the plank. You go out on this platform high above the Heartland,

and there you stand—wind whipping past, britches filled with the stink of sweat and piss. Then they hit a button or pull a lever and—*zip!* The platform shrinks back. Leaving you out there in the great big nothing." Pally claps his hands, makes a loud whistle. "And down to the ground you go! Probably exploding like a blood sausage soon as you hit. Blood makes the corn grow. Isn't that what they say?"

"I didn't murder Boyland."

"You tried."

"I did not." Cael sighs. "*He* attacked *me*."

"That's not what I saw. I saw him just standing there. Then I saw you go over there and hit him in the face with a two-by-four. Start beating on him something fierce. He fought back, almost had you, but then you tried to kill him. That's what my report's gonna say."

"You're a damn liar."

"Maybe. But between you, me, and the mouse in the corner? I kinda want to see you hang for this, Cael McAvoy."

Cael sits back on the wooden bench. Thunks his head dully against the concrete. Kicks at the tin tray sitting there on the floor.

All the while wondering just how in King Hell he's gonna get out of here.

• • •

It's been hours. Morning won't be long in the coming.

Gwennie and her family sit in a lounge area aboard the ketch. They all sit on plush sofas that are a cerulean blue that Gwennie's never seen before except smudged around the eyes of Empyrean ladies. They have small porthole windows—each rimmed with an elaborate scrollwork of gold—and occasionally Gwennie goes to the porthole and peers out.

"Everything's fine," Richard says. He's been all smiles, but now Gwennie can see that his excitement is starting to wear down like a ground tooth.

Her mother adds, "I'm sure it's all just administrative."

"I heard them talking about Arthur McAvoy," Scooter says.

Gwennie nods. "I did, too."

She doesn't know what any of this means. She only knows that they packed up her family and shoved them in here, and the door closed and won't open again. The mayor took off with some guards after they bandied around the McAvoy name—and not in a good way. If Arthur is in trouble, that means Cael could be, too. And Gwennie cannot abide the thought of that.

Things had been going so well.

But now Proctor Simone Agrasanto is still here, standing

on this dust-caked, pollen-choked dung-ball. Five hours later. *Five excruciating, miserable, soul-crushing hours.*

Her only pleasure was finding that the mayor and the guards had things in order. And Barnes was right—which galls her somewhat, as she looked forward to humiliating him for his falsehood. But they found the town, found the terrorist, and cleaned house. Most surprising was the *extent* of the treachery: a veritable *jungle* in the dead town of Martha's Bend. Still, everything looked as though it had been handled. . . .

But now she's holding her visidex in her trembling hand. Devon flits around her like a nervous titmouse. *Evocati augusti* Parl Refn has just told her something she can't even imagine:

Arthur McAvoy has escaped.

His file says he's crippled. Like half of the mutants down here.

And yet he escaped.

By the gods, how?

Ugh.

She looks into the visidex screen and speaks to the guardsman. "Do we know where he's going?"

The guardsman—a fair-haired gent, maybe in his late forties—shakes his head. "No, Proctor. We're digging out the tunnel now. Then we plan to—"

The visidex camera shakes; everything goes blurry.

Then the mayor's haggard face appears. Bloodshot eyes. Lips curled into a grimace.

"Go to his house," the mayor says. "His wife is there. Bedridden with tumors. He'll go to her. To check on her. To *save* her. That's where he'll be. But you need to go now."

He sends the proctor a pair of coordinates. They appear on the screen.

Agrasanto hands the visidex back to Devon. "Program the pilot. Prep the ketch. The coordinates are on the visidex."

"Proctor, about the Shawcatches—"

"Just keep them locked up on the ship and we'll be fine. Now *move*, before I leave you behind to rot in this godsforsaken mud hole."

Devon nods, as scared as a rabbit, and disappears into the ketch.

She waits for the ship to thrum to life, to rise and take them to the McAvoy house, but then—

A voice calls from the corn.

At first the proctor thinks she's imagining it. *This place is getting to me*. They say the corn moves of its own volition, but she knows it doesn't have thought. *It can't communicate*.

She hurries to enter the ketch but then she hears it again: "Wait!"

Alongside the thrashing of corn.

Someone Agrasanto does not recognize comes crashing through the corn. The proctor sticks two fingers in her mouth and gives a long whistle. Two *evocati augusti* emerge from within the ship, weapons drawn and pointed at this new interloper.

Then recognition strikes her. *Really? Another one?* She tells the guards to stand down. "It's the mayor's son."

He looks like hell. Cut up from the corn. Beat up from . . . some scuffle or another? She doesn't even know. It appears as if he went toe-to-toe with a Korybantic dancer—of course, they don't have the Korybantes here in the Heartland. They don't even have the Cybele rites. *Primitives, with their simplistic mythologies and . . . well, no matter.*

The teen—Boyland Jr., if she recalls—gasps for air and drops to his knees before her.

"Please," he says between great gulps of breath. "It's my bride. My Obligated. I don't want her to go. Take her family, but for the love of the Lord and Lady and the"—another gasping breath—"and the salvation of Jeezum Crow and the trials of Old Scratch and King Hell, please *don't* take her."

Gwennie presses against the porthole.

Boyland Barnes Jr. has come for her.

She's not sure how she feels about that.

He's thick. He's a bully. He's arrogant. He's ignorant.

But she sees how the mayor treats him. She sees how it trickles down.

She doesn't love Boyland. But she can see that *he* loves *her*. Gwennie doesn't know if that love blossomed on the day of their Obligation or if it's been simmering long on the stove, but it's there now when she looks in his eyes. His touch is gentle with her. Not as gentle as Cael's, and certainly far clumsier, but he tries.

He was protective of her.

He *loves* her.

And that's something.

Scooter laughs. "Boyland and Gwendolyn sittin' in a field," he sings. "K-I-S-S—"

"It's tree," she corrects him. "Not field. Tree."

"That don't make any sense. We don't have any trees around our house!"

She ignores her little brother, sees Boyland making some kind of heartfelt plea to the proctor. She thumps on the porthole glass to get his attention, to give him a smile.

He turns and sees her, a big, dumb smile plastered on his face.

Agrasanto makes a motion with her hand, and one of the guards steps toward Boyland and cracks him in the temple with the butt of the sonic rifle.

Barnes goes down, curling into a fetal ball, his hand coming away red.

Gwennie yells and pounds on the glass. She hates it—hates that her reaction is to want to reach out and grab him and pull him close and hold him tight. Boyland. That *thug*. Always making her life hell when she was with Cael's crew. But now there's a twinge, a little twist of something inside her like a fish taking the bait on a long line and—

Don't go there, not now, not ever; you don't love him.

Right?

By the time she snaps back to reality, the guards and the proctor are all gone, leaving Boyland alone. Soon she can feel the droning purr of the hover-rails beneath her feet—and the shift of the ship as the ketch lifts up in the air. Boyland doesn't look up. He just cradles his bleeding head.

Gwennie thinks he's weeping.

And she can't help it. She weeps a little, too.

Gwennie's gone. Gone to one of the flotillas—and how many flotillas even *exist*, Cael doesn't know. A dozen at least. Maybe twice that. *Three times* that. The Empyrean doesn't share numbers like that and so Cael can only guess.

With Gwennie up there, what are the chances he'll ever see her again? Even if Pop's garden takes root and spreads like a fire across the Heartland, even if everything falls to pieces and the Empyrean loses its grip, what are the chances Cael will ever smell her scent again, or kiss her neck, or just hold her hand?

About as much chance as winning the Lottery, he thinks.

He sits in his jail cell with that thought twisting in his mind like a worm trying to tie itself in knots.

Cael imagines a life with Wanda. She's awkward and strange and seems to love him—or at least appreciate him—in a way he cannot return. But she's not the one he wants.

But then it strikes him—

The chances of winning the Lottery were one in a million.

And Gwennie won.

Which means a chance is still a chance. Small as a speck of pollen caught on an eyelash, maybe, but there just the same.

And then he realizes that his life with Wanda isn't going to happen. Pally's going to send him to the Empyrean. To the flotilla. Up in the sky, same as Gwennie. He'll be sent for punishment, not as a reward, but that doesn't matter. He'll formulate an escape plan as soon as he knows what he's dealing with. Then it'll be time to rescue Gwennie, steal a skiff, and get the hell back to the ground.

It's a plan.

A crummy plan hanging its hat on a wobbly hook, sure.

But it's a plan.

It's then that the plywood door into the jail creaks open.

Cael can't see who it is—but he hears the low murmur of voices and recognizes the timbre of the other Babysitter, Grey Franklin. The plasto-sheen walls do a pretty good job muffling sound, but he does make out two words:

"McAvoy farm."

Maybe they want to take him home? Maybe Pop is on his way.

Grey raises his voice. "Let me at least give him another tray of food. We're gonna be gone for a while."

"Aw, hell, let the mongrel starve, Grey!"

"Pally, you pulsed him. He needs to eat. Empyrean's not gonna cater to you torturing a boy. He's locked up fair and square, and you're the hero. Don't turn it the other way."

Cael imagines Pally clicking his teeth together. Finally he says, "Fine, *fine*, take him a tray."

The blurry, warped shape of Grey Franklin approaches the cell.

He stoops, unlocks the hatch, slides through another tin tray—this one covered with a metal lid clipped to the edges—and then slams the hatch closed.

"Hope they take you far away from us, murderer," Grey says through the plastic. "Far, far away."

"Grey, I didn't—"

But Grey just turns his back on Cael.

It cuts Cael to thc quick. Grey's always been good to the McAvoy family. The words sting. That Grey even *believes* the tale spun by Pally Varrin is . . .

Well, it just shows that Cael's neck-deep in the shit-heap.

Both Franklin and Varrin leave. To go Lord and Lady know where.

Cael sighs. Rubs his eyes. Looks down at the tray. He thinks about eating—Grey's right; if you get pulsed by even a low-frequency sonic blast, it's not the worst idea to replenish your gutty-works. But he just can't muster the hunger. He taps the tray with a toe. Nudges it into the other tray.

Then he gives it a kick, makes it spin.

It rattles. Almost like a rattlesnake's rattle, but louder, denser.

Metal on metal.

Is this a joke? What the hell is Grey trying to feed him? Nuts and bolts? He grab the tray, finds that it has surprising heft, and pops the lid.

Well, look at that.

The tray is split into quadrants in order to separate whatever gruel they're feeding the prisoners. It's just like the other one that way. But in this tray's compartments, Cael sees no food.

He sees ball bearings.

He sees his slingshot.

He sees a rasp-tooth saw.

And atop it all a small, hastily scribbled note:

RUN.

Far, far away.

What's going on?

No time to worry about that now. No telling when Pally will come back. Cael drops to one knee and gets the saw in between the hatch that's cut into the plastic. He sets the saw-teeth against the hinge and starts working on it, back and forth, plastic shavings building a small cairn of squiggly clear bits on the floor. When he's done, he kicks the hatch out, and it falls against the straw-strewn floor.

He tucks his slingshot into his back pocket and fills his front pockets with the ammo.

Then he breaks out of jail.

THE WIND THAT SHAKES THE CORN

"CAEL!"

Pop's voice echoes across the homestead. Out past the house, over the corn-tops, night is giving way to the first embers of morning. He swallows hard, brushes himself free of the straw and dust from inside the stable, and then he hobbles to the house. His hip feels as if it's on fire, but his leg no longer hurts—instead, it's falling prey to a spreading numbness.

He limps toward the house, grunting and wincing and holding his hip.

"Bessie!"

No answer.

Maybe they're asleep. It is late. Or early.

He goes to the front door. He doesn't know how much time he has, but he knows it's slipping through his fingers like juice from one of those beautiful strawberries. They're going to come for him. And his son. *And Filomena.*

Inside the house he calls again. "Cael! Bessie!"

But still nothing.

He hears a creak upstairs. A floorboard shifting.

Bessie calls down, "Up . . . up here."

She sounds tired. As if he woke her up. Good. *Maybe she knows where Cael is.* Pop goes up the steps, formulating a plan. Filomena's not going to be easy to move, and they don't have a boat, not anymore. Burt and Bessie do, though. If not that, then the rail-raft. The magna-cruxes don't only fit the rail running between Martha's Bend and the McAvoy household. They also fit the rail two miles north of here—the ones on which the maglev auto-train travels to bring goods from town to town, delivering provisions and such to the likes of Bhuja and other deliverymen and women.

Hit the rails like hobos, he thinks. *Again.*

Arthur does his best to race upstairs, putting together in his mind a way to make a stretcher out of a couple oar-poles and a tarp from the barn. As soon as he reaches the stairs to turn into the main bedroom, he finds Bessie.

She's lying on the floor. Hands bound behind her. Bloody hair matted to her head.

"I'm sorry," she says.

Two figures step out of the shadows. *Evocati augusti*. More guardsmen of the Empyrean. They point sonic rifles toward him. The rifles hum; Arthur knows they're powered to full.

From behind him, Arthur hears footsteps emerging from Cael's bedroom.

"Arthur McAvoy?" asks a female voice. A voice he recognizes from the many Harvest Homes as that of Proctor Simone Agrasanto.

He hears Pally Varrin say, "That's the rat-bastard traitor."

Arthur turns. He draws a deep breath. He musters what dignity he can and offers his hand. "Proctor. Nice to finally meet you in person."

She smiles. Broad, red-painted lips. Pale cheeks made whiter with makeup. Peacock-blue eyes behind a pair of dark cat's-eye specs. She takes his hand. "So polite."

Then, a barely perceptible nod.

A rifle butt slams into the back of Pop's head.

Cael sneaks around town as the sun just peeks the top of its fiery head over the horizon. He darts behind the old fridge around back of Busser's when he hears a *hsssst!* coming from nearby.

He sees Lane and Rigo hiding between buildings. They flag him over.

"Cael! You're all right!" Rigo says, throwing his arms around him.

"Grey said he let you out. We've been waiting for you." Lane nervously smokes a crooked cigarette, then tosses it in the dirt as smoke vents between his teeth. "Everything's gone south, Captain."

"*Everything*," Rigo confirms.

"What? What's going on?"

Lane tells him. Tells him how they saw the Empyrean ketch-boat approaching the McAvoy farmstead and hightailed it out of there. How Bessie stayed behind. How they heard Busser and a couple of drunk field shepherds talking about the fight between Cael and Boyland and how Cael got stuffed in a jail cell for it. How they found Grey on the way to the jail, and he told them that Agrasanto wanted Pally and him to perform backup duties at the McAvoy farm in case things "got out of hand." How the three of them devised the Free Cael from Jail plan. "Took you long enough to get out here," Lane says.

"We have to go to the farm," Cael says.

"No!" Rigo waves his arms. "Grey told us to run, Cael. Said that things were way beyond the point of fixing. We have to *go*."

Lane draws a deep breath and bites a nail. "I think Rigo's right. I don't think we stand a shot."

"They want my father. They probably have my mother. And Gwennie might still be here." Cael stands up, draws his slingshot. "No force in heaven or the Heartland is going to change my mind."

Rigo and Lane share a pained look.

"Then we're in," Lane says.

Rigo gives a reluctant nod. "Lead the way, boss."

The ketch sits parked out behind the house and barn, a few hundred yards away—Gwennie thinks it's so the craft stays out of sight. So far away, though, that she can't see what's happening. It feels as if bugs are crawling under her skin she's so agitated and nervous.

The Empyrean Lottery is no longer a gift she wants. It's no reward. It's a curse. She's sure of that now. She doesn't want to be part of those people. She doesn't want her *family* to be part of those people, either. Besides, she's heard the rumors: Lottery winners are freak shows to the citizens of the flotillas. Curious strangers. A novelty to be used up and then later abused.

"We need to get off this ship," she tells her family.

"Just . . . sit tight," Richard says.

Her mother looks worried. "Richard, maybe she's right."

"The McAvoys are good people," Gwennie says. "We can't let Agrasanto do . . . whatever it is she's going to do to them. You saw what they did to Boyland Jr. They don't care about us. They could watch the Heartland dry out, or burn up, or drown in a hundred days' worth of rain."

Richard shakes his head. "We won the Lottery. We just keep our heads screwed on tight, and we'll be living a good life before you can bat your pretty eyelashes. Don't worry, daughter of mine."

Gwennie's had enough.

She goes to the door.

Waits. Takes a deep breath.

Then slams her body into it.

Once. Twice. Three times.

It barely budges. She screams. Time for something bigger. She reaches under the couch and unscrews the leg. Richard asks her what she's doing, but Gwennie no longer cares to answer. As soon as she has the leg, the couch tilts downward and Scooter laughs.

Then she goes back to the door and starts pounding it with the stubby couch leg.

Screaming.

Weeping.

Until she collapses against it, breathless.

• • •

They drag Arthur McAvoy outside and throw him on the driveway. One of the guards gets behind him and pulls a thin white plastic cord. He closes it around Arthur's wrists and then presses a button, and the cord tightens suddenly with a *vvvvvip*.

Agrasanto hates this man suddenly. Hates him with every inch of her icy marrow. He's ruined her trip here. This was supposed to be quick. Lickety-split. She'd fly down, snatch up the Shawcatch family, and then be back in her own bed by midnight, with her husband fast asleep. She'd turn on the oxy-mist. Crank up the white noise. Put on her lavender-scented face mask. And another sound night's sleep would be hers.

But now it's almost morning. And she's still awake.

She hates McAvoy. And she hates the mayor, too, for putting her through all this. Ignorance is truly bliss. Martha's Bend was not her problem, and suddenly it *became* her problem.

One of the Babysitters—the squirrelly, scrubby one—gets a mean smile and then stomps over to McAvoy and kicks him in the ribs. The man *oofs* and rolls over.

Agrasanto helps him to his knees.

"Mr. McAvoy," she says. "I regret to inform you that

you have been declared a terrorist against the sanctity of the heavenly Empyrean and the earthly Heartland. Do you have anything—"

"*You're* the terrorists," Arthur says, wiping his mouth on his shoulder. "You're the ones who come down here and terrorize us. You take away everything we have. You get to keep it all. When we want a taste—*just a taste*—you kick us like dogs."

"Like dogs," she says. "No. We treat you like the children you are. When you misbehave, we break your toys. It's just a lesson. *You're* just a lesson. A lesson to other Heartlanders to sit down, relax, and shut the—"

Devon clears his throat behind her.

"*What*, Devon?"

He coughs and places the visidex gently into her hands as though she might reach up suddenly and snap his head off his neck. Which is not an entirely unreasonable worry.

On the screen she sees the Shawcatch girl going spastic. Screaming and flinging herself against the door like a calf who realizes he's about to have a nail shot through his head.

"The ship alerted us," Devon says.

"Fine." She snaps her fingers to the two guardsmen. "Go handle this. We'll be along shortly."

"Ma'am—"

"I said *go*. I'm not interested in bringing back a ruined ship, so just subdue the girl, will you? Subdue the whole family while you're at it." The other guards are still at Martha's Bend cleaning up this terrorist's mess. *It'll all be over soon*. She's irritated, yes, but not worried.

The guards jog off.

She steps back to McAvoy. Then she looks to the other Babysitter—the thicker, squatter one. She puts out her open palm and claps one-handed. "Give me your pistol."

"Proctor, I think we should just wrap this up."

"I have *questions*," she hisses. "Pistol. Now."

He hands her the pistol.

"Let's talk," she says, and then she cracks Arthur in the face with the pistol.

A leafy finger of corn curls up under Cael's chin and snakes its way toward his mouth as if it wants to crawl down his throat and into his guts. But he blows it away with a puff of air.

He peers out through the corn at the house, his blood running hot.

Rigo hisses, "What do you see?"

It takes a moment for Cael to see anything at all.

But soon it becomes clear.

On the ground in the driveway, Pop kneels. Hands behind his back.

Pally Varrin is there, looking smug. Franklin, too. Pacing, rubbing his face.

There. Cael sees her. Proctor Agrasanto. Dark hair. Tight suit. She's got a pistol in her grip—by the looks of it, one of the Babysitter's sonic shooters. A small, dark-haired man stands nearby, tapping into some kind of computer.

Agrasanto says something.

Thens she hauls back and cracks Pop in the face with the shooter. Pop doesn't fall, but the blow looks to have stunned him. Cael sees red.

He scowls back at his friends. "We gotta get closer. *Now*."

Simone watches Arthur McAvoy leaning forward, spitting blood. His cheek is cut, but so are his gums. Her hand still vibrates a little from where she cracked him with the pistol.

The proctor makes another attempt. "So. The seeds. You grew a garden, an *impossible* garden. Too good to touch this foul, corn-throttled wasteland. I need to know from whom you procured these seeds, Arthur."

"I'm afraid I can't tell you that, Proctor."

More politeness from the terrorist. Cute.

She hits him again. This time in the side of the head. The sonic shooter she took from Grey Franklin isn't the same as her own shooter back on the flotilla. Her pistol is all curves: the gleaming chrome of a crafty, artisan-made Rossmoyne 70-99, a graceful weapon for an elegant operator. This crass pistol looks to be a—what? An Oswalt-Burmeister shooter from their Soundmaster line. With its boxy configuration, it's all hard angles and hanging nodules. Before, she regretted not bringing her own pistol. But now—watching how this crass weapon tears up the flesh of this Heartlander criminal—that regret has melted away like candy floss on a warm tongue.

The pistol leaves its mark. McAvoy's temple bleeds.

"We'll get the answer one way or another," she says. "Perhaps your son knows something. I hear he's in jail. One assumes that however much pain it will take to get you to crack, it'll take him *half* as much. That's my guess, of course. Always possible that he will have a secret cache of vim and vigor waiting and will outlast even you. We'll find out together."

"Cael," Arthur croaks. A torch-flame of anger rises in his voice. "You leave my boy alone."

"Not likely."

"You're awful. All of you. You're not gods looking down on us from above. You're not blessed by the Lord and

Lady. You're just monsters. The children of Old Scratch, looking down on ants with magnifying glasses, happy to watch us burn."

"That hurts my feelings," she says. And she means it. To be called a monster? To endure the suggestion that the Empyrean is anything but mankind's best intentions at work? Where would the Heartlanders be without the Empyrean watching over them? Without Empyrean science, without guidance, without a system of order in place? And here she is, an extension of that order, a hand carrying the best that civilization has to offer, and this animal, this *primate* with dirt in his hair, is going to tell her otherwise? It hardly seems fair.

The Overseer who looks like a bulldog steps forward, says, "Might be time to ease up on the stick and try a little carrot."

She wheels on him. "Overseer, this is a criminal whose only intent is to undo the Empyrean's good work. We do not negotiate with terrorists."

He offers up both hands and steps back. The other Overseer, still standing in the stomped wreckage of the last of the plants dragged out of McAvoy's workshop, appears gleeful. Grinning ear-to-ear through a beard that looks as if it would better serve as a nest for birds.

You get the hand you're dealt, she thinks.

Oh well.

Time to employ another trick.

They come through the corn to the back of the farmhouse. Cael, Lane, and Rigo hug the walls and sneak up along the side, ducking down by the set of cellar doors and peering around the corner to the gravel lot in front of the house.

Cael sees his father, still on his knees but now swaying. The side of his face is wet with blood. The proctor snaps her fingers and points to Pally Varrin. Right then, Cael wishes he'd taken that sonofabitch out on the road when he had the chance. It's the look of glee on the bully's face that gets him—Varrin is *enjoying* this.

From behind Cael, Rigo and Lane start talking about a plan.

But Cael can't help but watch.

"You know what to do," Agrasanto says to Varrin.

The Babysitter hunkers down next to Cael's father and pulls aside the waist of Pop's pants, exposing the cluster of bone spurs jutting out of his hip. Even that simplest of motions causes Pop to moan in pain, his whole body tightening.

"Your daughter," Agrasanto says. "Tell me about her.

Where did she go? I heard a rumor that she's on one of our flotillas. Which one?"

"I don't know" comes Pop's ragged answer.

Cael hears Rigo saying, "I'll distract 'em. Lane, you go inside the house from around back—"

"Is she connected to all this?" Agrasanto asks with a sweep of her arm. "Is she carrying your terrorist agenda onto our ships, into our homes?"

"I don't even know . . . what you're . . . talking about. . . ."

She nods to Pally, who takes the tip of his shooter and jams it hard against Pop's bone spurs. Cael doesn't know how it feels, but he can see his father twist up as if he was just shot with a crackling bolt of lightning. Hearing his father scream . . .

Lane whispers, "From inside the house I can get on the roof—"

"Is that still your answer?" Agrasanto says.

Pop nods, and Varrin again thrusts the gun barrel against his hip. Another scream.

"Just tell her something," Grey says, wincing.

Pop spits a gob of bloody spit on Agrasanto's uniform.

She barks to Varrin, "Again!"

Pally hauls back and kicks Pop in the hip with his boot. The cry that rises from the old man's throat is a warbling shriek, a sound Cael's never heard another man make before.

Cael hears the drumbeat of his pulse. A dull thumping in his neck, his temples, all the way down to his feet and his fingertips.

Rigo has his hand on Cael's shoulder. He's saying something about a plan. Lane is asking him again about the roof. But all Cael can really hear is the sound of his father in pain.

Varrin hauls back again with his foot. Pop topples over, and Varrin kicks him in the side.

They're killing him.

Agrasanto is yelling for Varrin to stop.

Cael pulls away from Rigo.

As he rounds the corner of the house, the slingshot is already in his hand. A steel ball bearing in the pouch, pinched there so hard it hurts Cael's fingers.

He screams as he runs toward them.

"Honey, please," Richard is begging her.

But Gwennie wants none of that. Her father's wrong. Plain and simple. This is not the time to be a docile little lamb. To roll over and let the shears take what's yours.

She flips the stubby couch leg in her hands. Hears the footsteps outside the door.

It's time.

The door opens, and one of the guards steps through. Gwennie rears back with her makeshift weapon—and a hand catches her.

It's her father.

"I'm sorry," he says. He gets his hands under her and holds her fast. "We need this. I can't have you doing this to the family."

"Dad!" she cries, thrashing, kicking out.

"Help me!" he says, and at first she doesn't know who he's talking to; but then the grim realization hits her: he's talking to the guards. The horse-faced soldiers grab at her legs. They produce plastic cords and fix them to her ankles, and then spin her over and bind them to her wrists. She screams. One of them drops her to the floor while the other dials back the power setting on his rifle.

He lances a muted sonic pulse into her back.

Gwennie's chin hits the floor and she tries to cry out, but she can't. Her words are lost as she begins to drool and dry heave. She looks up through bleary eyes and sees her father—face stricken with grief and guilt—sit down next to her now-weeping mother. Scooter, crying, crawls into Mom's lap.

• • •

Cael can't make a good shot while running, so he skids to a stop. He squints his eye over his hand.

Pally sees him.

Agrasanto sees him, too.

Aim straight, aim true.

Both of them draw their pistols on him.

Agrasanto reaches down to dial up the power. Pally just fires.

The shot misses Cael.

He lets fly with the ball bearing.

The sonic pistol drops from Varrin's grip as the ball bearing strikes him right in the throat. It collapses his windpipe. He staggers backward, clawing at his throat as though his wildly searching fingers can somehow put it all back together again. The only sound he makes is a wet gurgle.

The small man behind Agrasanto—her attaché—bolts for the barn, head down.

Agrasanto points the pistol, and Cael knows it's over. Maybe she has it on lethal. Maybe she'll just knock him flat. But he knows what's coming next.

Except he's wrong.

Suddenly Grey Franklin is behind her—his rifle against her throat, choking her. The pistol fires, and the air ripples as a warbling sound rushes by Cael's head. The shot hits one of the shutters on the farmhouse windows and blasts it to splinters.

Varrin drops to the ground. His legs start kicking, then stop.

I just killed a man.

He runs to Pop and begins dragging him toward the house.

She blames herself, of course, even as she fires off a shot that misses the kid by a scant few inches, even as her own throat starts to close as Franklin presses the rifle tighter against her neck.

She should have clamped down. Should have made a better effort to control this herself. Instead, she let these fool-headed Heartlanders get in the way.

Her fault or no, this won't do.

It's time to take control.

She stabs her elbow backward, catching the Overseer in the ribs. Then she pivots her hips and ducks forward, throwing the traitor over her shoulder. Franklin hits the ground on his ass bone, and the rifle goes clattering away into the dust and gravel.

Simone has to give it to him. By the time she's leveling her pistol at him, he's already rolled over and got his feet underneath of him, charging forward like a bull.

The thing is, he only knows how to fight like a Heartlander. The Overseers get a little training—mostly how to disarm some rowdy hick with a broken bottle or a sharp stick. But they don't learn the Heavenly Stance. Nobody teaches them how to fight like a proper Empyrean.

He comes at her, and she uses his momentum to throw his own body past her. Once more he loses his footing, and he face-plants into the driveway.

She takes a shot. The sonic blast hits empty earth as he rolls out of the way and kicks up a pocket of stone and dirt. Again Franklin's on his feet, but this time he's adapted. He doesn't charge in blindly. He comes at her from the side and hugs her like a circus bear—close enough that she can't get off a shot.

This is a distraction she can no longer abide.

With her empty hand she claps his ear and then rabbit punches him in the kidneys. When she hears his grunt and feels the air go out of him, she knows the job is done. Punch the kidneys and the liver, and the fight goes right out of a person.

He staggers back, and she snaps a kick into his jaw. His teeth slam down on his tongue, and blood wells instantly at the corners of his mouth.

"Betrayer," she hisses.

Then she shoots him in the face.

Grey tumbles backward. Blood erupting out of his nose. Eyes bulging. The back of his head hits the driveway hard, and a greasy froth oozes from his lips like soapsuds. The body twitches for a few seconds. And then it stops.

Now to finish this.

The boy with the slingshot—clearly the McAvoy heir, a rogue element she should have known was *not* buttoned up and taken care of, *thank you, Mr. Mayor and your ineffectual Babysitters*—is dragging his father toward the stoop and the steps of the farmhouse.

Easy pickings.

She levels the pistol and pulls the trigger.

Rigo doesn't know what happened. One minute there they were, ducked down behind the cellar doors, and he was acting as master strategist—and then Pop was screaming, Cael was gone, and the whole thing went to hell in a husk-bucket.

He stumbles out into the middle of the driveway, eyes wide, unable to parse what's going on. Is that Pally Varrin over there, his body jumping like it has an electrical current running through it? Why the hell is Grey Franklin fighting with the proctor? Cael's got his pop and is dragging him over to the house. Where did Mayor Barnes go?

Rigo turns to Lane. "What the hell should we—"

But Lane's already gone. His gangly legs are pumping, and he's taken off like a bottle rocket.

It's then that Rigo sees Grey Franklin's head fountain twin jets of blood from the nose. Just like that, the proctor points her pistol and Grey Franklin is dead.

Rigo feels his bowels go to ice. He thinks, *Run, just run, just get out of here, don't piss your pants, you might piss your pants, she's going to hurt you kill you run stupid run.* His head's like a switchboard of flight over fight, and yet his feet remain fixed to the Heartland earth.

Agrasanto points her gun. Not at him but past him.

At Cael. At Pop.

And before Rigo can think twice, he *is* running, bolting forward like a fat pony with a swarm of hornets stinging his ass. Except he's not running away from anything. Instead, he's leaping forward and making a sound like he's never heard himself make.

He barrels into the proctor just as she pulls the trigger.

The visidex.

Lane knows what that thing can do. It's not just a computer. It's a communication device. It can call the flotilla. It can bring reinforcements down on their heads like a hailstorm of hot coals. So when Agrasanto's attaché flees down the driveway with the visidex tucked under his arm, Lane knows he has to get that damn computer.

So he runs.

Agrasanto's pet has probably never run this far in his life—not from bullies calling you a sissy, not from Babysitters who caught you out after curfew, not after a fruit cart so you can get the sweet taste of a half-rotten apple. But if there's one thing Lane can do, it's run.

Privileged prick, he thinks. *Never had to work for anything.*

The lackey cries out as Lane flings himself forward, tackling the man to the ground. The visidex spins away. The man squirms from beneath him, and his face is a contorted mask of terror.

He's scared of me, Lane thinks as he raises his fist. *He thinks I'm some kind of damn savage. Like I might start eating his face off.*

All Lane can feel is contempt.

And then Lane hears the sound of the proctor's pistol, and his heart damn near quits.

Rigo thinks, *I've been shot.*

His ears ring. His head is like a bell someone just struck with a carpenter's hammer. He hits the ground, but his feet

won't hold him and he tumbles over like a stack of milk bottles hit by a rotten apple.

Even his vision isn't working right. Two images—same but different—swim toward each other and then apart again, as though trying desperately to become one. In both he sees Agrasanto slowly walking toward him, pressing the back of her wrist against her lips—a wrist that comes away red with blood—wearing an incredulous look on her dour face.

He expects his stomach to roil. He figures any moment blood will come boiling out from inside his skin—but he just blinks as the charge of adrenalin surges through him.

No blood. No death. Nothing.

"I'm not shot," he says, but his words are lost in the dull roar of blood and bell ringing going on in the echo chamber of his head.

Then Simone Agrasanto says something to him.

Again she raises the pistol.

"You little shit," she says.

She had a clean bead on Cael McAvoy. Until this little melonhead connected with her own head, and before she knew it, her teeth were cutting through her lower lip. The tang of iron and copper fast filled her mouth as the gun went off right next to the kid's ear.

The pudgy bastard looks up at her with pleading eyes. He feels his chest as though he's been shot.

She can oblige.

She licks blood from her lip and raises the pistol.

And her head snaps back. All she sees for a moment is half a starburst, a white field of flash that explodes in her vision. She screams and she thinks, *My eye! My fucking eye—it's gone!*

She brings her hand to her face and knows it's absurd. It's not her eye, everything's fine; it's just the madness of the moment.

But then she sees Cael McAvoy standing over his father, the slingshot held firmly in his hand, the tubing and pocket dangling slack. And when she pulls her hand away from her face, it comes away wet. Wet with blood.

Frantically, she feels for her eye.

It's there. But it's just a mushy bubble—it gives way to her finger like a stepped-on grape.

She cries out. This can't be. This won't do. McAvoy just stands there, jaw agape, looking horrified at her, as if she's some kind of freak. She senses somebody behind her, and she wheels on them, pointing the pistol—

It's the tall one with the shock of dark hair. He's got her visidex. She thinks to shoot him, but she doesn't know if she could make the shot. Her head is vibrating. She can only see out of her one eye. Everything else is a pulsing tide of darkness giving way to light and then again to darkness. The pistol drops from her hand, and she does the only thing she can think to do.

Proctor Simone Agrasanto runs.

Cael watches her bring her hand to her eye. An eye he ruined. When he let fly, he knew what he was doing. He knew where that steel ball would go. It wasn't that he didn't want her dead; in a sense, that was all he wanted. She's an emblem of the Empyrean, a symbol of their crushing grip and callous control.

But he's already killed one person. Someone he knew. Someone he didn't like and, given the state of things, someone who may very well have deserved it.

But still, Cael *killed* him.

He just couldn't do it again.

And now she stands, staggering about. She's got the pistol raised, but she's not even pointing it at Lane, who's coming up on her flank.

Her eye looks like a blackened mess. Blood trickles down her cheek. She feels for it. Cups her hand over it. Makes a sound like a wounded animal.

And then it's over. The pistol drops, and she runs.

Cael goes after her.

He can't let her live.

He can't let her leave on that boat.

Gwennie.

The woman staggers around the corner of the barn just as Cael lets a metal ball fly—it chips a splintery pucker out of the wood, missing her by a hair's breadth.

Pop calls his name. He can't listen. Can't care.

He hurries after her, rounds the corner, sees Agrasanto bolting for the ketch. Lines up his shot . . .

Two Empyrean guards appear at the base of the boat's stairs, their rifles drawn and firing. Two sonic pulses hit the barn behind him, the wood shuddering and cracking with the weight of the blasts. Cael screams, skids to the ground, crawls behind an old thresher bar lying there in the dirt.

He gasps, desperately struggling to get another ball bearing in the pocket.

Two more pulses come shrieking forward, striking the thresher bar—Cael feels it shudder with the blast, and it's just enough for him to drop the metal ball onto the hard earth. It rolls away.

He leaps forward, slapping his hand down on it. By the time he stands, he sees Agrasanto staggering up the steps of the ketch. The guards follow behind her.

The hover-rails glow and hum.

"No!" Cael screams. He bolts toward the ship.

But it starts to lift from the corn, the stalks shuddering and straightening.

Cael fires the ball bearing upward at the ketch-boat.

The metal marble plinks off the side and falls to the earth.

And then the boat lurches forward, shooting up over the Heartland.

Gwennie is gone.

OLD OBLIGATIONS

POP'S IN THE kitchen on the floor, leaning up against the corner of two cabinets. He winces, clutching his side with one hand and his hip with the other.

Cael comes into the house with a bucket of cold water from the well and motions for Rigo to hand him a cloth napkin sitting on the table. Rigo pitches him the napkin, and Cael dunks it into the water and begins to wash the mask of blood off his father's face.

"Thanks, son," Pop says.

"How's Mom?" Cael asks.

"Quiet." As if she could be anything else.

"Gwennie's gone," Cael says.

"I know."

"I killed a man."

"You did what you did because you had no recourse. You're going to have to let it go. At least for today. Let your guilt pursue you some other day, Cael."

Cael nods, but he's not so sure.

Pop winces as Cael runs the cloth over the wound across his temple and brow. He looks to Rigo and Lane. "I want to thank you all for your help. The way everything shook out today wasn't the way I expected it to. I'm still here because of the three of you, and I am very grateful for that."

"Anything, Pop," Rigo says.

Lane says quietly, "We're still paying you back for all the good you've done us."

"Listen here," Arthur says. "We're not safe. Not here. Not for now. We've hit a juncture in this road where one path is now closed to you, to all of us. What I'm telling you is to run home. Pack a bag—a light bag, just some provisions and clothing and whatever else you'll need out there. Then get back here as soon as you can. Race like the wind, because I can assure you, this isn't over. The proctor's going to send more people. The Empyrean does not brook this kind of trouble."

Rigo and Lane share a look.

"You boys trust me?" Pop asks.

They nod, all three of them.

"Then go."

Rigo and Lane clap Cael on the arm and give Pop's hand a little shake. And like that, they're gone. Off to do what needs doing.

"You okay, son?" Pop asks.

"I reckon all right." It's a lie, but Cael can't see any reason to speak the truth right now.

They sit there for a while like that. Cael doesn't even know how long. Long enough that the bucket of well water has gone from clean to pink to a little too red. But already Pop's looking better—less like someone who got mauled by a bear. He'll make it through okay.

"Everything's going to be different from here on out," Pop says.

"I'm starting to figure on that."

"Your sister."

"What about her?"

"She's going to be in danger, too. This is all my fault, Cael; I know that. This isn't over, and in fact it's just beginning. They say the sins of the father are repaid on his children, and I know now how true that is." He winces as he sits up straighter. "But regret doesn't change anything. Where we are is where we are. And your sister thought she could get away from all this, but now it's going to find her.

These people are going to track her down the way a shuck rat sniffs out a crumb in the corner. Which is why I need you to find her first."

Pop's words echo in Cael's head—*I need you to find her first*—when he hears it. Upstairs, a bend in the floor, a groaning creak.

At first he doesn't know what it is, and he sees Pop's gaze flit toward the ceiling, too.

"I sent Bessie home," Pop says, lowering his voice. "Can't be your mother. . . ."

"It's okay," Cael says. "She may have fallen out of bed again. I'll go check."

Cael heads up the steps, taking them two at a time.

Lane looks out over his own farm and sees how dilapidated everything is. In some ways it feels as if his father's still here, his ghost marauding about, bragging, boisterous, chest puffed out like he's ten feet tall and made of stovepipe. And his mother, too. But her ghost is different. Standoffish. At the margins. She never was all that nurturing, was she? How could she be, to leave them like this?

Still, he decides to let it be. He's not sure if he's laying their ghosts to rest, or taking them with him, or condemning them to rot with this place. Right now, after all he's seen today, he's not sure that he cares. He packs a bag, does like Pop McAvoy says.

And then he's gone.

He leaves the front door open, because what does it matter anymore?

Rigo's up in his room, packing clothes in a bag but also secreting away food he's been hiding under his cot for those nights when his old man doesn't let him have dinner.

A shadow falls across the bed.

Jorge Cozido stands in the doorway.

"Hell you think you're doing, kid?"

Rigo doesn't say anything. He just keeps pumping the duffel full of clothes.

"I said, what the—"

"I'm leaving," Rigo blurts.

Jorge laughs. "Yeah. You're leaving. That's real neat, Little Rigo. You're always full of stories."

"I'm serious," Rigo says in a small, quiet voice. "I have to leave. I'm in danger."

Another laugh. Jorge comes up behind him, puts a hand on Rigo's neck, begins to massage it.

"Uh-oh, my kid's in danger. He's on the run from pirates, maybe. Or the Maize Witch."

Jorge tightens his grip on his son's neck hard enough that pain shoots down Rigo's arm. Rigo twists away. "Get off!"

"Oh! Oh, dang, the boy's getting lippy. You speak to me that way with that mouth and I can split those fat lips of yours; don't forget it."

Rigo's eyes glisten. He blinks back tears. "I thought you preferred to hit me on the body, so nobody else could see the bruises."

Jorge's fist clubs Rigo in the side of the head, and the boy tumbles. But he doesn't stay down. He grabs the duffel and skirts around his father, heading to the door. The old man's drunk—Rigo can smell the acrid fixy breath hanging around him like a toxic miasma—and he reaches for Rigo but misses the grab.

But he's still faster than Rigo expects. Rigo gets through the door, and his father's right on his tail. His father reaches out and steadies himself against the doorframe just as Rigo slams the door as hard as he can. The door closes on his father's fingers. Rigo can hear the bones crunch. The fingers bend backward in a way he's never seen: the old man's hand looks like a splintered board.

It's still not enough. Jorge shoulders open the door and he grabs his son by the throat, snarling with rage, the veins on his forehead forming a cruel topography. Rigo knows then that he's not going anywhere. Then—

Crash.

His mother steps out of the bedroom and breaks a ceramic pot—a pot her own mother made years before, a simple thing ringed in blue—over Jorge's head.

The man drops, blood wetting his hair.

Rigo sees that the old man is crying. Not just crying but blubbering. He's got his four broken fingers cradled to his chin and mouth like a baby, and he's staring out through weepy eyes, the blood already running down his forehead in red ribbons.

"You're a shit kid," Jorge says, his voice trembling. "A *shitty* little prick of a kid. You want to get out, go on. Go. Nobody wants you." He looks up at his wife. "Nobody wants you either. *Puta*. Whore."

Rigo's mother looks at her son with glistening eyes. Brushes hair away from his ears. "You need a haircut, Little Rigo."

"I know."

"You need to go."

"I know that, too. Are you going to be okay?"

She kisses his cheek. "Go, my boy. Go."

Rigo hurries downstairs. As he escapes out through the front door, he hears his father calling after him. "Rodrigo! Rodrigo! Wait, son, please—"

He closes the door behind him, drowning out his father's cries.

• • •

As Cael ascends the steps, he hears another creak of the floorboards—and then it's cut short.

He reaches his mother's room.

Mayor Barnes stands over Cael's mother. The window is open behind him. He's already got her robe off, and when Cael comes in, he's humming a song and kissing the tumors on her feet.

"Get your damn hands off her," Cael says. "Or I swear to the Lord and Lady—"

The mayor stands. Woozy. A little drunk, maybe. He smiles. "She's mine. I'll give her the life she needs. Maybe get her a cure. At least make her comfortable." He sees the incredulity in Cael's eyes. "I *love* her. You wouldn't understand."

"The hell you talking about?"

"Things have changed, boy! You're a woman-stealer like your father. Stealing that Shawcatch girl. Him stealing Filomena. You're both a bunch of bastards, and now I'm fixing what I should've fixed a long time ago." Those words all slur, but this next batch is said with an angry clarity: "She's coming with me."

"She's not going anywhere. Not unless you plan on putting me in the ground." He feels his back pocket for the slingshot—

And it's not there. It's downstairs on the counter. He set it down when he went to get the well water to wash Pop's face.

He'll just have to make do. His hands ball into fists.

The elder Barnes reaches into his coat jacket and pulls a long, jagged knife out of a sheathe.

"Put that knife down, Mayor."

Cael takes a ginger step closer.

"I'll stick you like a pig, you come near me," Barnes says.

"Maybe so. Or maybe I can take that knife out of your hand before you do."

Barnes slashes the knife inches in front of Cael's face.

"I said back away! You want me to cut you a new smile?" Boyland the Elder offers his own smile to that. He laughs as if he's hearing his own private joke. "You know, you could have been my son."

The mayor's gaze flits away from Cael suddenly, toward the doorway.

"Cael, step back."

It's Pop's voice.

Then he hears it: a *chick-chack* sound.

He turns and sees his father leaning against the frame of the bedroom door, wincing in what must be miserable pain after climbing all those steps.

But what really floors Cael is that Pop is carrying a gun.

Not a sonic weapon. Not a popgun or a pellet rifle.

A genuine bullet-shooter. The kind the Empyrean outlawed long, long ago. The kind Cael's only read about in books, books featuring cowboys and soldiers from an ancient time.

This one's a lever-action rifle, all blued-steel and red wood, with iron sights like the devil's teeth.

"I knew it," Barnes says, laughing without mirth. "I knew those rumors about you were true."

"Get away from my wife," Pop says.

"I can't do that."

"Then I'll shoot you."

"You won't. I don't even suspect you have ammo for that old thing. And who says it won't jam? It's just an old toy by now."

"It's no toy. I keep it clean and working. It's loaded."

The mayor seethes. "You took something from me, McAvoy. You need to let me *have it back*, Arthur."

"No. No, I do not."

The mayor makes a sound in the back of his throat, a guttural cry like a rabid beast, and he clutches the knife and looks to Cael.

He leaps at Cael with the blade.

And a red rose opens in the dead center of his forehead.

The room stinks of gunpower, and the air rings with the report of the rifle. Whorls of smoke drift from the barrel's mouth.

The mayor falls against the drawers with a bang and a clatter, closing half of them with the bulk of his body.

THE TRAILHEAD

EVENING'S COME, AND with it crickets. A rare chorus for a warm night.

Pop lights oil lamps and hangs them in the stable door and waves the three boys over. Together they see a wider opening in the floor and then withdraw one of the rail-rafts from within.

"So now we ride the rails," Cael says. "All of us. Hobos. Who'd have thought?"

Then Pop drops the bomb.

"I'm not coming with you, son."

"What?" Cael asks.

"I'm going a different way," he says. "Your mother will

have a hard time traveling with you. And so will I, with the way my hip hurts."

"We've got two rafts!" Rigo says.

"We'll be fine. Besides, it'll pay to split up. And where you're going, I can't follow."

They're headed to the flotillas. To follow in Merelda's tracks.

And, Cael thinks, *to find Gwennie, too.*

Pop's plan is simple: go north to the rail. Take the rail west using the rail-raft. Pop reiterates what Mer told them: there's a Provisional Depot there—that's how Merelda got on board a flotilla, after all. And that's how *they're* going to do it, too.

Pop opens the floorboard with a stomp of his foot and lifts a bag out of the space. He hands it to Cael. "Here. Provisions. A few root vegetables I salvaged from the garden before . . ." His voice trails off. "Anyway. Some other odds and ends in there. Oh. And a box of .30-30 ammo. Half a box anyway."

"Ammo?" Cael says.

Pop snatches the lever-action rifle from the corner and thrusts it into his son's hands. "I don't have time to teach you to shoot it, and the shame of it is, you'll need to conserve your bullets. For most things your slingshot will manage. But sometimes you're going to need some real firepower, and this rifle will do you right."

Rigo and Lane stare at Cael.

"Pop, I dunno—"

"Cael, you got this. I know you do. I trust you. Maybe I should have said it before. And I should have told you what I was doing this whole time, because I *do* trust you." He takes his son's hand and shakes it. "Go. Find your sister. Bring her home. I'll find you when the time is right. Come hell or high water, come Old Scratch on his skeleton horse."

Cael hugs his father.

Then he and the others grab the raft and take it outside.

They're out in the corn, pulling the raft through the stalks, suffering the cuts and paper-thin slices from the grabby fronds and twitching leaves when Cael stops.

"Can you guys handle this?" he asks.

"What?" Rigo says. "What the heck do you mean?"

"I mean, can you keep carrying it? I . . . I have something I gotta do."

Rigo whines in the back of his throat and mumbles, "Aw, Jeezum Crow . . ."

But Lane waves him on, as if he knows what Cael's gonna do.

"Go. We'll meet you at the tracks."

• • •

Cael doesn't have anything to write with, and he feels like an ass for not thinking about this sooner. So instead, he takes a sharp stone and clambers up to Wanda's window and begins to carve into the soft, paint-flaked wood of the window frame outside her bedroom.

He writes: *Wanda, I am leaving for a long time. Sorry, but I don't love you. You'll find a better*

He's going to finish with *man than me*, but he doesn't have a chance.

The window opens, and Wanda pokes her head out. Her hair's in a ginger tangle. Her freckled face sees him and lights up brighter than the moon above. Before he knows it, she's raining kisses down on his cheeks and forehead, and he has to pull away.

"Cael," she says, breathy. "I'm happy you came. Oh! I heard the proctor was in town; and, Lord and Lady, I am so glad that didn't have anything to do with you or your father. Oops, I know I shouldn't say anything, but the town's been saying things and—"

But as she's speaking, her eyes drift down, down, down, and soon she sees what Cael was doing. Wanda's eyes spy the words written into her windowsill, and she cocks her head so she can read the words, upside down for her.

As she reads, she lets her finger drift across them.

And when she looks up, Cael's already receding from the house. She calls to him, reaches for him, but he's fleeing into the dead orchard, into the dark corn.

It's not far past midnight when the auto-train roars by. It's a mean beast of long steel, the cattle catcher on the front paired with the glowing green headlights giving the look of a ghostly skull charging through the darkness. As it passes, Lane and Rigo tilt with the wind.

"Note to self," Lane says, the attaché's stolen visidex tucked under his arm, an unlit cigarette pinched between thin lips. "Do not be on the tracks when an auto-train is a-coming."

"That thing would turn us into pudding," Rigo says.

"I'm gay," Lane says.

Rigo blinks. "I thought we were talking about pudding."

"I know. I'm just sitting here thinking, Dang, who knows how this whole thing is going to go? Are we going to make it out okay? Are we going to end up dead, or worse, in some Empyrean prison up in the sky? I figure we could die, and all this time I haven't told my friends the truth about me—which is, I'm gay. So. There you go. Gay as the day is long."

"It's okay," Rigo says. "I didn't know you were gay, but I don't really care."

"You don't?"

"Nope. I got my own problems. I'm fat and short, and my dad beats me. I figure we are who we are and we ought to be okay with that."

Lane laughs. "You made up for it by making the proctor bleed."

"That was pretty cool."

"It really was."

Rigo finally says, "So, you gonna tell Cael?"

"Tell me what?" Cael says, coming out of the corn, wiping a bead of blood from his brow where a sheaf of corn got him.

Lane clears his throat. "Uh. Just that I'm looking to stick my thumb in the eye of the Empyrean. Then piss on their heads. Then push them down a flight of stairs. Then pee on them again."

Cael nods. "A little dramatic what with the urinating and all, but I think I'm on board."

"You finish whatever it was you had to do?" Rigo asks.

Cael stares off in the distance. "Yeah. I guess."

"Then let's get moving. Morning's not far off, and we've an adventure ahead."

They ease the raft over. The moonlight reflects in long

bands across the metal train tracks. They set down the raft and jiggle it so that the magna-cruxes line up right—

The raft floats on the tracks. A slight wobble, but stable. Mostly.

"We don't have oar-poles," Cael says, "so you two hop on, and I'll get to running."

Lane and Rigo ease atop. The raft shifts and dips, but then it stabilizes.

Cael begins to push—slow at first, but then he picks up speed, running behind it. He lets go and runs alongside, as fast as he can. Lane and Rigo grab his arms and haul him aboard.

The raft slides along the tracks, silent and swift.

With the moon above and the wind in his hair, Cael can't help but think, *I'm flying*.

Toward what, he cannot say.